Further Praise for *Sight Hound*

"The much anticipated debut novel from the marvelous short-story writer Pam Houston. . . . Animal lovers will understand completely the bond she has with her dog. As fans of Houston's writing have come to expect, her characters are outspoken and original."
—Barbara Lloyd McMichael, *Seattle Times*

"Entertaining. . . . It's a poignant and joyous novel, a tear-jerker certain to appeal to those of us who suspect, foolishly or intuitively, that our pets' emotions are tightly bound to our own. Without excess sentimentality, Houston offers proof that fickle humans are capable of learning a lesson or two in devotion, even if the teacher has four legs and bad breath." —*Miami Herald*

"Houston has an exquisite understanding of animal-human relationships. Maybe she's creating a new genre of fiction: the cross-species romance." —*Atlanta Journal-Constitution*

"Will convince you that Houston is at least a wonderful novelist and maybe also a full-fledged witch capable of advanced spells. . . . A voice so genuine you'd know it in a dark alley."
—Kimberly Marlowe Hartnett, *The Oregonian*

"[Rae] sorts out the good people from the bad in her life in time to face Dante's death with bravery and love in several tender scenes that will touch even the least animal-besotted reader. . . . [An] amplitude of heart." —Jenny Shank, *Rocky Mountain News*

"Houston writes well, with a wry knowledge of the human condition coupled to an admiration of the absurd. . . . The novel is compelling. . . . As if on a mission from God, Pam Houston repeatedly reminds her readers of life's multiple teachers, the possibility of healing and a word she uses often: 'hope.' "
—Wendy L. Smith, *San Diego Union-Tribune*

Sight Hound

ALSO BY PAM HOUSTON

A Little More about Me

Waltzing the Cat

Cowboys Are My Weakness

Women on Hunting

WITH VERONIQUE VIAL

Men Before Ten a.m.

Sight Hound

a novel

Pam Houston

W. W. NORTON & COMPANY   NEW YORK LONDON

Lines by Jane Hirshfield from the poem "Hope and Love,"
in *The Lives of the Heart* © 1997 by Jane Hirshfield.
New York: HarperCollins, 1997. Used by permission.

For information about permission to reproduce selections from
this book, write to Permissions, W. W. Norton & Company, Inc.,
500 Fifth Avenue, New York, NY 10110

Manufacturing by Quebecor World, Fairfield
Book design by Chris Welch
Production manager: Anna Oler

Library of Congress Cataloging-in-Publication Data

Houston, Pam.
Sight hound : a novel / Pam Houston.—1st ed.
p. cm.
ISBN 0-393-05817-4
1. Human-animal relationships—Fiction. 2. Women dog owners—Fiction.
3. Irish wolfhound—Fiction. 4. Veterinarians—Fiction. 5. Actors—Fiction.
6. Dogs—Fiction. I. Title.
PS3558.08725S56 2005
813'.54—dc22   2004024759

ISBN 0-393-32739-6 pbk.

W. W. Norton & Company, Inc.
500 Fifth Avenue, New York, N.Y. 10110
www.wwnorton.com

W. W. Norton & Company Ltd.
Castle House, 75/76 Wells Street, London W1T 3QT

1 2 3 4 5 6 7 8 9 0

This book is dedicated to the greatest dog that ever lived,
to the man who came along in the nick of time,
and to veterinarians, everywhere.

Acknowledgments

The author wishes to thank Carol Houck Smith for her belief in this project, her absolute understanding of the canine-human connection, and her line-editing skills which are second to none; Liz Darhansoff for her enthusiasm and ongoing support, Kelli Ziegler for her internet skills and her friendship; and Emily Bernard and Tami Anderson for their keen eyes in the final hour. Boundless gratitude to Dr. Peter Walsh, Dr. Alan Leach, Dr. Robyn Elmslie, Dr. Phyllis Glawe, Dr. John Howard, Dr. Carroll Loyer, and to the staff and students at the University of California Veterinary Medical Teaching Hospital, the Veterinary Referral Center of Colorado, and the Creede Animal Clinic. Special thanks to those who heard or read early drafts, especially my U.C. Davis colleagues, my Phase Two students, and one young man in Greeley, Colorado, who said I ought to give the cat a chance to speak for himself. Sincere appreciation to Toni Morrison and Jackson Browne for lighting the path with kindness and grace, with artistic and personal integrity. Warmest thanks of all go to Martin Buchanan, who in so many ways makes this book possible.

Contents

I know that
hope is the hardest
love we carry.
—*from* "Hope and Love"

JANE HIRSHFIELD

One

•

Mona's Dream

Rae #1:

We were driving along Colorado 64, somewhere between Meeker and Rangely—the Milky Way bright above us and Dante and Rose snoring softly in the back of the 4-Runner—when Mona told me about her dream. It was the early eighteen hundreds, she said, and we were going west together.

We had eloped. I was a man, she said, in that life, and I had stolen Mona from the man she was supposed to marry in Boston. She was pregnant with my child, and when she tried to deliver the baby it died, and then so did she, and I buried her, the baby in her arms, next to a slow-moving river.

I don't remember that life, though ten years earlier in this life I had insisted upon floating every single mile of the Green River, through oil fields and farmlands and sections of flat desert no one had ever boated just to say I had, and I never knew why.

In the life I do remember I died on a battlefield, in the Civil War, I think, or maybe the Revolution. There were bodies all around me, I was a man that time too, bullets and blood. Battlefields come up for me in dreams more times than I dare to count. More often this year, because of all the war movies I won't go to see.

Mona said, "Rae, is that really true, you think you might have been a man in your last life?"

I said, "Oh Mona, I'm just barely a woman in this life," and we had another good laugh like we'd been having for weeks. A *Denver Post* journalist once said I had the soul of a man, but I don't think he meant the same thing as Mona did.

I don't know yet what any of this has to do with love between women, or the way I've always thought the safest place in the world is a darkened theater, right before the curtain goes up, or the way the young actor's white collar against his chin made my guts pull so tight I almost fell off my chair.

I was so happy after the show that night I couldn't keep my feet from knocking together. I was almost making a successful run at living in the present moment, my mind sliding into the future only now and then. Thich Nhat Hanh said if you take care of the present the future will take care of itself, so that's what I was trying for, trying to feel every bit of it and not to look away when the young actor said any number of things that were daring me to meet his eyes. I was too old for him and too old for new love, but I'd finally gotten around to cultivating something I might one day call faith and there seemed no time like the present to test it.

I'd spent my whole life convinced that one sure way *not* to get what I wanted was to hope for it, out loud or even to myself, and it didn't seem to matter whether it was something simple like rain on the parched pasture so the wild iris would have a chance this year, or something bigger and softer I could fall back on, like a man who would stay, or a friend.

Now that Dante had had all the chemo an Irish wolfhound can have in one lifetime, there was nothing to do but share a bottle of vitamin E and miracle mushroom gel caps and live each day like it might be the last—since it might. Dr. Evans says it's a good thing dogs don't walk on their X-rays and I took him to mean that a statistic is only a statistic after your dog is already dead.

That Alanis Morissette song was playing on the radio all that spring, *thank you terror, thank you disillusionment,* and I got it long and loud. Peter had left me with a note in October that said, I really did love you, and it took me exactly two hours to make an appointment with Theo, my therapist, 24 hours to start the paperwork for a visa to get into Tibet. Theo had told me once that the only way Peter could handle our relationship was if I dimmed myself down to about forty percent of full wattage, and in Theo's office that day it became clear that the first thing the well-rested sixty percent of me wanted to do was head off to some far-flung corner of the world.

It's a desire that never wears out in me, to go as many miles as possible to a world that resembles my world not at all. Theo says loving the unfamiliar is a convenient way to avoid loving myself and he may be right, but whenever I'm in the Himalayas I tell the villagers how happy I am to be there so many times they think I am drunk or retarded or both.

At the Sera Monastery on the outskirts of Lhasa, the monks in debate out in the courtyard sounded, from a dis-

tance, like a raft of migrating snow geese rising off the surface of a lake, but when I got up close I could tell that half of
the monks were asking questions—*What is Big?* my guide
translated—and the other half were answering back.

"What is big?" I asked my guide, and he shook his head the
way he'd been doing all week, a combination of I-don't-
have-the-language and you-don't-have-the-capacity-to-
understand.

My dog is big, I wanted to say, and in all the ways you
mean it. But who was I to presume such knowledge, so I kept
my mouth shut and leaned my back against the big bodhi
tree in the center of the courtyard and closed my eyes to listen better to the sounds.

I once traveled a long way with my boyfriend at the time
to visit the concentration camps at Dachau, and miles before
we got there I knew there was no way in hell I was going to
go in, so I sat at the train station while my boyfriend and his
friends toured the ruins of the camp. And it was not as if I was
such a sensitive soul in those days—in fact I was cultivating
coldness—but years later when I told my friend Jonathan
about my reaction he said, "Well, you were probably one of
the souls who died there, I mean think about it, a hell of a lot
of people did."

On the hike to Delicate Arch, Mona said, "The baby's
name was Nell," and then the trail went around a corner and
damned if there wasn't a mother nursing a newborn who
looked about four hours old. We had left the dogs in the car
with all the windows open, because a four-mile trip was too
long by then for Dante, and because Rose couldn't be counted
on to hide from the park ranger when we told her to.

I asked the sun to just please give us an hour at the top of the trail and it did, and then it went away for good right before all the sunset photographers arrived, and I thought about Jonathan again and how he once asked me why I was always giving the power to people like Adam and Peter and Henry Miller and God, when was I going to realize I was the one who could make the sun come and stay.

My cell phone rang after we got back in the car, and it was Howard, the young actor, telling me that while he was driving he felt as if he might turn at any second into a tiny beam of light. And it was right at that moment that Mona pointed up out of the sunroof and said, "There, look, there, that's two golden eagles, that's us. What are the chances that there would be two golden eagles, right on the highway like that?" And I thought, well, the chances are good enough that the highway department put a sign up that says BEWARE OF EAGLES ON HIGHWAY, but I knew inside that if the eagles came to tell me anything that day, they came to talk about Howard and his little beam of light.

And I couldn't stop thinking about the battlefield, looking for Howard's face among the bleeding and dead. Maybe we died there together. Maybe it was his job to take care of me. I meet so many people, but I've never met anyone like him. I've never met a man before who would spend his last five dollars on floating candles.

In therapy the other day we focused on my battlefield, which Theo thinks is a metaphor and that's fine, if that's what he needs to do. And then we did EFT where you rub your sore spot and say your affirmation, and it was no problem to say, I accept myself fully even when I'm supposed to be taking care of someone else, but when it got to the part where I was supposed to say, I accept myself fully even though I want someone to take care of me, well, I just couldn't say it.

"Try it again," Theo kept saying, as if we were talking about the balance beam or the high jump and not the simple task of putting several words together in a line, and eventually I did manage to say it but not without my heart beating hard in my throat.

The guy who came to Mona's door last month said, "Someone from another time lives in your house," then he said, "You lived in another time too, you were a pioneer."

Then she was thinking he looked just like John Candy, and he said, "Yep, that John Candy, he's my man." He sold her a magazine subscription and then he went on his way.

But somehow after he left she knew that I would die in a fiery crash the next month when I was going to Italy for the opening of Jonathan's play. As if the guy had given her that information telepathically.

And Mona's husband, Daniel, said, "You have to call her, it's too important not to," and I said,

"What, does this mean you don't want me to go?" and she said,

"Of course I don't want you to go because then you'll be dead."

When Jonathan and I got to Italy, Vincenzo, our driver, said he was dating a woman named Pina and her best friend, Tina, simultaneously, and when I asked him wasn't he afraid he'd say the wrong name he said, "I've never slept with both of them at one time!"

I tried to tell him in my pidgin Italian, which is really more like passable French with O's stuck on the end of everything, that "my amiee-go in Etas-Unito parleyed of an accidento terrifico, grande fuego! Morte, Morte, por moi."

Vincenzo nodded and smiled when I said this, and then whenever he'd pass two cars at once on the double yellow line Jonathan and I would yell, "Fiery crash! Fiery crash!"

In Italy I rode a big grey horse that turned his neck all the way around to eat figs from my hand, and Gino, the heart of Teatro Spagnola, said, "I have so much charisma, but Jonathan, he is not simpatico. I play the guitar when people are sad, everyone is jealous of Gino."

Gino showed us the image of the Madonna in a knot of a tree. He said God tells him who are the good people. Then he got out his photo albums full of stills of himself in all his starring roles since Teatro Spagnola opened in the 1970s.

And all the time I kept thinking about the young actor, how when he took off his ball cap to reveal his hairline I thought, *Oh, thank God,* because otherwise he was just too, too handsome, and how I thought for the first five minutes that he was gay, and for the next five minutes that he was with the leading lady, and for the next five minutes that Victoria had her hooks in him somehow. But when he walked me to my car that night and said,

"Well, at least I've met the dogs now,"

And I said, "Yes, well, that's the important thing,"

I knew that I would see him again.

The next morning I drove up to Boulder to see Madame Roslinka and the first thing she said to me was, "The spirit has helped you out, not *one* time, but many times. There are two people in your hand," she said, "only one in your heart. One is a little lighter, one is a little darker, but don't worry, you will make the right decision."

She said I had had big pain in my life three times, seven years before, three years before, and last October, and it took me a moment to realize that she had hit them all perfectly—Tucker, Adam, and Peter—and I was pretty impressed. She said I would live to be eighty-six or eighty-seven, that I would earn and spend money easily, and that in general I would always do the right thing.

I know there's not a woman who's ever been in love who didn't think some kind of fate was at work in the background. What I'm saying is, I understood that my connection to this young actor was deep and true and old, and we had only just unearthed it. What I'm saying is, there was no chance that I would have driven off into the sunset with Mona into whatever life we might have had alongside the Green River. What I'm saying is, this was a time in my life when the big questions collided with the small ones, when the smell of sage coming up through the snowmelt could seem like a bona fide promise, when what is big was all around me, demanding patience and courage in alternating doses, singing this is the beginning of beginning to understand.

Two

·

The
Meeting

Dante #1:

The first point of confusion I'd like to clear up is that there are three legs left, three good legs that are perfectly capable of lifting the entire lithe grey body over a single-strand barbed-wire fence from a standstill, especially if the human you love is standing next to it, crying about your osteosarcoma, about your lost fourth leg, about your impending decline and premature death, about how she will never live without you.

You jump over the barbed wire to show her that your death is still a long way off, that for a wolfhound three legs is a kind of koan, that your one true goal is to stay alive long enough to help her find another human who will love her properly after you are gone, and that finding that human is at once as improbable—and as effortless—as a three-legged wolfhound sailing over a four-foot barbed-wire fence.

She has been such a slow, yet eager learner, and that has given the assignment a sweetness like none that has ever come before, tinged with the fear that time would run out. Tucker, Adam, and Peter. I could waste a lot of your time trying to put them in some kind of order from bad to worse.

She and I would be spooned up in bed together after one of their untimely departures, she'd be trying to take comfort—as most people do—in the cinnamon smell of my ears. I'd roll over to face her and press the ends of my big black nose flaps right up against hers and try to stare everything I know right into her eyes. Sometimes she'd get it and fall asleep, dreaming of sea turtles and prayer flags, other times she wouldn't, and she'd sleep dreamless just to know someone was keeping watch.

It's funny how love is both harder, and easier, without language.

I watched the moon, those nights, roll from one of her windows to the other. I never went to sleep myself until the light behind the mountains marked the dawn.

A wolfhound isn't afraid to die. A wolfhound isn't afraid to suffer. A wolfhound practices nonattachment—with only modest success when it comes to the organic beef roast she cooks for dinner, and very little success when it comes to her.

The tail, a very important part of a wolfhound's musculature in terms of carriage and balance, made all the more so by the amputation of one leg, reveals this failure by thwacking rather violently, as if it had a will of its own, against walls, doors, windows, every time she walks in the room. Tail to washing machine provides the best resonance, a booming beating heart.

It makes her smile. Twenty times a day, two hundred times a week, two thousand times a season, how many smiles hath the thwacking of one tail wrought? Countless, though more to the point, counted upon, and therefore forgivable, since counting upon anything has been an ability she has not heretofore possessed.

She barely has the covers up in bed and I am there, rib to rib against her. She only has to think about sitting on the couch, and I am there, curled up at one end, ready to warm her feet. She has hardly made a trip as far as the clothesline without me. There has never been a time when she has extended her hand into the car's back seat that I haven't licked it. I go each week to the therapist's with her, and I drink the water he offers me, whether I am thirsty or not.

There are three principles to remember if you are to teach a human being anything, and they are consistency, consistency, consistency. They are such fragile creatures to begin with, with poor eyes, poorer hearing, and no sense of smell left to speak of, it's no wonder they are made of fear. Some centuries ago they moved inside and with that move went nine-tenths of their intuition. It is almost unmerciful to make them live so long when they spend their lives in so much pain.

Yesterday she and Howard and I walked in the mountains behind her ranch, which were covered with purple lupine and skyrocket gilia, and little blue-grey butterflies fluttered among them, the color of barn wood at dawn. The streams are fat and full this summer, Rose was tumbling in them, scattering rainbow and golden trout. Everything brimming with life and health, except me, of course, which now is of even less concern than ever before, and even I was keeping up better than usual, the crisp dry day giving my overworked hip joints a reprieve.

I heard my human singing a little song under her breath, I don't think there were words, just syllables, *Doop-y-doo,* she sang, *doop-y-doo.* The grief she carries—always—in her face was gone. She leaned over and kissed my wet whiskers, and Howard kissed her hand. Then I stumbled a little, nothing serious, nothing any four-legged healthy-hearted dog couldn't have done, and when I looked at her again, she was still smiling brightly, yet behind the smile the sadness had returned.

Perhaps that is the most the humans can hope for, a moment on a blue Sunday morning when grief closes its eyes and dozes off for a while, when it relaxes its old arthritic hand. If that's true, I'll die proud of having helped her to a few of those moments. Of the day two years ago when I leapt the fence for her—though my heart wouldn't allow it yesterday—of the way she gasped and clasped her hands together as my body reached the top of its trajectory, clearing the barbed wire by half a foot if it was a millimeter, and I kicked my back legs even a little higher into the air.

Dr. Evans #1:

I see a lot of animals in here. I mean sometimes twenty-five in a day, all of them critical in one way or another, all of them with perfectly nice owners who each try to make me understand that their little Rover's or Morris's mind-boggling uniqueness is matched only by the depth of their bond with him, and should I not be able to pull out of my hat some highly experimental cutting-edge surgical procedure to save him, their hearts, their psyches—not to mention their marriages—will never be the same again.

I'll be sitting with them in the consultation room and their little Rin Tin Tin is ten minutes away from being dead from tumors the owners have somehow let grow undetected to the size of basketballs and they are literally throwing thousands of dollars at me with big glassy tears rolling down their faces and saying *anything, try anything, it doesn't matter how much it costs.*

I want them to know so many things at once, then. First, though I may not appear to be, I am on their side; and if I weren't, I wouldn't be here. I'd be behind some big oak desk in an advertising firm figuring out ways to sell people even more Coca-Cola, or driving a landscaping truck full of begonias around the wealthy suburbs, or making my father happy cutting out and replacing human organs over at the medical center on the other side of campus. But where I am is here, at what is arguably the finest college of veterinary medicine in the country, sixteen hours a day, fighting the good fight on behalf of the animals.

The second thing I want them to know is that I'm not God, though I impersonate Him daily, and am delighted when He lets me get away with it. I can't save every dog and cat that comes in here and no amount of money or tears or wishing will make it so I can.

The third thing I want them to know is that I believe every word they tell me. I believe that long-faced Henry is the smartest basset hound in the state of Colorado, that silky Vishnu picks out her own flavor of cat food each evening, that fluffy little Foosball comes to the door of her rabbit hutch whenever she hears her mother's car in the driveway.

I believe that Maggie and Guinness and Decker and Sarvis and Walter and Moxie and Toto and Dumpster and Spot is each one of them the greatest dog that ever lived. And that Stanley and Monkey Boy and Trader and Scat and Road Kill and Tigger and Josephine and even fat Apostrophe is each one of them the most wonderful cat. That's what you learn here, and every ferret and hedgehog and potbellied pig and now all of a sudden even every flying squirrel—perfection on four legs.

Please do not mistake my tone for sarcasm; there is not one ounce of derision in what I say. In ten years I have opened the bodies of more than ten thousand animals and what I have seen there lying around and among their organs are souls as deep and authentic as anything in creation.

You don't have to convince me, I want to tell the owners, I will try equally hard for each of them. So hard that I will lie awake the night before every surgery making lists in my head. So hard that my wife is ready to divorce me because I've had to return home from two family vacations in a row when one of my patients became critical and because I do tend to sleep in ICU with a dog the night after a particularly grisly surgery, and while it's true that aside from watching Detroit Red Wings hockey, veterinary medicine is the only thing that makes me happy and it makes me happy every single day, I literally cannot afford to get even more attached than I already am to this hospital or to any one particular case.

I don't say any of these things to the owners, because I am not, I am told, a people person. So I sit there and look at my hands while they cry. I offer them X-rays and life-expectancy charts and statistics from recent veterinary journals. I try to rub an ear or scratch a belly in a way that shows them I'm more than just the guy with the knife. They take me on faith and I take their faith seriously. I try to save the miracles for the operating room.

Having said all this I have to admit there was something special about Dante. I saw it right from the beginning, though I tried not to acknowledge it. He knew things—I wouldn't want to have to say what all they were—but he knew a lot of things. His mom—his human mom—used to say he knew all the secrets of the universe. She said that when a high Tibetan lama does a really good job at being a high Tibetan lama, he gets to come back as an Irish wolfhound.

At first I thought she was talking about real llamas of course, which I found confusing because we've got half a herd of them out here behind the clinic, and I was pretty sure they came from Peru, and while they definitely weren't dumb they were mean as snakes when it came time to vaccinate them, they'd spit right in your face if you gave them the chance.

Then one day in the shower—which is where I figure most things out—I realized she meant the priest kind of lama and I only have limited experience with priests too, but I can tell you this dog knew more than any priest I ever met.

Let me give you a concrete example. When this dog developed the mother of all postsurgical infections and I had to scrub . . . SCRUB . . . the dead tissue out of his wound three times a day, a wound so deep I could look down in there and see the plate and the bone and the screws, see all the work it had taken my interns and me thirteen hours under anesthesia to accomplish—eleven of those being microscope work where we tried to repair all the veins and the capillaries, the most sensitive tissues—and that now some bacteria that wasn't responding to anything, even to the eleven-hundred-dollars-a-dose-antibiotic, was threatening to eat completely away . . . he didn't move a muscle. He didn't yelp or jump. He didn't even twitch.

I have experienced nothing in my life that would hurt one-tenth as much as that scrubbing must have hurt Dante, but this dog knew I wanted to help him. He understood what we were trying to do better and more completely than a person would, no matter what I might have said or what they might have said, if both of us spoke the same language. Which is another reason you find me here, at the vet school and not across campus working on human beings.

I've got nothing against people, except for all the ways you can't trust them. I'm a veterinary surgeon, and a good one. Some people say I'm the best goddamn veterinary surgeon in America right now.

My father, who went to war instead of med school and wound up delivering the mail for forty-five years, still leaves the *veterinary* part off of my title when he tells his new friends about me. Everybody's a disappointment to somebody I guess, and I'm his, and my mom's, and my wife's if you want to know the truth, and her mom's too.

I ask you, has there ever been a dog who hasn't approved of his master's career choices? Or one who would make you sleep on the couch because you missed a stupid barbeque with your stupid neighbors who only want to talk about golf and the Home Depot, two subjects you know absolutely nothing about and hope never to?

You should have heard the cheer that went up in the operating room during that first operation when the blood started moving back into Dante's left front paw. Eleven hours of work under the microscope and all those reconnected vessels were holding! Bringing blood and oxygen and chemotherapeutics and anything else they needed to bring through the entire system.

He didn't like the morphine. It made him howl like a banshee, so I stopped using it. That's when I recognized his

Gandhi-like tolerance for pain. Everything I put that dog through and still he wagged his tail every time I opened the door to the kennel. He missed his mom every minute, but he put his trust in me, and that's one of the things I'm most proud of. The dog put his trust in me.

It didn't take the students long to figure out what kind of a dog Dante was, and a rumor began around the hospital that a kiss from him would bring good luck all day. He was an inpatient from three days after the long first surgery—when the infection kicked in—until we got down to one wound flush per day, and that was nearly two months. Brooklyn Underhill, my intern at the time, said if you ever doubted that Grace was mightier than Fear, one look in Dante's eye and you'd be reminded.

Grace isn't a thing I spend much time with one way or the other, and I never knew how to take Brooklyn, who was a Mormon and a member of the U.S. Armed Forces to boot, but I couldn't deny the fact that even if I didn't know exactly what Grace was, Dante was a dog who had it.

His mom came to visit him every day. Came and sat out on the lawn with him, rubbing his belly and looking at the sky. She said it was the best part of her day, that she'd gotten her workaholic gene from her old man and she couldn't turn it off, especially when bad things happened, and this was just one more gift Dante had given her, a chance to sit still for three hours a day and instead of *doing* every second, to give *being* a try. Rae has a place up in the mountains, another down here in the Front Range—so she must *do* pretty well for herself. Playwriting gave her a way to see the world, she said, taking her plays to festivals in California and Italy, winning grants to study the lives of people in Laos and Tibet. The travel had always seemed like a good thing, until the day that Dante got sick.

When all the decisions had to be made after that, whether to fight the infection with superantibiotics, whether to go ahead with the chemotherapy, sixteen hundred dollars a dose for a dog that size, nothing to sneeze at when the survival numbers aren't all that good, and the biggest decision—the three subsequent surgeries where I tried to make the mess I'd made of his leg turn into something he could actually walk on—she'd turn to me and say, "What's your gut?"

My gut was always the same, that I could save the leg and the dog. My gut was, this is the reason I was put on the planet. So I'd tell her so and she'd say, "So you're not nervous?" and I'd say, "Rae, I've been nervous since the first day I met you," and that became our little routine, but it didn't make it any less true. We probably said all of three sentences to each other that didn't contain medical terminology during all those months, but we understood each other, Rae and I, and with that understanding came trust.

You should have heard her voice on my pager the day Dante fell twenty feet over a retaining wall into the Platte River. It was three days after the third attempt to save the leg. We'd just gotten a brand-new cast on and he was probably off balance. Probably a little woozy from the chemo, which we had gone ahead and administered the same day. They'd gotten out of the car for a minute so he could take a whiz on a telephone pole. She was standing right next to him and saw him lean, in slow motion, and she reached for him. His fur brushed her fingers as he fell.

She was over that wall in no time flat and into midstream, fully clothed, screaming for somebody to get a throwing rope, holding Dante's head above water while they both bumped along the rocky bottom, headed downstream. She screamed some more until a guy walking his English mastiff spotted her and ran down the two hundred yards to where the retaining wall disappeared into a grass bunker, and used his locked Extend-a-Leash to fish her out.

When they showed up at the hospital, soaking wet, Rae was in tears, sure she'd ruined all my hard work, sure she'd rebroken the leg and fatally wounded the dog. We replaced the cast and kept him overnight to watch him. I don't know how a dog falls twenty feet with a ten-pound cast on his left front leg into a rocky river bottom and then gets carried downstream half a mile without injury, but as I've said—probably one too many times already—Dante was no ordinary dog.

In the end though, my gut turned out to be wrong about the leg. He was too damn big, had too much weight up front. We'd used Dante's own leg bone for the graft, what was left of the section of ulna we had cut out, turned upside down and put back to replace the tumored part of the radius we had to cut away. It should have worked, but we cut too high, too close to the elbow.

You always want to cut as high as you can, always want the largest possible margins around the tumor you can get away with, but I cut too high, and Dante couldn't put weight on the leg, not after that first surgery, nor the second, nor the third, nor the fourth. He needed two bones there and the ligaments between them to keep the elbow from popping, and all the bands and screws and contraptions I could come up with didn't do a thing. The truth was, he never put weight on that leg again.

This was the first surgery of its kind in the world. Now, three years later, we do it every couple of weeks like rolling off a log, but at the time we didn't have any idea what we'd see till we got in there. How much bone the cancer had destroyed. How complicated all those severed veins and capillaries were going to be to sew back together. Whether or not the reconnections would hold when the heart started pumping blood.

I might tell you that his mom hid her anger well, but I don't think she had any. She had a look behind her eyes I recognized, one that says, *Go ahead and hit me with the worst news possible and I'll stand here and ask you if you're sure it's not any worse than that.* Maybe that's how she knew—like I say, I'm not much of a talker—that I wanted that dog alive and on four legs exactly as much as she did. She knew I was the best and that I did my best. She knew I stayed awake all night in ICU with him after every surgery. She knew I got down in the cage with him when he was hooked up to seventeen different monitors. She knew I lay there all night and stroked his handsome head.

We learned so much from him. I'm not sure Rae fully understands that a lot of dogs are going to live a whole lot longer because of what she and Dante let us do. We've saved twenty-four limbs since Dante's failed surgery, and all but two of those dogs are still cancer-free. I wanted to make a book for her filled with all their pictures. That has been my good intention, which as I mentioned, I am chock-full of.

•••

HAVE YOU EVER been in the waiting room of a veterinary hospital? It's not like a Home Depot at all. In the middle of the night sometimes there's an hour or two between emergencies and then that room is just a big space full of stained Formica and cracked vinyl chairs with chewed legs. But most of the night somebody is sitting there, flipping through a magazine without seeing the words, trying not to cry, trying not to look at the clock, trying not to ask the receptionist for news she doesn't have on the Afghan hound whose stomach flipped over or the Siamese who had her first grand mal seizure or the great dane who has finally fallen into congestive heart failure.

During business hours there can be as many as fifty or sixty people in there, waiting for Abner to finish his chemotherapy, waiting to see if Blacken has developed any secondary pulmonary metastases, waiting to hear if the lump on Fiona's back is malignant or benign. Sometimes I walk through there on my way to recovery and there's a soft humming in the air like what you hear sometimes in a church, like all sixty of them are holding their collective breath, all sixty of them are murmuring their prayers.

There's no mistaking the restrained sniffling that occasionally gives way to sobs, no missing the hopeful little Tupperware containers full of broiled chicken breast that might tempt Sadie even though she's seventeen and hasn't eaten a thing in days, no avoiding the hands that clutch the favorite toys, the beloved blankets, the empty carriers, no escaping the fear in the human eyes—so much more complicated than the fear in the eyes of the animals—as they follow my footsteps along the corridor, waiting to see if I am the one who comes with the news.

I once watched a big man, a Marine, a man who if you passed him on the street you might believe didn't care for anything in the world, fall to his knees when my intern told him his cockatiel had inoperable brain cancer. It's okay for the people to cry in here. More okay, I think, than over at the med center because here, there's nobody they have to be strong for. For years they have been jilted, cheated on, rejected, fired, and their pets have come to them and placed a warm nose on their thigh, a knobby three-toed claw on their shoulder. Would a dog ask his master not to cry over him? Would he ever misinterpret the grief?

Every now and then a silence will fall over the waiting room, and you know a family has decided to take a deceased pet home. We offer cremation, at no extra charge if the owners want it, but sometimes they'll want to bury their pet in their backyard. When the room gets that kind of quiet, as the family crosses the tiles to the elevator, pushes the button and waits with the big zipped-up blue body bag wrapped in their arms or thrown over their shoulder, sometimes even carried between them, it makes a person long for the sound of the sobbing again.

I hate doing amputations. I mean, they're the simplest operation I do, about as complicated as cutting up a roasting chicken just before you sit down to eat it for dinner, but with the exception of begging the suits in Administration for research money, amputations are my least favorite part of this job.

I know what people said after I punched the operating room wall right after Dante's amputation and broke a couple of the smallest bones in these very well-insured hands. They said that God's gift to veterinary medicine was pissed off because his miracle reconstruction was a failure, because he wouldn't be written up in the journals, because he wouldn't be flooded with offers that would get him out of this meat market and into private practice, working two days a week and spending the rest of the time playing golf.

Have I mentioned how I feel about golf? Have I mentioned how anyone who holds that opinion of me can shove a graphite-compound nine iron straight up his ass?

I wanted Dante to have four legs. I wanted Dante to live forever.

We show our amputee "parents" a video of a dog named Wagner, a golden lab with osteosarcoma who had first one leg amputated, and then another, and they were both on the same side. Cruel, you say, an abomination. But in the video, when Wagner's mom and dad come home, the dog gets up on his remaining two legs and runs—in a manner of speaking—over to greet them. Wagner is a happy dog, an active dog, a loved and a loving dog.

I still wanted four legs for Dante.

Darlene #1:

I was there the day he took off, the sneaky little bastard. And even though you couldn't have told her *then* that it was the best thing, I think if she could have known herself better in those days, she would have said it was exactly what she wanted.

The night before, another very relaxed evening around the dinner table, I look up to see Peter, who's just helped himself to some salad, picking all the tomatoes out of his salad and putting them on her plate, so I say, "I take it you don't like tomatoes," and he looks up at me, sort of cross-eyed and vaguely menacing through those Coke-bottle glasses and he says,

"I like tomatoes just fine, it's just that she likes them more than I do," and he smiles in that way he has that makes you think smiles are some exclusive property of the hateful, and I say,

"Oh, let me get this straight, you actually really like tomatoes, but if you give them to Rae you'll have one more reason to be angry," and her eyes fly up from her plate with a smile in them for a second.

He was an angry son of a bitch, that one, a big step down even from Adam if you ask me, but nobody did. She was ashamed of him from the very beginning; I could tell that the first time she brought him home. And he knew that's exactly what he was, a thing to be ashamed of, and that's why he was always madder than spit.

I couldn't understand how she got mixed up with him in the first place. He'd seen her on TV one time, and he'd tracked her down like an animal in the beginning, begging her to see him, always claiming to be in the neighborhood, and let me tell you something, if you find yourself in this neighborhood, you've come a long damn way.

I've lived here at Rae's ranch for six years now. I look after things while she's down at her apartment in Denver, or any one of the other million places she takes off to when she goes on the road. My goal is to keep things running around here so her mind is set at ease when she's traveling.

She's got a worry Rolodex inside her skull that's so thick she can barely spin it. I keep the pipes from freezing, the dogs fed and the trees watered. I keep an eye on the propane leak and make sure that the creek the horses drink out of doesn't run dry. I keep plenty of wood cut and I bang on the side of the refrigerator when it starts to do that screaming thing it does. My cat Stanley stays on top of her rodent problem.

But when she decides to bring home somebody like Peter, there's not a goddamned thing I can do to save her.

He was a man with a story. She's a sucker for a man with a story. His was full of foster homes and minor league base-

ball and a brief stint with a traveling circus before a bad marriage led to hospitalization for male anorexia where he met a
bulimic costume designer who became wife number two and
who first got him interested in building theatrical sets. His
heart had shriveled somewhere along the way to the size of a
Delta peach pit, and his soul had never gotten any bigger than
a kernel of Olathe corn. He had those little identical she-troll
twins for daughters who came around for three weeks in the
summer and would only eat Cheerios, Pop-Tarts, and Velveeta
cheese. They had fits so loud even the dogs didn't want in the
house anymore. The one threw herself from the guest bedroom window one day in a rage so deep she didn't stop to
think how her sister would laugh when she hit the woodpile,
less than a foot below the sill.

Peter hid in the basement with his plastic models and his
tools and his drawing table while his girls told us stories
about their mother's all-girl pool parties, while they refused
to eat the fresh blueberry pancakes I'd gotten up at the crack
of dawn to make, while they smashed all the little art projects
we'd spent half the night thinking up.

When Peter took off he left behind every gift Rae had
given him. The high-tech ski coat, the really swanky leather
jacket, and a ten-inch hunting knife with a handle carved out
of elk antler that I had salivated over a time or two. Rae gave
me that knife without a moment's hesitation, then I put the
ski coat on and went out and rolled around in the manure
pile while she took pictures. Howard's got the leather coat
now and it fits him like a dream.

Howard's a fine-looking man. He looks fine in that coat
and he doesn't give a damn where it came from. I don't know

too much about men in the new age but that seems like a pretty Zen thing to me.

The first time Rae brought Howard home, well you could see right away how different it was. Her face all lit up like I'd never seen it before, and they were laughing their heads off and dancing in the living room, acting like drunkards without having a thing to drink. Every time I'd come home there'd be that freshly fucked look on both their faces. We were laughing at dinner, I can't remember over what, and all of a sudden she bursts out saying,

"Well, Darlene, doesn't this remind you of the old days with Peter?" and then she about falls off her chair she's laughing so hard, and I say,

"You're so different with Howard I don't even recognize you," and he gets all ahead of himself and tells me how good that makes him feel but I say, "Look. I don't give a damn about you. But I do give a damn about her, and you seem to be making her happy."

He kept it all tucked in a little better after that.

My cousin Dorice says that "men are a luxury item," by which she means they are nobody's necessity, and she found out how true that was when she was pregnant with little Beauregard and big Beau couldn't make up his mind whether or not he could leave his aging mother in Waco to come up to Colorado and take credit for what his dirty deed produced. It all worked out, of course. Men come to their senses eventually, faster if you pretend you don't give a damn.

I was married one time, for about ten minutes. Didn't take.

Right before he left for good my husband said, *Darlene, everything you want in a man you could find easier in a good half-*

ton Ford. I'm not one to ignore a piece of advice that solid so I went down to the dealership the next day, and found out just how right that boy was.

Dorice also says a man's no good at all if he can't make you laugh. And that's another thing I like about Howard.

Rae and I are sitting around here one night playing rummy and eating a key lime pie I whipped up that afternoon when the phone rings. It's Howard, down in the city, doing some actor's thing, they haven't seen each other for about a week, and he asks her if she wants to hear his Oprah fantasy, and she says only if Darlene can hear it too.

Now I'm not a person who's got much use for television, except maybe those videos they have on the country music channel now and again, Tim McGraw, or Garth Brooks, and I have been known to watch the occasional hockey game. And while it's also true that the only thing that will get me to leave this valley and go anywhere near Denver are family funerals or similar acts of God, I do know who Oprah Winfrey is, so we put the phone on speaker and got comfortable.

In the fantasy, Oprah has asked Rae to write an article for her magazine, and the article is called "The Most Amazing Motherfucker on the Planet," and, naturally, it's all about Howard.

I should probably mention that Rae writes plays for a living and while she has had her plays up at some very respectable theaters in Denver and elsewhere, and while she does get asked to write the occasional article or give the occasional talk now and then, there's nobody like Oprah Winfrey calling the house here on a regular basis. And that's probably a good thing, because people around here are so suspicious of Rae already, the words she uses, and the strange kinds of food she cooks, the minute somebody like Oprah starts calling they'd probably run her straight out of town.

But in Howard's fantasy, Oprah loves the article so much that she invites them both to come to the show. Rae's on stage with Oprah, of course, and Howard is sitting right in the middle of the audience, which happens to be made up entirely of women. He's wearing purple, his favorite color, and he's just had his hair cut, fresh.

"What's left of it," I say to the speaker, but Rae hits me in the gut to shut me up.

The cameramen are all women too, and so are the security guards, and the grips and the assistants. In Howard's fantasy, he's the only damn man on the entire ABC lot.

Oprah asks Rae what it is that Howard loves the most about her, and she says, "Why don't you ask him yourself?"

And the camera pans across the audience until it lands on Howard, sitting there all done up and purple, and he says, "Really Oprah, what's not to love?" and the audience starts booing and hissing and throwing tampon cases at him and so forth, and so he says, "No, really. She just makes me happy, and it's a happiness that's taking over my entire life."

Well, now all the women in the audience are crying and clapping, the cameras are shaking slightly because the camerawomen are weeping, the security guards are throwing down their guns into the aisle because it's all too beautiful, and I have to admit it, even this old cynic is having a laugh.

Then the camera sweeps back to Oprah, who is wiping a tear from her eye, and she says, "Howard, I think you should have been the one to star in that movie *What Women Want*, the heck with Mel Gibson, and anyway, you've got a much cuter ass. And we cut to commercial."

When Rae hung up the phone I said, "Honey, I ask you, what man that you have ever come into contact with would have a sequence of thoughts like those? And if he did, what man would ever have been brave enough to say them?"

"I know," she said, "but is that a good thing?"

That's the reason I worry about her. She's felt bad for so long she don't know good when it's bubbling right out of her. And even when she catches up to it, she's waiting for whatever bad thing is about to happen next.

Take Dante.

And before I say anything about him, I want to say that on the rare occasions when she goes out of town and can't take him with her, I don't miss one step of their routine. First thing in the morning he gets two cans, one lamb, duck and pasta and one chicken and gravy. He gets the digoxin and the enalapril in the lamb and pasta, because they are the most important, and he gets the vitamin E and the L-carnitine in the chicken, because sometimes he gets fed up with pills and if he's going to get fed up he can afford to miss those. He gets all of this brought to him on the couch, with a tea towel under his chin, and he eats it off a stainless steel fork.

You can probably tell by looking at me that I was not put on earth to fork-feed a dog his breakfast, which should give you some measure of my dedication to Rae. When Howard's here and he performs this ritual he speaks to Dante with an English butler's accent, and that I will not do.

At noon Dante gets the special lamb roll imported from New Zealand. At night he gets his dry food—which he manages to eat all by himself—and the second set of pills, in little balls of cream cheese I roll with my fingers.

He gets one walk a day, no less than thirty minutes, no more than sixty, a turn around the biggest pasture is exactly the right length and has the virtue of a creek right before the end so he can dip his overheated chest. He sleeps on whatever part of my bed he wants to, usually diagonally across, leaving me one corner, and Stanley the other.

I call her cell phone nightly, though there is nearly always very little to report.

"Put your hand on his chest," she says to me from a hotel room in a city I can't even visualize. "Tell me the noise his heart is making."

And I do it. "Bump, ba, pa, bum, ba, pa, bum, bum, pa, bump bump."

"Really?" she says. "Bum pa bump bump?"

"It's the same as always," I say.

"I thought it was more like ba pa ba pa bum pa, you know, there at the end," she says.

"Rae," I say, "I know what a dying dog looks like. This dog isn't dying."

She doesn't hear me. She says, "Run your hand down his chest right below that place where his hair gets thick. Do you think that's a new lump?"

"No lump," I say. "This dog chased a rabbit today for a quarter of a mile without breaking stride."

She says, "How many breaths do you think he's taking a second right now?"

I say, "From the side he looked exactly like a four-legged dog, I think he felt like a four-legged dog."

"But really, Darlene, is it more than one a second?"

"Honey," I say, "listen to me. Turn on the TV, find a Lucy rerun. The dog is well. He's in my bed. It's my health you should worry about because I never get any covers."

This is what I mean about her. The dog is a miracle. Twenty-four months after chemo and still cancer-free. All those surgeries and he's chasing rabbits like he's fresh off the track. The heart, enlarged to the point where on paper it's not even pumping anymore. "Fortunately," Dr. Evans always says, "dogs don't walk on their X-rays."

You don't have to spend five minutes with Dante to know how big his heart is. I don't go in much for religion of any kind, and I wouldn't say this to just anybody, but I think making his heart bigger and bigger until it bursts means somebody up there is winking down at her saying they need him back. Or maybe, if there is such a thing as reincarnation, somebody needs him someplace else. The way she needed him before Howard came along.

She told me once, right after Dante was diagnosed, about a theory she has that if a person is living right, keeping their eyes open, the exact right dog will come to them, the dog that will teach them whatever set of lessons they need to learn right then.

"We're so lucky," she said, "to live so long, to get to know so many dogs, to learn from them."

It was late at night. She talks about stuff like that late at night, and I'm the kind of person if I'm not in bed by nine-thirty I can't be responsible for anything I think or say, but that night I remembered the dog my mom and I had when my dad left.

It was before she got the cancer, but not very long. My dad would come home from work at the plant every night, put down his lunch box and head straight outside and throw a tennis ball for that dog until it got dark. Our house backed up onto a steep ravine and he'd haul off on that ball and it would roll forever and the dog would bring it back, as many times as he would throw it down there.

In the winter he'd only be out there about a half an hour till it got too dark to see, but in the summertime they might be out there for two, three hours, him chucking that ball, the dog bringing it back.

When Dad left, the dog tried everything to get my mother and me to throw that ball for him. He'd put it down between our feet, in our dinner plates, on our pillows before we went to bed. Neither of us could bear to throw it. My mother started to take walks with the dog in the ravine instead, and a few weeks later I bought him a Frisbee, which he loved, but he never stopped trying to make us throw that ball.

Even when my mom got sick and I had to quit school and go to work at the Conoco, even, years later when the dog got sick, he'd drop that ball at my feet every single day when I came home.

I was sure, at the time, he was doing it for his own sake, his small dog brain unable to let go of the obsession, unable to let go of my dad, but that night when Rae started talking about the one right dog I wondered, what if he had some plan that we couldn't pick up on? What if that dog knew that all we had to do was go outside and throw that ball one time and we would have seen how much we didn't need my dad? Maybe we would have known then that we were strong without him. Maybe if my mother had thrown that ball she might have intimidated all those cancer cells straight back into remission. Maybe I would have stayed in school, met a man who had more going for him than a half-ton truck. That night I started to wonder what would happen if I started throwing that ball right then.

Criminy. They'll lock me up if they hear me talking like this. And anyway, I'm a cat person. Name 'em all after power tools. Decker, Makita, now Stanley. He's a fine cat. Lets Dante and Rose toss him around like a stuffed toy and leaps up and kills a pack rat half his size faster than you can say exterminator. Leaves a little pile of guts on the welcome mat for a present.

We get along just fine on our own here, Stanley and me. We get along just fine.

Howard #1:

It all started in Denver, in February, if you can believe it, not a month when I'm exactly at my best. The miracle was that I got out of the house at all that night. I've got what some people might call a little problem with videos. I watch about forty a week, and no, thank you very much, the majority of them are not X-rated.

I watch Shakespeare, and Jane Austen, everything from *Secrets and Lies* to *Dr. T and the Women*. There are a couple of Thai places and a Chinese in the same block as the video store, which is only three blocks from the house on Republican. What I'm saying is that in February, it's not that common an occurrence, me getting in my car and actually going somewhere.

It was Carmen who talked me into seeing the play. Carmen, my roommate and current mother substitute. It was opening night and Carmen was playing the crazy daughter —no crazier than any of us were in that house on Republican anyway—but in the play Carmen offs herself with a bottle of pills.

In real life Carmen says, whenever she sees that look in my eye, "You will not do that in my house, you will not leave me with that particular mess to clean up," and so far it's been enough to keep sending me to the corner for another five or six movies instead of anywhere else I might go.

I'm an actor, did I mention that? So you could make an argument, if you wanted, that all that time I spend watching movies is research, that's what my accountant calls it.

My therapist calls it agoraphobia, but I think that's fucked, because the truth is, I like to be looked at. I mean really, I . . . need to be looked at. I require it. Like a plant needs oxygen, I breathe in attention, from your eyes to my pores. Sometimes, if a mirror is tall and wide and clean enough, I can even feed myself. Even on my worst days, I take a lot of comfort in looking at my own reflection.

My wife, Rae—I still get a kick out of saying that—she doesn't really mind how much time I spend in front of the mirror. She says I'm pretty enough for both of us. Which is not to say that she's not pretty. Because she is, she just doesn't think so.

She is bigger around than anyone I ever dated, not fat . . . and I know what you're thinking, but she's not any of those other words either, Rubenesque, or pleasingly plump or matronly, words she says were made up by the same people who put those ads with the anorexic models right next to the articles on anorexia.

Her mom was anorexic. Died from it she says, although the death certificate officially said heart attack. She weighed 125 pounds every day from the time she was sixteen until she died at age sixty-nine, and she was tall, like Rae, but caved in a little in all the pictures I've ever seen of her.

Rae is sexy and round, and looks like she was meant to have babies, which she says we might do one day, once we figure out how to live with each other, and if we don't have our hands full with the dogs.

She has this belly, I call it the Buddha and I think it's the sexiest thing in the world, sitting up on top of her tight tan legs. She walks around all the time looking just a little bit pregnant, which must be one of those perpetuation-of-the-species instinctive turn-on things 'cause it gets me over and over, day in, day out.

She's got great legs. I've actually got pretty great legs myself. Rae says she especially likes my flanks . . . that's what she calls the sides of my thighs here: flanks. I love that. I like to dress up in Rae's bras and underwear and frilly night things sometimes. I know what you're thinking and you're not right about it, and that's the difference between my wife and every one of you, and every member of my family and every other girlfriend I've ever had. Rae understands me.

She says it's okay if I keep dressing up like a woman sometimes even if we have kids one day as long as we don't try to keep it a secret from them. Anyway, it's not what I live for or anything, cross-dressing, if that's what you want to call it. I'm an actor, you know, and we've all got a little of that.

You know what I live for? I live for the time of night when she comes to bed and turns toward me and bumps her Buddha belly up against me and puts her head on my chest.

Did I tell you about her hair? Silkier than any slip or camisole Victoria's Secret ever made, or at least any one I have personal experience with. As soft as the nose on a baby horse, that's how soft it is. She's kind of half wild anyway.

Just the other day she turned to me and asked why I thought human babies were so ugly, and I said they weren't all ugly, and she said, "But I mean like, compared to a lion cub for example. If I could give birth to a lion club," she said, "then I'd sign right up to have a baby. I know I could fall in love with it then."

I said I thought there was a good chance a baby we made would be as cute as a lion cub, and she looked at me kind of pityingly and said, "Oh Howard, the cutest human baby in all the world isn't as cute as the ugliest lion club," and there was something about the way she said it, I had to admit she was right.

On one of our first dates we went for fancy coffees and when I ordered mine with soy milk, she said, "What's that all about?" and I said,

"Oh, I'm lactose intolerant," and she said,

"HA!," a single note, high and fine, and I said,

"What, you don't believe me?" and she was still a little shy with me then and pushed my arm and shook her head as if I'd told her I could speak sixteen Chinese dialects. And even though I had experienced bloating and gas pains in my stomach on several occasions after drinking coffee with real milk I started to doubt myself right then and there on the subject, a doubt that stays with me even now.

I'm not gay. I'm going to say that one time, and I'm also going to say that it would be perfectly fine with me if I were gay, but it happens that I'm not.

Rae always said it would be okay if I changed my mind somewhere along the way, unless we decide, one day, to get pregnant. When we started to talk seriously about that she said, "Howard, I need to talk to you about something. I know you like to dress up in women's clothing and I know I've also said in the past that if you decided somewhere along the line you needed to experiment sexually with men it would be okay, and that I would even understand if you liked it better and I'd let you go, and the dogs and I, we'd find a way to carry on without you. But now you are talking about wanting to be a dad, and I've read too many books by the children of men who left their kids for that or a thousand other reasons and how it was the leaving that fucked them up, however good the reason. And I won't have my child fucked up that way, so if we ever did have a child, I might have to go back on what I said before."

Can you see why I love her so much?

I mean I don't know about you, but in the family I grew up in, we didn't ever talk to each other like that. In fact we hardly ever talked to each other period.

I mean if my sister Frances was mad at my other sister Connie, Frances would call up Dad on the phone and tell him about it, and then he'd discuss it with our stepmother Blanche, and then she might run it by her son Wally down in Florida, and then she'd get back to Dad who had in the meantime talked to Connie, and maybe somebody would pass it by me, although most likely not because I was the baby, and then by the time Dad got back to Frances she'd have forgotten what she was mad about and Connie had gone off to college or something.

And speaking of mad, Frances is, at me, right now. I mean really mad, like not-speak-to-me-in-months-and-months mad.

It happened the weekend Rae and I went back to Columbus, when I took my wife—of course she was only my sweetheart then—back east to meet my family. We had met so many people, and I was exhausted and I knew she was too, so I said, "Let's go over to Frances and Ed's," because that had always been the place where I could relax and watch TV or just lie on the couch and stare into space.

They live in this really cool house; I mean on the outside it's a normal suburban house in Upper Arlington, but on the inside it's all fish tanks. Giant fish tanks in every room, sometimes even forming the walls between the rooms. I think it's what they have instead of kids, thousands of tropical fish. And Ed—that's my sister's husband—he does tae kwon do, all the time.

He's some kind of master, whatever belt that is, and he does it at the dinner table. Everybody will be eating, maybe talking a little, and you'll see Ed's hand shoot out and do some move, some curvy kind of move. It's a thing of beauty, really.

I know their house is not what some people would think of as ideal for relaxing, but it always did it for me. All those air filters bubbling away and the fish swimming, Ed off in a corner doing his hand movements, nobody hardly saying a word.

But then Frances started to tell me about all the calling going on behind my back, the family calling, as Rae puts it. Blanche had called Louise, who had talked to Connie, who had called Frances, and it seemed that Blanche was—Frances's word—*concerned*. Connie had in turn talked to Dad, who talked to Blanche, who called her son Wally down in Florida, who had called Frances to reveal that Connie was—Frances's word—*nervous*

Then Frances launched into this huge diatribe on the seriousness of marriage, talking to us like we were teenagers, and I could see it wasn't going over too well because in the first place Rae's been married twice before and in the second place she's two years older than Frances and probably quite a bit smarter, and I could tell she was thinking about all the ways she could take Frances apart right there, and finally she made a decision I think was in the interest of continued familial relations and she just flopped over into my lap and went to sleep.

Then Frances tore into me, same old shit about me always needing to be the center of attention, and I said I thought that if there was ever a time it might be okay to be the center of attention, it might be on the weekend I'd chosen to bring my future wife home to meet my family, and that's when my sweetheart woke up all of a sudden and said, "Howard, we gotta get outta here," and I could see that she was right so we did.

I USED TO HAVE anxiety attacks. I used to take a whole lot of medication. Paxil for depression, and Amitriptyline to sleep, and Xanax for anxiety, and of course with all that I also needed Viagra. And sometimes something to settle my stomach, and caffeine to get me going after all those other drugs put me to sleep. You get the picture.

But here's the thing. I'm an actor. I can act like a person who is having an anxiety attack. I can appear suicidal. I know all the lines. I could get myself a prescription for lithium if I really wanted one. I could get myself locked up. I could convince Doctor Ruth, Doctor Drew, even Dr. Sigmund Freud himself that I was bonkers. I could even convince myself.

I told Rae about my anxiety attacks on our first full weekend together. Then, right after I proposed to her I told her about the nervous breakdown I had had in Portugal the year before. I even read her all the surrounding entries in my journal, an act that she now calls the stupidest thing anyone has ever done in the world history of relationships. That may have been going too far, but I thought it was only fair that she knew.

Knew what? That I had successfully convinced everybody including every member of my family, every member of the house on Republican, and three licensed psychiatrists that I had had a nervous breakdown when really I was just pissed off because Jennifer, the girl I had gone to Portugal with, wasn't as serious about me as I wanted her to be?

I read Rae every journal entry. All the sex—real and fantasized—all the whining—all the pathetic vengeful wanderings of my mind. She looked at me steadily while I read. Any normal person would have run screaming from the room.

Maybe I could tell she wasn't convinced by the journal, so I decided to give her a sample of the real thing. I had primed her a little earlier when we were driving back to her apartment from dinner. It was pouring, I mean hellacious the-heavens-are-open-wash-all-those-Colorado-sinners-into-the-sea kind of rain, and I opened the moonroof and stood up between the two seats and with the upper half of my body out of the car getting what felt like bucketsful of water thrown in my face on the I-25 at seventy miles an hour I started screaming about writing with my own piss and excrement and when that didn't seem to be having any effect I sang, in its entirety, "Love Rears Up Its Ugly Head," a song by Living Color I happen to like, the lyrics go, well, just how you'd think they'd go, and I could see by the end of the song that she was getting pretty wet down there so I yelled, "Am I scaring you yet?" and she looked up at me like it was a normal day, like we weren't in the middle of a storm that would send all the Methodist farmers in Columbus, Ohio, back to church for at least a couple of Sundays, and she hadn't just recently agreed to spend the rest of her life with me, and she said, "No, are you trying to?"

So I came down out of the moonroof and curled up against her arm and cried for a while for the little boy whose mother was perpetually about to die, and for the not quite grown man who had just found the second person on the face of the earth who actually understood him. "Don't die," I said between sobs, and she said she'd try not to.

And you would have thought that would have been enough for one night, but then I got the idea to read the journal aloud and when that didn't even faze her, I launched into a full-scale panic attack right there in the apartment. Whining, crying, hair-pulling, rocking, and then comatose, I know all the steps.

She kept looking at me, sitting on the other double bed while I lay on the one that was against the wall, my breath slow and ragged, my eyes half closed.

"You know," she said, "I'm sorry, but I'm not really convinced."

I probably opened one eye then, a little more than the other.

"This guy with the panic attacks," she said, "I'm afraid he's not a very good actor. He doesn't really say anything original or specific. You'll have to forgive me if I'm in error here and you really are in dire pain, but I'm just not buying this guy."

I had both eyes open now and I turned my head sideways so I could see her straight on. "Would you believe I'm lactose intolerant?" I said. She gave me the briefest of smiles and went into the bathroom and turned on the shower.

When she came out of the shower I said, "I want you to bite me, and I want you to leave a mark." And I did. I wanted this big girl to mark me. I'm gonna be honest here. I had never really even looked at a girl who wasn't skinny. I mean all the way back to middle school, when I had all my hair and I was the hottest thing going.

My friend Terryl tried to tell me, "Hey man, you gotta get yourself a round woman, you want to know about loving. Round women, they got generosity down to their cells."

Take Carmen for instance, she's really round. Extremely. And when I first moved into the house on Republican she went around telling practically every goddamned person in the Denver theater community that if she hadn't been married to Duke she would have gone after me, which is good for the ego in a certain way, I guess, but I mean we all had to live together in that house, and what anybody could see who even glanced in our direction is that both Duke and Carmen needed me in the middle of their marriage to lust after in their own little ways, and I wonder if the marriage will have a glass of water's chance in hell now that I'm gone.

But I'm getting off the subject. I asked Rae to bite me and she did. Hard, and not just once.

At first she had that look on her face like, *what next*, you know? But then she really started to get into it. I mean she'd clamp down on some flesh, say, on my belly or in the middle of my back and I'd yell, "Is that the best you can do?" And she'd clamp down harder, slow and steady, like an animal who wants to feel the pleasure of the exact moment of the kill. And I wouldn't yell out until I was sure she was about to break the skin and then she'd always let go, but it was fun to think about what would happen if she didn't.

DID I TELL YOU about my mom? Her name was Mary Elizabeth and she was so beautiful. I have her lips, which Rae says—even including my legs—are my very best feature. Rae says the day after she met me at that play, she and Victoria—who is a director I work for and Rae's oldest friend—spent the whole next evening talking about my lips. They're my mom's lips. And it's my mom's diamond I gave Rae when I asked her to marry me.

Frances was keeping it for me, because it's true I've never been all that good at hanging on to things, and she gave it to me that first night Rae and I were in Columbus but after the next night, when Rae fell asleep in the middle of her diatribe, I got a phone message from Frances asking for it back.

I called Frances then and suggested that if the idea that I might be destined for a life of love and happiness was giving her such a hernia she might want to sign up for a little ther-

apy herself. Which I have come to understand is not a suggestion that most people take kindly to, even if it is delivered
with the best of intentions. She hung up on me when I said
it, and I haven't heard from her since.

Someday I'd like to name a baby after my mother, and it
would be okay with me if it was a baby wolfhound instead of
a baby human being. We could call her Mary Ellen, which is
close to Mary Elizabeth, but not quite. Rae says it's better to
do close but not quite in case somewhere down the road I
recover some locked-up childhood memories and find out
that my mom was really some kind of bitch from hell.

Rae says it might not be the right thing to have a kid,
because I still have a whole lot of kid in me, and she says she
does too, but in a slightly less optimistic way. She says the
worst being married to me ever gets is when it feels like she's
the single parent of the greatest thirty-two-year-old kid in
the world, which really isn't all that bad, she says, and the rest
of the time it's even better than that.

Rae says my family is stuck in some kind of Twilight
Zonesque lifelong mini-series in which I play the mercurial
and mildly dangerous young son whose actions give all the
other characters an opportunity to be grateful for their own
powers of denial, and I know it's true. When my father proposed to Blanche Remington, not six months after my
mother was in the ground and I wasn't, perhaps, quite as
eager as my siblings were to embark upon a series of family
bonding vacations with my new Remington brother and sisters, I got shipped off to the psychiatrist who put a big old
prescription bottle of pills in my hand, and that was how that
vicious cycle got started.

Not too long after that I packed all my things into a Honda hatchback and left Columbus, Ohio, once and forever. I landed in Denver, where I managed to work in the theater often enough to pay the bills, where I had a handful of, not so much friends as fellow commiserates, and where more often than I'd like to admit, especially in winter, I didn't come out of my house for days at a time if I had movies and Pepperidge Farm cookies and leftover Chinese food.

But now that's all changed. I'm somebody's husband. I might even be the dad of a little two- or four-legged Mary Ellen one day. You might be somewhat worried about me in that respect, and I don't blame you, but I think I'm starting to figure it all out. See, I can act just like somebody's husband. I can act just like the best daddy that anybody ever had. And I can keep acting that way for a hundred years.

You could too if you wanted. I think pretty much anybody could. I can act like somebody who is going to love my wife forever, and then I can act that way some more. And don't think that means for a minute that I don't love her, because I do, and I will, forever, but she would say that's a separate thing.

She says there are always two worlds running side by side, one's called the truth, or the way things should have happened, and the other's called what really happened, and most of the time the two don't converge, but every now and then they do and she says those are the times we call moments of Grace.

She says some people only get a few of those moments and other people get a few more, but the important thing is to live toward them, to be ready for them, to act as if they are always about to happen, and in that acting, make them so. She says that's how the stage can work, when the actors bring the truth into being, though it doesn't happen in life very often, which I suppose is the whole point.

One time in my life I acted toward the truth of those panic attacks. Even though they weren't what was really happening, they were true, they were the truest expression of how I felt inside. Then they became untrue, and Rae saw that they were untrue and called me on it. Now I act toward a different truth, the truth of a good life with her. I sleep like a baby with her and one or another of those great big dogs on top of me. I'm down to one pill a day and it's not even a very big one. I can drink a whole glass of milk now and not even fart.

I see a future now that the guy who was all locked up with his VCR in the house on Republican couldn't have conceived of, a future with large dogs and small children, garbage to be carried to the curb on Wednesday nights and a new refrigerator to buy on a weekend in June. Slow seasons that tumble in to each other until we can no longer agree on how many years we've been married, the rest of my hair gone, her crow's feet deepening, two lamps on in the living room illuminating the pages of two separate books.

It's its own kind of hubris, I know, to wish for such simple rapture. Whether that will be what really happens I can't say, but I know it's the truest thing, the thing that ought to happen, and maybe I can make it happen just by the way I act.

Brooklyn Underhill #1:

My belief in service is what brought me here. Service to my family, to my country, and to God.

I was raised in the Church of Jesus Christ of Latter-Day Saints, my grandfather and his only brother were killed on the beaches of Normandy. My family lived on a farm outside of Walden, Colorado, in the prettiest valley this side of Zion, and my grandmother lived with us all our lives. She was a strong woman who gave my five brothers and me the kind of love you take straight to the bank for a lifetime's worth of dividends.

In Walden we had working horses and a small herd of beef cattle, outdoor dogs and indoor dogs, cats in the barn and goats for milk and for cheese, a pen full of exotic chickens my mother loved because they laid blue and green eggs. A trout steam ran right through the middle of the property and we made a trail through the national forest to ride our bikes to town and to school. There was nothing on all sides of us but plenty to be grateful for, and if we ever forgot that, my grandma had us cleaning out the shower grout or scrubbing poop off the carrier pigeon hotel until we remembered.

Colorado Mormons are different from the Utah kind. My mother was a painter, and my dad would never have dared call what she did a hobby. "No one twisted my arm to make me have six children," she was always saying, "I just seemed to get more and better painting done with one baby boy or another hanging in a Snugli around my neck." She named me after the one place besides Walden she could imagine herself living. She had once read a novel that was set in the borough of Brooklyn, and she said it sounded like a good place to set her imagined parallel life.

My dad had the only reliable snowplow in Jackson County in winter, raised enough vegetables to feed half the county in the summer, no small thing at 8,099 feet above sea level, and made sure my brothers and I spent at least as much time with schoolwork as we did with farm chores and fun.

I went to college in Greeley on the GI bill. Then I went to the Gulf War with the 24th Infantry Division to pay my country back. When I got home from the war my grandmother was ill, so I went back to Walden to be with her till she died, to find out what she might have left to teach me.

All that summer my grandma and I would sit in the shade of the big aspen grove that overlooked the garden. We could see my dad pulling the weeds from rows of turnips, parsnips and rutabagas. We could see my mom moving around in the big glassy studio my father had built for her to celebrate her first exhibition in a downtown Denver gallery.

It was back before the drought began, and the meadows were green and tall enough to swallow the big Bouvier that my father favored, as well as Cronkite, the miniature pony that some gypsy healer had come to town and left behind.

My grandmother asked me what I wanted to do with my life and I told her I was thinking about going to vet school.

She smiled and nodded. "Your great-grandfather had a way with horses," she said, "you'll have genetics on your side."

"The school isn't far," I said, "I'll come home every weekend and see you."

She shook her head and turned away, but didn't disagree.

I took her hand then, traced the freckles that made a Big Dipper on the inside of her wrist.

"What is it, Brooklyn, do you think makes people happy?" she asked.

I refilled her glass of lemonade from the pitcher my mother had left with us that morning. The ice was long melted, and the smell of the tiny lavender blossoms she always mixed in with the liquid had gotten stronger in the heat.

"I would think," I said, "that would depend on the person."

"That's what they think too," she said, smiling, "but they're wrong."

I looked down at my own hands, which had aged in the war and now looked more like my father's. I didn't want to waste another answer, but my father was walking toward us with an armload of mustard greens and chard and radishes, and when he got there he would ask me to take them inside and clean them, get them ready to be braised for dinner that night.

"The land?" I said, since that's what she was looking at, the Eden she'd lived on or near since she was a girl.

"Not the land," she said, "not fame, not money, not work, not art." She glanced over at my mother in her studio. "Not even love."

"Though love is nice," I said, and she gripped my hands tighter.

"Very, very nice," she said. "All of these things can be nice," she said, "even money. They will make you happy for ten minutes each, but ten minutes isn't long, held next to a life."

I had spent a lot of time that summer thinking about how to earn money, and even more time thinking about how to find love. My father had stopped to wash his hands at the garden well.

"I don't know then," I said, "tell me."

"You do," she said, and I wracked my brain.

"Maybe you're giving me more credit," I said, "than I deserve."

"Maybe," she said, "you're afraid to admit what you know."

My father was moving toward us again.

"Service?" I said, because that had always been the word in my head. When I was a child I thought it was God actually speaking it. I still thought that might be true.

She nodded. "Generosity," she said, "is the word I would use, but if service is your word, I think we mean the same thing."

My father approached and handed her a lavender and white columbine. "I broke it accidentally," he told her, "I know you'd rather see it on the vine." He handed the bundle of greens to me and I rose to take them to the kitchen. Across the field a Cooper's hawk was calling to his mate.

"I was thinking," I said, "of reenlisting, of being an Army veterinarian when I get done with school."

"That sounds like a good plan," my father said, though he had already heard it, had said the same exact words in answer the night before.

"This has nothing to do with paybacks," my grandmother said, "nothing that you owe, nothing you are owed in return."

"I know that," I said, because I had learned it in the Gulf War. I knew that on earth there was no fairness other than whatever we created. I knew how the logic of an eye for an eye failed the minute a 1.15-billion-dollar airplane dropped cluster bombs on a village whose people didn't have enough to eat.

"What you don't yet know," she said, "is that the reward is immediate, consistent, reliable." She shook her head. "Some days it seems the whole world has forgotten."

"Forgotten what?" my father said.

"Kindness," I said.

"That too," she said.

"I'm kind," my father said.

"Mostly," my grandmother said.

"Other people say so," he said, and I marveled, as always, at how quickly in her presence the patriarch became a little boy.

"Happiness that lingers is not the face the world turns to you, Benjamin," she said. "It is the face you turn to the world."

"I think you have an excellent face," I said to my father.

"Go wash the greens," they said in unison, and I left them there, watching leaf shadows move across the grass.

MY CLASSMATES HAD a harder time seeing my logic. Vet school is no picnic. It's everything that's hard about med school, with the added complication that your patients can't tell you what hurts.

Anybody smart and determined enough to get into one of the top vet schools is looking at specialization. Cardiology, Radiology, Oncology, Nuclear Medicine. If you can get yourself invited into an established group, you're talking three hundred dollars minimum for fifteen minutes of your very highly regarded opinion, a three-day work week, and if you have the sense to hire somebody to do your investing for you, retirement at age forty-five.

There are a handful of people who hang around the university after vet school, either because they believe that research dollars will help them discover some new way to prolong and improve life and thereby achieve notoriety, or simply because they are the type of person who sees a need and fills it. Dr. Evans, I think, was a little of both.

It's not like he and I hit it off personally—I don't think he actually hits it off with anybody—but I can't ignore the power of his work ethic, the power of his dedication to the animals. He spends more after-hours hours at the hospital than any other doctor. If he's got a patient in ICU you won't get him out of the building with handcuffs and a straitjacket, but even when he's off-clinics you're likely to see him over in Accounting arguing down the bill of some old lady who makes six thousand dollars a year and has seventeen cats—eight of them with cancer. Or he might be sneaking in a vanload of Humane Society dogs for X-rays and shots on the weekend.

Fourth-year students like me spend a series of six-week rotations working side by side with a lineup of different specialists, and I drew his name for my surgery assignment.

It's all old news now, of course. How this young upstart doctor with too much attitude and not enough social skill started doing limb-spare surgeries on dogs with osteosarcoma using a method no one had ever thought of before. That's what medical advancement often is, an obnoxious kid with a good idea and somebody else's money behind him.

Dr. Evans's idea was to remove the tumored ulna, leaving large margins of course, and then cut out the radius and flip it upside down, so it would fit back in the place where the ulna used to be. This took thirteen hours under the microscope because it was also his idea to reattach every vein, every capillary that was not so small that it dissolved in his fingers. He wanted to fashion a highway in the reconstructed limb that would carry the chemotherapeutics in and around and below the original tumor site, increasing the odds that the cancer wouldn't return.

What he never counted on was the "infection affect." And even after the international veterinary community made a hero out of him, even after he'd been to twenty states and sixteen countries delivering papers on Dante, even as the limb-spare was failing, and the graft succeeding—I'm not even sure that Rae knows this and I hope it won't upset her, but they kept that leg alive with machines and refrigerators for three months after they eventually cut it off—he still couldn't mention the postsurgical infection in his talks. There had never been a controlled study, and without a controlled study in medicine, you're a fool if you don't keep all your theories and results to yourself.

But we saw what we saw, and we knew what we knew, and what we knew was that Dante, and the six limb-spared dogs that came after him that spring, all developed postsurgical infections of some kind, and have all lived far longer than the statistical average, some of them, like Dante, two and three times longer.

"I hate to be crude," Dr. Evans told Rae, "but his leg was essentially hanging off his body for an entire day."

When the inside of a body is exposed to the air for thirteen hours, even in a "sterile" environment like an operating theater, you're going to get some kind of infection. What you hope is that you can treat the infection, so that you haven't saved the leg and killed the dog.

But what if the body's reaction to the infection, an exponentially increased immuno-response coming immediately on the heels of the removal of the tumor, actually keeps the cancer cells from regaining their hold at the site of the original invasion?

Then it may have been that nasty infection that gave Dante one, and now two years of cancer-free life.

"Or," I hear my grandmother saying, "maybe it is God or good works." And nobody argues with my grandmother.

There were plenty of people engaged in good works on behalf of Dante. He was the Veterinary Class of 1999's good-luck charm, and when he got septic and lost all that weight there wasn't anybody, not even the dermatologists, who didn't look in on him, bring him a liver treat, offer him a little wet food the way I discovered he preferred it, on the end of a stainless steel fork.

Dr. Evans did his best to keep Rae's expenses down, using the ends of ten different bandage rolls for Dante's rewraps, and issuing his pain medication on Sunday morning when nobody was there to see him come and go from the supply room. Dante's big leg looked like a rolled-up rainbow sucker half the time.

"It's a rare owner," Dr. Evans would say to me, "who puts up the money to support this kind of research." I didn't tell him that he was preaching to the choir, that I myself gathered all the leftover cotton and alcohol from the first-year students' ER classes for Dante's four daily wound flushings, that every time I found a fleece in the ICU dryer, I added it to the floor of his cage so the cold of the concrete would never seep up and chill his skinny hips.

Rae had two big scars I finally asked her about—on the same limb where Dante had his tumor: left front.

"I had my own limb-spare," she said, rolling up her sleeve. The scars ran from her wrist to her elbow, one over the radius, one over the ulna. "I lost an argument with a young horse over that one," she said. "In my case it took two years before they knew whether I was going to keep my arm or not."

DANTE'S INFECTION APPEARED when Dr. Evans was off-clinics for a couple of days, in Hawai'i with his wife. Old Dr. Morganstern decided he was going to save everyone a lot of money and heartache and take the leg off right then and there. It was a common thing, the older doctors ganging up on Dr. Evans in those days. Of course they'd be lucky to dust the awards on his desktop now.

Doctors Morganstern, Stone, and Wallace had Rae cornered in the waiting room when I got there. Dante was at her feet with a big candy-cane bandage over the leg.

"The leg is septic," Dr. Morganstern said. "In a matter of time, the dog will be. It's time to cut your losses. Lose the leg. Save the dog."

"Dr. Evans said that beating the infection might save the dog," Rae said.

"There is no empirical evidence to support that."

"We haven't even talked about osteomyelitis," Dr. Stone said. "That seems inevitable without the amputation."

Rae looked over at me, and I smiled at her but I didn't dare speak up.

"Dr. Evans said this surgery was important," she said, "not just for Dante, but for research, for the future."

"That's a lovely idea—" Dr. Wallace began.

"Dr. Evans said that even if the graft only stayed alive for a few weeks, they would learn a lot. There's a Malamute with Osteo, Colossus, I think her name is—"

"Sepsis," Dr. Stone said, "can kill in a matter of hours, Miss—"

"Rae," she said, without looking at him.

"Rae, then," said Morganstern, "I know that the limb-spare surgery was very costly."

"This isn't about the money," she said

"And that a simple amputation," Dr. Wallace said, "would have cost thousands less."

"Did you not hear," Rae said, "what I said?"

"Sometimes," Dr. Stone began, "young doctors have an idea that drives them to make decisions—"

"Save it," Rae said, "please," and for a couple of minutes, everybody did.

"You will neither believe nor understand this," Rae finally said, "but Dante has . . . has made it clear to me that he wants to keep fighting the infection, that he wants this experiment to go as far as it possibly can."

At this point, among the doctors, looks were exchanged.

"As I understand it," Morganstern said, "Dr. Evans feels that Dante would do very well on three legs."

"That's right," Rae said.

At first, Dr. Evans had been afraid that Dante was too tall, and not entirely sound in his hindquarters. But then he took note of how Dante's eyes never left Rae when they were together, of how he picked up that big bulky cast only twenty-four hours after the first surgery and crossed the hospital lawn to get to her. After that we all knew Dante would find a way to make it work.

"I'm aware that it takes a little time to get used to a three-legged dog visually," Dr. Stone said.

Dante sighed and began chewing on his toenails that stuck out of the bottom of the cast.

"I don't know how to make you . . ." she said, but stopped herself.

I didn't know either, but I did know that the last person on earth they were going to listen to was a fourth-year vet student on his way to a general practice on behalf of the U.S. Army.

"I couldn't have put him through all this," she said. "I wouldn't have put him through all this, if I thought there was any chance that I would come into this room and all of you . . . whoever you are . . . would just decide to give up. . . ."

"Medicine is an inexact science," Morganstern said. "Dante might have died on the operating table."

"Exactly," she said. "But at least he would have died try-ing." She was crying now and I could feel their satisfaction, feel their sense of closing in on her.

My grandmother had passed away three months after I started vet school. *What face you turn to the world,* was what she had said.

"Maybe," I said, "Rae would like to speak to Dr. Evans on the phone before she makes this decision."

The doctors turned on me like some white-coated Cerberus, barking out all the disclaimers I already knew by heart, about the team effort at the vet school, about Dr. Evans's hard work and deserved time off, about the impossi-bility of securing the phone number, about the irregularity of even considering such a thing.

"I have the number," I said. "He gave it to me for just this reason before he left."

It did my heart good to watch them stumble a bit over that one. In spite of their seniority they were all a little frightened of Dr. Evans, his combination of skill and bravery, the way he moved through the halls like a hammerhead shark.

"Excellent!" said Morganstern. "I thought it would be impossible to reach him."

Rae went in the other room and called Dr. Evans on her cell phone. The conversation was short and in my imagina-tion took place in very short sentences, a language designed more for dogs than for humans, their own unrecorded code.

When she came back Rae said, "I've decided to stay with

Dr. Evans's plan. As soon as Dante goes back to his cage, Brooklyn will start him on the new superantibiotic. If his condition hasn't improved by morning, Dr. Evans will arrive by three o'clock tomorrow afternoon."

"Well, Dr. Evans is an excellent surgeon," Morganstern said. "I'm sure he told you what a rough road this is going to be, how the prognosis is anything but good."

"Actually," Rae said, "he asked me if I wanted it to be simple, or if I wanted him to be honest. Then he held his breath and waited for me to say I would stick to his plan."

I took Dante back to his cage and gave him the new antibiotic. In honor of Dr. Evans, I slept in the cage with him all that night.

THAT WASN'T THE LAST time Rae had to stand behind Dr. Evans, and as the surgeries mounted up and kept failing, it got harder and harder for her to keep her resolve. After the fourth failed surgery even Dr. Evans was defeated. The graft pumped along like a champion, but even with nails and screws and artificial hinges, the elbow could not stay engaged enough to support Dante's hundred and fifty pounds.

The amputation took place at three-thirty in the afternoon. Dante's condition was nowhere near critical, but Dr. Evans slept in post-op with him, for old times' sake.

At three-thirty in the morning Dr. Evans said, "You want to go outside?" and Dante jumped up, tail wagging, hopped across the linoleum and down the hall to the exit door as though he'd been a tripod since birth. He'd been carrying around that rainbow cast for almost six months. It was a relief for all of us to see it gone.

But when Rae came to pick him up later that morning nobody wanted it all to be over. Dante was finished with chemotherapy as well, and they were headed to Rae's ranch in the mountains for the summer. As long as the cancer remained in remission, we'd have no reason to see them again.

"I want you to be the one," Rae said. "I mean when the time comes—"

"Of course," Dr. Evans said, before she'd gotten all the words out.

Dante looked from one to the other of us, wagging his tail softly. Nobody seemed to have anything else to say.

"Brooklyn," Dr. Evans finally said, "be sure to get a pint of blood from Rae before they take off today." He looked at his shoes, so Rae and I did too, as if whatever he was talking about might be found there.

"I've decided I'm going to try to clone her," he said. "Make our job a lot easier around here."

I could tell by the look on Rae's face that it was the first compliment he had ever paid her, and by the look on his that giving it had practically undone him.

"We'll see you again," he said to her, "but let's not make it for a long, long time."

Three

•

The
Courtship

Rae #2:

The first thing I see when I look all the way back is my mother examining herself in her magnifying mirror, plucking out what few eyebrows she actually had and embarking upon her very extensive, but not tackily excessive makeup regimen.

She was a beautiful woman, and she was both adored and doomed in all the ways that beautiful women are. Her favorite car was an MG Midget, dark green, that my babysitter Esther Robinson always called the Pretzel Bender. Her drink was Tanqueray and tonic—easy on the tonic—with a twist. Her favorite color was yellow, her favorite season was summer, her favorite ice cream was homemade peach.

She was anorexic before you ever heard the word, and to hear one doctor tell it, it was the combination of her high blood pressure and her habit of trading breakfast and lunch for cocktail calories that eventually killed her. But she could rip through a jar of dill pickles in five minutes flat (sometimes drinking all the juice when she was finished) and if she got her hands on a rack of lamb—even in a fancy restaurant— she'd chew on the bones until they looked like they'd been bleached in the desert.

Her audition songs were "Moon River," "How Are Things in Gloccamora," and one a famous composer wrote just for her called "I Said to Love" about a young woman who turns love down one too many times and winds up old and alone. Her favorite TV shows were *What's My Line* and *To Tell the Truth*, and eventually *Wheel of Fortune*. Her favorite singers were Frank Sinatra, Linda Ronstadt, and oddly, Bob Seger, right around the time of "Night Moves." She especially liked his song "You'll Accompany Me," though I knew if she knew what he looked like, she would never approve of his tattoos.

She was so deathly afraid of water that she always took baths instead of showers, but she loved the beach and if the sand was flat and hard enough she'd do handsprings, even into her sixties. She'd been a cheerleader, an acrobat, a dancer, when she was young. She hated school, and after her Aunt Bette, who raised my mother, gave her the five dollars she was promised if she found a way to pass her ninth-grade history class, my mother used it for a bus ticket to New York City, and never looked back.

"Of course, New York was a much different place in those days," she'd always say when she got to that part of the story. She loved to tell about her *Uncle* Tom and *Uncle* Don, dancers themselves, who pulled the scared, but undeniably talented fourteen-year-old off the streets. The way they found her an agent, gave her singing lessons, discovered she was quick on the uptake and marketed her as a singing dancing comedienne.

She loved to tell about working off and off-off and every now and again on Broadway with Walter Pidgeon and Nancy Walker. WWII came along and she went overseas with Bob Hope, and when it was over, she went to Vegas, to open the act for Frank Sinatra in his long engagement at the Desert Sands. She liked to talk about what an ass he was, how they would pass behind the backstage curtain—she going off, he going on—and he wouldn't even glance at her, how in two and a half years he never once said, *Good show.*

"A sexy broad like I was," she'd say, "and he looked right through me. There's just no accounting for some people's taste."

It has always fascinated me, the way people don't talk to one another. A lot of times they don't listen either. Like two radios tuned to different stations, shouting over each other across a flat empty yard. That might be the thing that started me playwriting, how fast people stick to their own agenda. How they never say what they mean, how I don't, how the world teaches us not to.

That and Esther Robinson, who taught me to read and who gave me a Dr. Seuss book called *On Beyond Zebra*, about the twenty-six letters that came after Z and all of the creatures you could make from them. Esther gave me a penny for every road sign I read and a nickel for every billboard, and a dime every time I jumped in the city pool, and a quarter for a dive and a fifty-cent piece for the high dive and like that, until I could swim like a fish. *On Beyond Zebra* gave me the first inkling that language was infinite, though I'm sure I had yet to learn the word. *The Adventures of Mrs. Pigglewiggle* made me believe in magic, and *The Secret Garden* made me understand that it might be a good thing to be lonely sometimes.

My mother loved to sew and until I was a certain age made nearly all of my clothing. I learned to stand in front of the mirror for what felt like hours, while she moved straight pins from her mouth to the hem of my shirt or skirt or sleeves. She believed in the A-line skirt, the tapered pant leg, dark, slimming colors, and above all else shoulder pads, but she did once make me a hot pink bellbottom jumpsuit with rhinestone buttons that I wore proudly with purple platform shoes to my seventh-grade *Summer Breeze* dance.

The only person my mother hated more passionately than Richard Nixon was Pat, taking the most offense at the cloth coat she wore as evidence of her humility. My mother was outspoken about her politics which were liberal and heartfelt, if somewhat ill-informed, and always the exact opposite of my father's. Her obituary in *Variety* said that she had been blacklisted during the McCarthy hearings, and it pleased me to imagine that she might have had more of a secret life than I realized, more depths than those life with my father would allow her to plumb.

What my mother never told people is that her mother (my grandmother, though I have never learned to think of her that way) died in childbirth with her, and that her father ran off before either the ink on the death certificate or my mother's birth certificate had begun to dry.

Looking back now, it seems obvious that my mother would have considered my passing from her body and into the world a sentence that brought the end of everything: her happiness, her marriage, her freedom, her life. And though she lived until six months past my thirtieth birthday, though her marriage lasted that long too, history is a starfish that grows an extra arm no matter how many times the original limb is severed. It is no accident that I have lived nearly forty years now without having a child.

My mother spent decades trying to convince herself that being a mom was exactly what she wanted, and I spent at least the first decade of my life trying to make it true. I spent way more nights than I can count and far too many school days backstage in some dusty New York theater or nightclub, all dressed up . . . a little more Caroline Kennedy than Shirley Temple. I would sit on a big black baby grand in Mary Janes, socks with ruffles, and a black and white corduroy pinafore, waiting for my turn to sing "These Boots Are Made For Walkin'," which I did with some regularity from age four to age eight. I called Walter Pidgeon *Pee-pidge* for short and when I was five he was my escort when I was the poster princess for the Trenton, New Jersey, Easter Parade.

In eighth grade my parents sent me off to Wales as an exchange student, and my host family took me to Stratford-on-Avon and I saw *Henry V* performed on an empty stage save for Kenneth Branagh standing on a three-step stool giving his St. Crispin's Day speech. I didn't understand that the play was about war until years later when the movie came out and I saw all those horses and wagons mired in mud. I thought *Henry V* was about language, and love, and in a way I still do, and I decided right there in Stratford that I wanted to be a playwright so that someday, somebody like Kenneth Branagh would say my words for me.

My friend Jonathan says that I'm a bad appreciator of fine art because no matter what the form, I'm really only interested in the words. At art museums I can hardly keep my eyes from the title plaque and on the painting; when I buy a new CD I miss the music for the lyrics. Sometimes I'd rather read a play than see it, which Jonathan says is unforgivable, but I'm the one who had to tell him that Springsteen's latest album was entirely written from the point of view of 9/11 survivors, and if there is one thing that Jonathan doesn't like to be wrong about, it's anything to do with the Boss.

Jonathan says he started writing plays to give the voices in his head somewhere to be when he didn't want to pay attention. He's always said he is mildly schizophrenic and I didn't really believe him until that time we were riding those draft horses that belonged to Teatro Spagnola near Brindisi, Italy, and the little red fox dashed between two olive trees and sent both the horses galloping at such a pace there was nothing to do but hold on for dear life. My horse stumbled and I dropped the reins and leaned down to put my arms around his big neck, which threw my balance all out of whack, and I kept shouting to Jonathan to turn his horse hard to the left and he just kept staring straight ahead as if he weren't hearing me. Later he said he was doing his best to block me out the whole time because he didn't think it was me, he thought it was the voices.

"Wait," I said, "you mean one of your voices sounds like me?"

"One of my voices is you," he said, and I said,

"What's that supposed to mean?" and he said,

"Forget it."

WHEN PEOPLE ASK ME how big an Irish wolfhound is, I tell them, big enough to eat off a plate in the center of your dining room table with all four feet still on the ground. We had a bring-your-favorite-French-food party up at the ranch one night to celebrate the end of a long run of a play I wrote that was set in the Dordogne. On a platter I had arranged four French cheeses in a circle, with a round of bloc de foie gras in the center, the last tin I had carried back with me after my time in France.

We were sitting in the living room sipping Pernot when I heard a barely audible slurp. I ran to the kitchen to find nothing but a yellow stain in the center of the platter and Dante sitting quietly, wagging and wagging his tail. What impressed me most that evening was Dante's discerning palate, the way his tongue must have maneuvered up and over the pont l'évêque or the cabecou and then under the foie gras so deftly that he was able to lift the entire six ounces of goose liver, and swallow them all in one gulp.

Dante was nothing but arms and legs when Zelda, his breeder, handed him to me in the parking lot of a Yellow Front discount store in Delta, Colorado. Two months before I had ridden on a plane next to a long-haired young man who spent most of the flight crying, and when I finally worked up the courage to ask him what was wrong he pulled a picture out of his coat pocket of a huge and wiry-haired dog standing with all four paws on the kitchen linoleum, drinking water straight from the kitchen-sink tap.

"The late great Zaphod," he said, recovering a little. "Irish wolfhound. Greatest dog that ever walked the earth."

We talked until the plane touched down in Denver, and though Mike wasn't the type of guy I would take a book or restaurant recommendation from, there was something in the way he talked about that dog that stayed with me. When I saw an advertisement for Irish wolfhounds in the *Denver Post* I called the listed number.

Zelda lived in Grand Junction. She had one puppy left from the litter, a boy, who was, she said, *pet quality,* which sounded like a good thing to me. She agreed to meet me halfway between the ranch and Grand Junction, and when she handed him over to me—he was twelve weeks old and weighed thirty-five pounds—he buried his nose in my armpit and kept it there until Zelda had driven away.

Once we got into the 4-Runner he was so insistent about being in my lap that I finally gave in, pushing the seat as far back as it would go and straining my feet to reach the pedals. I named him after Colorado Rockies outfielder Dante Bichette, because I'd been to a game the day before I went to pick up the puppy and I liked the way it sounded when the announcer said his name. Dante learned his name in a day, was house-trained in less than a week, and the only things of value he chewed up in his entire puppyhood were an autographed *Seven Plays* by Sam Shepard and the left rear leg of my piano bench.

When Dante was a little more than a year old, when his muscles had developed to their full strength, but he had not yet begun to feel the effects of age (this is a slim window, even for a wolfhound who doesn't contract cancer, as their average life expectancy is only seven and a half years), we would hike up to the top of the Continental Divide which stretches out and up behind my ranch. After several hours we would come to a high alpine meadow, as wide as ten football fields and twice that long, that I always guessed to be just under twelve thousand feet. The altitude and the mountain goats kept the grass tundra-short, the way it is on a golf course or in a formal garden.

On the way up the hill, Dante would take his favorite position right behind me, wet nose occasionally brushing the back of my knee, but when we got to the meadow I would sit in the center of that grass-and-stunted-wildflower carpet and he would run giant circles around me, his body impossibly extended, his paws barely brushing the surface of the earth, like a Thoroughbred on a racetrack, like a dervish making some kind of ultimate contact with God.

When he was finished he would trot over, lower himself to the ground beside me, and we would watch the clouds move across the sky together and wait for him to regain his breath. I always felt, walking home from those outings, that I was somehow the recipient of his efforts. That his grace and his speed were slicing—scalpel-like—an opening between the earth and the sky, and if only I had faith enough, I could rise and step right through.

Tibet is the only other place I've had that feeling. And it is also a place where people fully understood both the power and the danger of language, the only place where nobody's afraid of dead air. The first time I found myself walking across the wooden floor of a monastery that had been polished by the bare feet of five centuries' worth of monks and looked up into the primary colors of the thankas and prayer flags, into the black eyes and serene expression of a Buddha twenty times my height, I thought, *If these prayer rooms had been my prayer rooms, I'd believe in God too.*

If there were no such thing as cancer, if a dog's life were as long as a human's, I'd find a way to take Dante to Lhasa, so he could feel the calm that is in the air there—even in the wintertime when the Jokhang Temple is thick with pilgrims. It's the only place where I've found that particular serenity, other than in Dante's golden eyes.

Mona used to say she doesn't understand why, if I'm so fascinated with language, the only thing I'll let myself get close to is a dog, and I would have told her how obvious the answer was if I hadn't known what she really meant was, "I want way more than you are willing to give me."

It was Brooklyn Underhill, the vet student who worked with Dr. Evans, who said if you find a way to get free in your life your next job is to free somebody else, if you have some power your job is to empower somebody else, and I know there is a way art can do that, but I've never been sure if mine does.

Victoria, who has known me almost from the very beginning, says I wound up writing plays either to please or get even with my mother, and that gets even more complicated now that I've married Howard, but Victoria always has an explanation for everything, and most of the time it is wrong.

My mother was happy in the theater, happy putting on costumes and makeup, happy when she was singing, most of all. Each night I would watch her turn into somebody else, a madam, a waitress, a mother whose diabetic daughter makes the fatal decision to try and have a child.

The theater was a micro-universe, a world where people loved each other, where they touched each other, where before they said good night they always hugged and kissed, not just on stage, but off as well. When I was a little girl the stagehands picked me up and tossed me high toward the stage lights and the dressers fussed over my hair, the ushers bought me candy from the concession stand and Pee-pidge, or some other kindly actor like him, showed up—more often than was good for me, my mother said—with a giant stuffed dog from FAO Schwarz.

Then we'd drive in the wee hours all the way back to Trenton and my mother would slink into the house as if she'd done something wrong, even though I now understand that in some of those years her career was bringing in more money than my father's.

My mother wanted more than anything for me to be an actress, and I went to the auditions she set up where I had to pretend that some red-haired kid with too many freckles was my little brother, or that I loved the ruffled potato chips way beyond reason, or that I would fall to the ground and expire if the guy I was supposed to call Daddy wouldn't take us all to McDonald's that night. I've never called anybody Daddy, and the word doesn't feel right in my mouth. I called my father Papa, with the accent on the second syllable, until I understood that it sounded pretentious, and then I called him Father, and eventually even that felt a little scary and so if I needed to talk to him I would just stare across the table and will him to raise his eyes.

My mother would spend the whole car ride into the city trying to explain to me the difference between acting and faking it. She was an expert at both of those things and I was never very good at either.

But I wasn't too bad with words, Esther Robinson had made sure of that, so when I went off to college I studied every kind of writing I could. I fell in love first with the rhythms of formal poetry, spent two years writing pantoums, villanelles and sonnets that were perfectly awful, and then took a run at a novel that was even worse. Eventually I got a job writing travel articles for a couple of the better in-flight magazines, a gig that showed me just enough of the world to make me want to see the rest of it.

Somewhere along the way I realized that if I had a gift at all it was not in my voice, but in my ear. I could hear the way people spoke to each other, more often how they did not. Dialogue had a rhythm similar to what I loved in formal poems, as well as a steely street logic I could understand. I had a teacher once who said that once you go to the trouble of creating characters in Act One, you shouldn't be surprised if sometime in Act Two they start running away with the story; that if you've done a half-decent job of enlivening them, it's only natural they should have a will of their own. I wasn't sure if I believed him, but I had noticed that most times when I got a character talking, he never wanted to shut up.

I thought back to Kenneth Branagh and Stratford-on-Avon, and less far back to the eleven hours I had spent breathless at a marathon performance of *Angels in America,* and worked up the courage to find my own way back into my mother's big dark spaces. Those theaters that got transformed late at night by chain-smoking carpenters who climbed catwalks like superheroes, and where every night was a new beginning, where every show demanded everything that everybody had. I had some success with a couple of early plays, one set in a research station in Antarctica, one in the farm country of southwestern France. *The New York Times* called me a playwright of unfamiliar landscapes, and lucky for me, there are a lot of foundations out there who love to finance the unfamiliar.

What I got addicted to first was the process of discovery. The way a foreign place gives up its stories, slowly at first, then more quickly, the translation of that story from the mouths of the people—often through a translator—to my ear, to the page, and eventually to the stage.

What I got addicted to next was the adrenaline that flew around backstage. The way the night before preview is always a disaster, how dress rehearsal hangs together by the skin of its teeth, how the only chance of pulling off an opening is if about a hundred people—some of whom would have no reason to speak to one another outside the walls of that black box—decide to cooperate, decide to dedicate themselves to each other and to their shared project with such ferocity you would think what they were doing was saving lives.

Some days, it is easy to believe that they are.

Jonathan #1:

It's possible that my first mistake was that I never married. But if you're born and raised in California, there's something inherently wrong with the whole idea of marriage. The same kind of disconnect can happen if you are born Episcopalian and then you try to become a Buddhist, which brings me to my second mistake.

My first love was Ricky Nelson. After that Roy Orbison. After that the incomparable David Byrne. Ricky Nelson led me to Mick Fleetwood, Roy Orbison led me to Bruce Springsteen, David Byrne led me to Michael Stipe, and so on and so on into this new century.

I myself am a mostly unappreciated playwright by trade, a screenwriting hack by necessity, a poet in my heart, and in these unrequited loves I find inspiration. I wrote a hundred coronas of sonnets to John Lennon, some of them double coronas, which represents, as you may know, nearly a thousand poems.

I write them, I mail them, I hear nothing in return. There is no art without suffering, and it gratifies me to know that the intended recipients of my letters pay another person, in some cases perhaps a whole team of people, to put my poems straight into the trash.

I have managed to acquire addresses for all my living mentors. My friend Rae says the Internet is a dangerous tool in the hands of someone like me, but I do not abuse my knowledge. I send them things—artist to artist—poems mostly, sometimes newspaper articles I feel would interest them, an obscure book or CD that they might have missed. They are busy people, rock stars, and I've got nothing but time on my hands.

I would like the record to show that I have never dropped by any of their houses, have never thrown myself into any of their paths even if I happened to have found out, say, where they buy their groceries or get their dry cleaning done.

I like to imagine that in a few cases my letters get through somehow and they enjoy them. That I am, for some of them, the ideal fan. I am, after all, a dedicated scholar of their music, and I bring to it a deep and complicated understanding, deeper sometimes, I'd wager, than they bring to it themselves.

My third mistake, as it turns out, has been investing the last ten years in my memoir, *I Was Born in the USA, Too*, in which I attempted to show, using Springsteen's last seven albums, that my life and his life have run an almost perfectly parallel course. That aside from a few logistical differences: he's been married, divorced and married again, he was raised looking out at the Atlantic and I the Pacific, he clings to his Christian upbringing, while I have tried to inhabit a different faith, he's in a different economic bracket, naturally, and he does have that gaggle of children from the woman with the puffed-up hair . . . but when you're talking about pain, about the kinds of suffering life dumps in your lap again and again, the Boss and I, we're blood brothers.

I don't know, I thought he would want to see it. I thought I owed the guy that much. Then all of a sudden one Tuesday morning the phone rings at my cabin and I pick it up and I say, "Hello," and the guy says,

"Hello, is Jonathan there?"

And I say, "This is him,"

And he says, "Hey, Jonathan, it's Bruce."

I was sure it was somebody trying to fuck with me, and it took me a minute to respond.

"It's Bruce," he said again, "Bruce Springsteen."

"Yes sir," I said, "Mr. Springsteen, how can I help you today?"

He told me he was doing a concert in Sacramento in a couple of weeks and he wanted me to be his guest. I knew about the concert and told him so, told him I already had my tickets, that I had taken my sleeping bag down to Arco Arena and spent the night there with a couple dozen New Jersey ex-pats so we'd be the very first ones in line.

The Boss said, "But I bet you don't have a backstage pass, do you?"

To tell any more would be too much like bragging, how I got to tour with the band to their next three gigs in Portland, Seattle, and Vancouver, how restaurants would reopen after the shows, just for us, and make the Boss's favorite dishes, pot roast and barbeque and homemade meatloaf with heaps of mashed potatoes; and how Clarence and Nils Lofgren and

Bruce would sit around these restaurants after dinner with their backs against one chair and a leg up on another, acoustic guitars in hand, singing all the not-for-prime-time verses of the songs they'd been singing on stage since I was a boy in short pants, and how Patty, who hung around for all these years until Bruce finally saw the light and married her, would get tired of all the old stories and all the old songs and she'd curl up like a little girl in one of the booths and go to sleep, how the Boss had a star over his name on the door in Portland and how he tore it right down and gave it to me, *for your scrapbook,* he said, and the best part of all, how when I first got down to Sacramento and traded the seats I bought at Arco for a backstage pass, and a bouncer showed me the line of electric tape I had to stand behind, right up there on the side of the stage, and after I watched Bruce start off with a bluesy solo acoustic version of "Born in the USA" that was designed to remind all those asshole car makers who appropriated that song what it had really been trying to say in the first place, and after the end of "Born in the USA" fed right into "Who'll Stop the Rain"—the only cover he did all night by the way—and made his point about our current political situation all too clear he looked right out into the audience and said, "Did my friend Jonathan make it?" and for just that one second my whole strange life made sense.

But the problem with three days like that is that you have to come home from them, and what happens after your little wet dream of a rock and roll fantasy comes true is that all of a sudden there is no more longing, there are no more poems, there is no more art. I couldn't listen to the Boss's albums at all after that, and turned my attention to Hendrix and

Morrison and Stevie Ray Vaughan, guys I knew would never call me up.

Rae told me about one time she was flying from Denver to Kansas City—they gave her the upgrade at the last minute—and as she slid into seat 2A she looked at the guy in seat 2B and was pretty damn sure she was sitting next to Joe Montana.

Joe Montana seems like a guy you'd know if you saw him, especially Rae who's a sports fan down to her toes, but she said he was so much smaller than she thought he would be; his wrists looked too thin to chuck a ball eighty yards.

So the seat belt sign went off and this trembling businessman came up from 4B and said, "Joe, I still have your jersey over my desk at the office," and Joe was polite to the guy but Rae could tell he wanted to be left alone.

When their meal came Joe seemed willing to chat, and Rae apologized in advance for being an Elway fan, and Joe seemed to like that approach better than the guy who trembled.

"Sitting next to someone like Joe Montana can *only* be disappointing," Rae said, as if it were obvious. "You want to kneel down and kiss the earth around him, you want to say, *There's no way I can express how much happiness your existence on earth has brought me,* but there he is in front of you, just another guy in first class in an expensive golf shirt, and there you are, on your way to talk about some play that you can't quite remember writing, both of you gnawing on dried-out chicken sandwiches with stainless steel forks and plastic knives, and you are struck suddenly by the fact that it won't make any difference whether anybody remembers either of you ten minutes after you're dead."

I sent Rae tickets to see the Boss when he went through Denver. I can do that now with one phone call; get Springsteen tickets for any show, any night, anywhere in the world.

"That guy," she said, "has the most amazing work ethic of anyone I've ever seen."

"Jesus Christ, Rae," I said, "you are getting so fucking old."

I LIKE HOWARD. But no one in his right mind would want to live at Rae's pace—God knows I couldn't even write at it—and he'll get tired of her moods and her fear and the way she chases back and forth across the globe, running to, or running away, she's never been clear about which.

Don't get me wrong, I mean I *get* travel. I *get* what it does for your head, for the work. It's become Rae's thing now, to set plays in places nobody's heard of: Punakha, Bhutan, Ulaangom, Mongolia, Gyantse, Tibet. They are performed in English, of course, and there is often a Western character or two on the fringes of the plot. She says the Far East is what the American West used to be a century ago for theatergoers, a blank slate of imagination, a place where anything at all might happen, a place where no one from your family can see what you do.

I could save her all the money she spends on her shrink by pointing out that her mother's been dead for a decade, the cops took her ninety-two-year-old father's driver's license away a couple of years ago when he plowed through the front door of his favorite restaurant back in New Jersey, and she's as safe from them up at that ranch of hers in Mineral County as she could possibly be. She's there to hide out, she'll admit that much, and because the mountains make her feel calm, and because she had never felt calm in her life. "Who does?" I said, and she said,

"Yeah I know, but I want to."

Years ago, before either of us had gotten a play up any-where that counted, a friend of Rae's got us a gig team-teaching at the Sundance Playwriting Workshop where it was Redford's unspoken rule that all the work we looked at was supposed to have an outdoor slant.

Now I won't deny that I like to cast my fly into the stream as much as the next guy, but when it comes to climbing and backpacking and all that other shit, well, I prefer to get my endorphins up the old-fashioned way, with Kentucky bour-bon, cocaine, and sex.

That summer at Sundance we headed back to our cabin after sitting through way too many scenes of a play called *Catch and Release* about a woman who takes fly fishing lessons in response to the dawning knowledge that her husband is having an affair and thereby learns how to . . . Well, you get the picture. I'd like to think even Rae was a little mad at nature that day, the way it hung over us out there in Utah with exaggerated grandeur, justifying its presence in all those badly written plays.

We were decompressing on the sofa, not talking really, just staring out the open plate-glass doors, when the fattest rac-coon in America waddled up onto our deck and rubbed his little hands against the screen.

"Someone has been doing you wrong, my friend," I said, and went to the kitchen to get the enormous bag of cool ranch Doritos I'd bought at the 7-Eleven on the way into town.

In unspoken agreement we invited the raccoon into the living room of the vaulted-ceilinged ski cabin that some rich Mormon had no doubt donated on behalf of the future of arts in Utah, and took turns feeding the little monster the entire bag right there on the carpet, one salty chip at a time.

In all those times Rae and I traveled together, we never once had sex. She always said I was too pretty and I always said she was too smart, but what she really meant was *short* and what I really meant was *fat*. Still, it was an intimate thing that night, silently feeding that big raccoon, getting even with nature.

Dante #2:

Buddha said, "Your work is to discover your work and then with all your heart to give yourself to it." My work, this time around, was to teach my human that she deserved to be loved. And faith, of course, because you can't have love without it.

I don't know any better than you do whether this is my sixth or tenth or four hundredth time here, but I can't believe they hand out such sweet and critical assignments to the new souls. Which brings me to Jackson, my predecessor in her life.

Jackson was half old English sheepdog, half Airedale. Need I say more than that?

Perhaps. He was a good old boy if ever there was one, which was fitting, as good old boys were all she was capable of listening to at the time. He was a scrapper, something to which I can testify from personal experience, capable of things like ear-tearing and given to nips below the belt.

Jackson had a record a mile long, dog-at-large convictions mostly, but he was accused of biting a frostbitten Texan's leg one time when the man came down out of the national forest and up to the ranch door wearing a face mask, wielding a shotgun, and hoping to find a fire and a cup of hot coffee. And though there was very little love lost between the two of us (my puppyhood overlapped with his dotage for nearly two years), I'm pretty sure he got a bum rap.

Jackson was capable of many things: of antagonizing some dog he never should have even sniffed butts with, a prize Doberman pinscher for instance, and coming home bloody and broken and needing three thousand dollars' worth of vet care, and that in our human's impoverished grad school days; of staying out all night when the neighbor's Arctic wolf/Siberian husky cross was in heat and making our human sick with worry; of stealing the neighbors' Thanksgiving turkey right off the front stoop, the sheriff's record-book mule deer head out of the back of his truck, a five-gallon container of vanilla ice cream from God only knows where . . . But I don't believe he was a dog who would—unprovoked—bite the leg of a human, not even a Texan dressed as a serial killer.

Jackson's assignment was to see her through the real losers, the drunk ones and the stoned ones and the ones who slept around and the ones who threatened to kill her after she finally got the nerve to leave. He even intervened a time or two when one of them started to get nasty with her. He'd provide a distraction by pulling the guy's hat off or grabbing his shirt, and then when the guy lunged for him Jackson would get hold of his arm or leg, never leaving marks of course, but sending a clear message.

He might have been no match for a prize Doberman, but drunken ski bums and mechanics generally didn't have much of a chance. Rae's judgment improved under Jackson's watch to the point where I've never found myself in a similar situation, though I'd like to think my brains would make up for my lack of brawn, should one arise.

I respect Jackson's dedication. But I also need to point out that he had fifteen years to do his job, whereas I'll have, if I'm lucky and my heart and lungs are willing, seven or eight. And while you might think my work has been all fine-tuning and finesse, everybody knows that the learning curve flattens out toward the end of every cycle.

I think of it like this. Jackson stood watch during the years Rae learned how not to keep falling headfirst down the well, I taught her how to come back up, to stand strong above the well, to ask herself whether or not she is thirsty, and if she is, how to take a long satisfying drink.

It didn't happen overnight.

A BRIEF HISTORY of events:

Tucker was a recovering alcoholic who had saved every liquor bottle he had ever drained, and there were so many that he rented a second apartment just so he could walk in and witness the vehicle of his demise.

Adam spat when he got angry, which fortunately was not often, little showers of venom from some deep source that seemed to redden his face and enlarge his eyes and make his mop of hair seem even bigger than it was already. Nine out of ten maître d's mistook Adam for Yanni.

I came on the scene in the waning hours of Tucker, alcoholics were among Jackson's specialties, and even though he was showing the first signs of the canine Alzheimer's that would eventually take his life, Jackson held it together in mind and body long enough to see Tucker's departure.

I tried to be optimistic about Adam, who was substance-free, educated and employed, though he had a cloying way of trying to please everyone that made him impossible to trust. Adam treated both my human and me with kindness for the better part of two years. He lived in Denver, and drove the four hours to the ranch to be with us each weekend. Sometimes, during the week, we'd drive to Denver to be with him. When he began to have an affair, I could smell it, but I tried to pretend otherwise.

A wolfhound, apparently, is as capable of self-deception as the next creature, and the fact that the affair was with a man was the thing that threw me, allowed me to pretend that Adam was playing particularly intense games of basketball, or had suddenly taken up wrestling.

When the question is common, the answer is also common, a wise man said. When the question is sand in a bowl of boiled rice, the answer is a stick in the soft mud.

We never met the stick, as it were. Adam just announced the end of the relationship one night in October when my human had to fly to New York on theater business and I couldn't even rest my head on her ankle for comfort, or spend an hour licking between her toes.

It took my human a good long time getting over Adam. It took yoga, and massage, and all the sashimi she wanted. It took a dark silent holiday season that found the two of us mostly in bed. It took a great deal of cross-country skiing. It took Alanis Morissette and the Indigo Girls, and even, in the worst of times, Liz Phair. It took hours of watching the Weather Channel, in which my human finds mysterious comfort. It took the Denver Broncos winning the AFC Championship and the Super Bowl.

It took a trip to Ireland where she'd been asked to bring one of her plays to a festival. She insisted that I be allowed to come and I became the only dog ever to stay at the hotel owned by the rock group U2 in Dublin. It took ripping both sideview mirrors off of an Irish rental car making right turns into two different stone alleyways. It took yoga in the U2 hotel and much too expensive phone calls to Darlene and Victoria, and the Westminster Dog Show reruns all night on BBC1.

It took playing Thich Nhat Hanh tapes, over and over and over in that same rental car. *Breathe in, I am a flower. Breathe out, I smile to myself.* It took her rewinding the part where he says, "The miracle is not to walk on water, the miracle is to walk on the green earth, dwelling deeply in the present moment, and feeling truly alive" sixty-seven times on the road to Galway.

It took the present moment.

It took the February sun breaking through the clouds and shining on the mottled fieldstones, wet with rain. It took watching the Ireland/France national rugby match in a bar on Grafton Street, the only woman there by herself, and it took not one of the three hundred men in the place trying to hit on her.

It took leaving Ireland behind.

It took convincing U.S. immigration that I had been to Ireland to get in touch with my heritage, and that I should be entitled to the same quarantine waiver that new wolfhound puppies are granted when they are imported to the States.

It took going home, where, thanks to Darlene, the ranch was finally empty of Adam paraphernalia. It took the snow melting, the grass greening, the wild iris finally blooming. I think the wild iris may have been the final thing.

She was happy again. She was, if the truth be told, happier than she had ever been. She bought throw pillows, for example, and buying throw pillows is in my experience the single best indicator that a female human being is feeling pretty good.

Friends would call and she'd say, "Oh, you know, hanging in there," and the next thing you know she'd be bounding ahead of me up a hiking trail or singing in the car at the top of her lungs.

Buddha said, "Do not think you will necessarily be aware of your own enlightenment." He said, "Enlightenment is not a sunrise, it is a firefly," so I was prepared, at any moment for regression.

I was not, however, prepared for Peter.

One ex-wife who's born again or worse, living on one of those Kool-Aid-drinking colonies somewhere in Texas, and another living in a utopian community modeled after Charlotte Perkins Gilman's novel *Herland* outside of Mexico City, the rage so thick on Peter's skin I could smell it when he got out of the car, before he even walked in the room.

I thought, *One way or another, this man will kill her.* But it just goes to show you that a wolfhound might know a lot, but he

can't foretell the future. Together we indulged Peter's part-
time twin daughters, his inexplicable love for dinner at
Applebee's, and the aroma he carried around with him from
munching all day long on raw broccoli.

He left us without a word one day in October—a year and
two days after Adam's departure—while we'd gone to town
to buy sausages and worm medicine. She came home, took
note of the empty garage, the bare hangers in the closet, and
we went straight down to Denver to see Theo and gorge on
sashimi.

She was over it in forty-eight hours. Which was forty-eight
hours too many, as far as I was concerned.

"Thinking is more interesting than knowing," Goethe said,
"but less interesting than looking," and I think the relief from
the oppression of Peter's anger made her look at the world in
a whole new way. She decided she'd been hiding out too
much at the ranch and so we rented a tiny apartment in
Denver, which, let's face it, is not Prague, and yet we found
beauty in it together.

The early snow on the not-yet-fallen leaves on our morning walks through Washington Park. An evening walk downtown, a stop into the Body Shop to buy cranberry lotion that
made her skin sparkle, a short dip for me in the man-made
waterfalls along Cherry Creek, a single scoop of sweet cream
ice cream at Josh and John's with a peanut butter cookie on
the side. Some nights she'd take in a hockey game, buying
only one ticket, which I thought especially brave.

We went back to the ranch for the holidays, a much less
solemn affair than the year before when Peter was there.
Victoria brought a bunch of orphaned actors up from Denver

to help with ranch chores and fill up the rooms with sound. In February, we met Howard.

VICTORIA HAD INVITED my human to Denver for an opening of a show at Victoria's theater. After the show, my human met Howard in the lobby where a conversation began that carried them out to the parking garage where I had been waiting, as always, in the 4-Runner.

He was a little overenthusiastic at first. Any book about wolfhounds will tell you that while we have an intense need to be with our own people, and we will put up with all manner of discomfort and inconvenience to achieve this, we tend to be somewhat standoffish with strangers and can be quite affronted by overfamiliarity. We prefer to initiate quiet introductions ourselves, to be perfectly frank. We are not a breed that lacks discretion.

Most of us, that is.

Rose, whom I may have forgotten to mention, was also in the 4-Runner that night, where she always is, in the *way* back. She leapt out and was all tail-wag and butt-wiggle in a matter of seconds. She then ran immediately over to a drain in the center of the floor and relieved herself, an act I later thought of as quintessentially Rose, displaying the very tenacious pragmatism, however uncouth and often embarrassing, that defines her.

All this had happened as I was untangling my stiff limbs from the back seat, and when I did finally manage to hop down, Howard showed us the excellent social skills that he no doubt acquired from his lovely mother—may she rest in peace—in Ohio.

He divided his time equally between Rose and me, complimented us both on our best features, Rose's platinum blond Tina Turneresque coat, and my bone structure, particularly that of my face, which has been the model for more than one sculptor over the years. He neither ignored the fact of my missing limb, nor did he focus on it. He let Rae tell him whatever version of the story she cared to in a chilly underground parking garage.

They were standing around the way humans do when they are nervous, and interested, not allowing each other so much as a sniff. The conversation wasn't much to write home about, but I do remember him saying,

"I'm glad I met the dogs." And her saying,

"Well, yes, that's the important thing."

It's so mystifying to those of us who have only rudimentary—albeit subtle—language skills, why a breed with such advanced skills so often fails to use them.

They just kept standing there, silent, neither of them acknowledging their attraction, Rose wagging her tail for all she was worth, me more reserved of course, but offering little grunts of enthusiasm as Howard rubbed in the deep cavities behind my ears.

"Lightning flashes," said Shiva, "sparks shower, in the blink of your eyes you have missed seeing." Howard drove off first and turned left at the top of the ramp. Rae turned right, but only after a hesitation that was far from lost on me.

But she hadn't missed seeing, and the next day she called information and got Howard's number.

Rose #1:

I like Howard. I know my opinion doesn't count, because I'm the next dog, and I'm probably just agreeing with everyone else, because as we all know, "Rose has no real thoughts in her head." Even so, here it is. Right from the beginning he let me put my tongue all the way inside that big toothy mouth of his and lick off any remaining food particles, and I've got to respect that in a human being.

I'd also like to point out that Dante, *the evolved one*, was just evolved enough to be a little skeptical of Howard at the beginning. That may not be the story he's telling now, but I could smell the skepticism all over him and I had already touched Howard's uvula with my tongue several times by then.

And while it's also true that yes, I did enjoy the company of Peter, who everyone else could apparently see through as if he were made of Saran Wrap, I was hardly old enough to be very discriminating at the time.

After all, I'm the next dog. I'm not here to say one person is better or worse than another, and while it's true that "Rose isn't going to win any major intelligence contests," especially compared to *the evolved one*, and while it's true that if Howard is trying to make me come inside at night and I don't want to all he has to do is lie down in the middle of the street and play dead and I fall for it every single time, maybe that's just a different kind of evolution.

I told you, I'm the next dog. My assignment is to teach her how to play.

Theo #1:

You'd probably like me to start with how Dante began coming to therapy with Rae. I'm going to pause here for a minute to express my concern about saying too much publicly when the work Rae and I have to do together is far from over. There is no question that her life has taken a few major good turns lately, and while it is also true that the credit lies primarily with the dog, I'd like to point out that it was my idea in the first place to let the dog come to the office.

I'd also like to offer this caveat: someone who has suffered as many childhood abuses as Rae has will occasionally find herself struggling no matter how much improvement she shows overall, and I don't want anything I say here to get in the way of my ability to assist her with those problems in the future.

Therapists practice confidentiality obsessively, the way a concert pianist might run through scales while he drives or sleeps. We can't actually stop doing it, and now that you're asking me to, it doesn't come easily.

Dante's first visit to the office was accidental, as things that affect profound psychological growth often are. It was summer in Denver, and unspeakably hot. Dante had an appointment with his oncologist right after her therapy appointment. Rae would not have had time to go back to the house for him, and he would simply have roasted in the car.

Let me flatter myself a bit here and say that he seemed to like me right away. He drank the water I offered him at that first appointment, and continues drinking heartily at every appointment since.

The first day Dante came I noticed that whenever our work got to a difficult place Rae would look down at him sleeping on the carpet . . . pause a moment, and then continue, as if the sight of him gave her strength to push on. When the hour was over I understood that she'd been both braver about her responses that day and more comfortable with them.

We had been talking about her conviction that if she isn't absolutely vigilant, terrible things will happen to her, to Dante, to everyone and everything she loves. She feels that some undefined portion of sadness is her due, in spite of all she's already suffered, and she's made some kind of agreement with the universe whereby if she proves she can handle a lot of small doses of trouble, perhaps she can stave off the larger doses.

From my office that day she and Dante were to go directly to the veterinary hospital to find out if Dante's osteosarcoma had returned. It will give you a window into our work if I tell you that as they were leaving I said, "Maybe you'll have a little accident on the way over there," and she smiled.

"A fender bender would be perfect," she said.

I suggested that Dante should come with her the next time, and he hasn't missed an appointment in the two years since. Soon he assumed a more active role. When it was impossible for her to see a way to defend herself from someone trying to hurt her, I could ask her to substitute Dante for herself in the situation. What would she do if it were he who needed protection? And then her course of action was clear as day to her.

I know what you're thinking, it's not exactly rocket science, but in my office we look for what works and are grateful. I am grateful for Dante. He became, for her and for the purposes of our work together, her frightened childhood self.

I'm not afraid to tell you how much I value my work with Rae, how I count her progress as one of the great successes of my professional life, insofar as I allow myself some of the credit, most of which, as I've said already, belongs to the dog. Our work together has brought out, I feel, the best in both of us, and with one glaring exception, I have been with her precisely the therapist, precisely the person, I most wish to be.

My one failure happened some time ago, after Adam, I think, before Peter, although at this point even I have a difficult time keeping them straight. It was early spring I remember, one of the first truly pleasant days in Denver, and Rae's appointment was in the middle of the day.

She was fragile then. It is some measure of our success that if the same thing happened today, Rae would probably burst into my office and say, "You asshole! I cannot believe you just said that." But at the time, I came as close as I ever have to losing her, and I shudder to think what it would have meant for both of us if I had.

I was in the back room between patients, boiling water for tea. Claire, my associate, said, "God, what a beautiful day it is," and headed back down the hall to her office.

"I know," I shouted after her, "I'm hoping my eleven-forty-five doesn't show, and I can maybe get in a run."

As the sentence came out of my mouth, my first thought was, *You lying sack of shit.* The second was, *Oh my God, what if Rae is in the reception room?*

I waited until the tea water was hot to see if she was out there. She was, but her face showed no indication that she had heard what I said.

Once in my office though, she wouldn't look at me, which is not so uncommon if she's ashamed or uncomfortable about what she is about to say. I let her hedge for a few minutes before I said, "Is there something going on today between you and me?"

She looked, for the first time ever in my office, as if she were measuring the distance between the couch and the door. She wrapped her fingers tight into Dante's thick mane and cried for a while, her eyes fixed on the dog, and then said, in a voice so small if I hadn't known what she was going to say I never would have made it out,

"I heard what you said back there."

Dante sighed and gave a tiny moan.

"That I would like to go for a run?" I asked her.

"That you hoped I wouldn't show up," she corrected, with just enough anger and exasperation in her voice to give me the strength and hope I needed to push on through the moment.

"That was a terrible thing for me to say," I began. I took a deep breath and pushed away every cautionary voice I had ever heard in med school. "Especially because it isn't true."

Her eyes shot up to mine, revealing that for a second this scene had become more interesting than painful for her. It is this, her unending interest in the human dynamic, that has kept her moving forward in this work when so many others would retreat.

"The last thing I need right now is to make this about me," I said, feeling precisely in the middle of the minefield I had created for myself, "but you should know that I have a habit of denying the importance of the very things that are the most important to me, and our work together is one of those."

She was squinting up at me, trying to assess, I knew, whether or not I was feeding her some line from my therapist's bag of crap.

"That's one of the main things I talk about when I see my own therapist," I said, "and I will talk about it this week for sure." I looked at my hands, thin and white from all the time they spend folded in my lap. "Going for a run is actually the last thing I want right now."

She looked at me, suspicion and satisfaction in her eyes. I had just revealed more about myself than I had in our three years of working together. She couldn't tell how she felt about it, and neither could I.

"But let's talk about how it made you feel," I said. She glanced back down, partly disappointed, partly relieved, that the against-the-rules part of this session was over.

"If I thought I could have left the waiting room without

anyone seeing or hearing me," she said, "I would have run and run, and never come back."

I probably deserved that, and I didn't doubt it was the truth.

"Thank you for telling me that," I said. "I think it's an excellent place to start."

It took most of the hour to make up for what I'd done, but with fifteen minutes left Rae said, "I've been wondering a lot lately, if my mother were still alive, would I confront her with all this stuff we talk about in here, would I ask her why she let my dad hurt us?"

"Why don't you do that," I said, "and see if Dante would like to go along?"

Rae sat back against the couch and closed her eyes; ten minutes later she opened them and told me what had happened. She had called the meeting to take place in the kitchen of the last house her mother had lived in before she died. It was a house where Rae had never lived, so she figured they'd both feel pretty safe for different reasons.

Rae said she sat down at the kitchen table, and Dante lay down at her feet. They waited for her mother to settle in, but her shape shifted into a big dark bird, a raptor of some kind, first an owl, then a hawk, and the bird made big loops around the open kitchen/dining/living room. Dante and Rae exchanged glances. *Give her time to settle in,* Dante seemed to say, *she's even more nervous than we are.*

Eventually her mother turned back into a woman, and Rae started talking, relating the memories one at a time, starting with the most benign and working toward the most awful. Her mother's face was set in the smile she reserved for

Rae's father and the stage. She was smiling too much and too steadily and after a while Rae reached over and pulled her face off and it turned out to be a mask, a Screen Actors' Guild happy face in the image of her mother.

She stared a long time at what was behind the mask. Her mother was made of stone, her face had no features, only indentations for the eyes and mouth and nostrils. Dante stood up and walked around the statue a few times sniffing and then, with an attitude neither playful nor violent, nudged it with his nose until it fell out of the chair and onto the floor, where it broke into several pieces. To each piece Rae tied a balloon strong enough to lift it out the open kitchen window and into the sky.

COMING CLEAN ABOUT the "going for a run" day affords me, I hope, the indulgence of pointing out that a character in Rae's most well-known play is based on me. He doesn't actually appear on stage, and he doesn't have any lines. He is a voice on the other end of a telephone, so you can figure out what he is saying by what the character on stage says. But in a certain way it is my—his—advice around which the entire plot turns. I'm a shadow on the wall of the play—as I hope to be in her life.

I heard her talk about that play once at the Denver Center. It was a difficult time for her, not long after Dante's initial diagnosis, and I thought my presence might cheer her.

I have a fountain in my office, the standard-issue therapy fountain with the water bubbling soothingly over the rocks, but as Rae would be the first to tell you, a metaphor is what you make it. I've given my patients rocks from that fountain from time to time as a way to carry the good work we do in the office around in their pockets.

It was the first time I had seen Rae anywhere outside the office, and when her talk was over, I wanted to leave quickly, before anyone could ask me who I was. I jumped to the front of the line of mostly women who wanted Rae to sign their programs. I gave her a hug and pressed one of the rocks into her hand.

"You were wonderful," I said. "I'm going to take off."

She gave me one of those smiles she gives me in the office when we've been on some particularly gnarly childhood battlefield and she's emerged victorious, laughing and exhausted, and I gave her my best smile in return.

As I reached the door I heard the first woman in line ask, "Is that your boyfriend?"

"Even better," I heard Rae say. "It's my shrink."

"I WONDER WHAT it would be like," she said to me on one of those days that make you feel that you have chosen the right profession, "if I could once and for all get my mother out of my head."

"Picture it," I told her. "Tell me what it looks like."

"It's a big white room. Massive. Sunny," she said.

"Anything in the room?" I asked

"Just me," she said, "and about a hundred thousand crayons."

Darlene #2:

Rae was the only person who had ever been honest with Mona. All the other girls just fell in love with her and told her everything she wanted to hear, and the next thing you knew they were living on her couch. Mona's husband Daniel was real tolerant about that . . . of course he's another one of those people who will say or do anything to keep her happy, and it was finally always Mona who kicked them out because between them and Daniel she never had a moment to herself.

Like the night here at the ranch when she told Rae how it works with Daniel and her—about Kerry, and then Star, and then Rachel—how Daniel understands that one person isn't ever going to be enough for her, how he lets the girls move in. Daniel says it even turns him on in a way. He likes, in point of fact, to cook dinner for Mona and Rachel while they are having a little romp on the living room couch.

Mona has probably told the same story a hundred times, to a hundred different women, and every time, just when whoever she's telling starts to get that look on her face—half incredulous and half seduced—she says with great solemnity what she said to Rae—*Of course I would never do it if I thought I was hurting Daniel*—and the women nod their heads to show they understand completely, and it's only a matter of time before there's a pile of girl clothes on the floor and some serious carpet-munching going on.

But when Mona tells Rae the story she doesn't look incredulous or seduced. She says, "Well you certainly *are* hurting him."

"You think?" Mona says, and Rae says,

"You'd have to be a total idiot to think you're not."

Mona lives in Steamboat Springs. She calls herself a serious snowboarder.

When Mona told us that the first time Rae said, "That's an oxymoron," and Mona laughed because she knew it was supposed to be funny but I'll bet she had to go home and look the word up. She's got boundless energy, a personality trait I immediately distrust. She drives all the way up to Aspen sometimes just to go to something called a Tozo, and she's got this e-mail thing going on where every day somebody sends her something or other that the Buddha said. Something wise. She says I'm stuck in my second chakra, which I might find insulting if I had any idea what the hell it meant.

"Well," I said, "I'd rather be stuck there than where you're stuck," and she said, "Oh, yeah, where's that," and I said,

"Up your butt."

Eventually she started calling me TAB, which Rae eventually told me stands for tight-assed butch little mama, but I suspect the *b* actually stands for bitch.

Experimentation has never been my thing.

Rae says that in a world where we have Thai food on Wednesday and Italian on Thursday, where we have a scoop of Chunky Monkey and a scoop of Brownie Batter on the very same cone, where we like folk music as well as hip-hop, the plains as well as the mountains, baseball as well as hockey, it doesn't make sense to have to choose whether we want to have sex with women, or sex with men.

At least that's what she said before Howard. She's gotten very heterosexual all of a sudden, and given Howard, the irony of that is supreme.

I don't care much for Thai food myself, or Korean, or Vietnamese or even Chinese really, except sweet and sour pork. I order twenty-five-pound bags of flour and sugar from the Co-op so I can put to use all the gadgets Rae brings home from Williams-Sonoma and her fancy theater friends say I should open my own bakery, make my fortune from muffins and tarts.

Mona's grandfather invented the spray that the fast-food restaurants use to keep their salad bars looking fresh and crisp, so none of the grandkids have to work for a living. Mona has a double major in English and theater from Colorado Mountain College and works as a T.A. up at the community college, which gives her an excuse to read a play or a book every once in a while, and a whole slew of pretty girls to pick from.

She originally came sniffing around here right when things were starting to fall apart with Peter, right before the holidays kicked into high gear. At first I thought it might be a good thing, all that energy dragging Rae to the ski mountain, out dancing at night, the kind of effort she'll never in a hundred years get from me. Excuse me for being so simple-minded that I thought *married to somebody named Daniel* might be equivalent to *likes men.* Excuse me for being so many years removed from the dating game that I can't comprehend how hard it is to turn down a romance at Christmas. Especially for Rae, or anybody else who grew up the way she did in the land of Suburban Gestapo Christmas. When the handwriting was on the wall I told Rae the last thing she needed was to get herself mixed up with a mixed-up married female snowboarder, and she told me I was absolutely right.

Even so, I come home one day to find Mona's truck in the driveway. I walk in, and—hello kitty—Rae's glittering. She's gone to the Body Shop in Denver or somewhere and bought some of that lotion that smells like cranberries and she sparkles—she's glittering from head to toe.

They went down to the Hungry Logger to dance to a band called Highway 149. I was in bed long before they came home, and I assure you, I took no notice of who was sleeping where in the morning.

What Mona hadn't expected was the shit fit Daniel threw the next day. She called him right from the phone in our kitchen, and we could hear him shouting from all the way across the room, and by the time Mona hung up she had promised Daniel that was *it*, no sleepovers with Rae ever again.

Rae didn't say *I told you so*, but it was all over her face when she asked Mona to leave.

"We can still be friends," Mona said.

"Yes we can," Rae said. "But not today."

Making that phone call from our kitchen was probably the first thing Mona wishes she hadn't done, but I bet there are others. I bet she wishes she hadn't woken up all those poor Tibetan men, women and children two weeks later, trying to reach Rae by phone when she should have known Rae wouldn't have been staying in a normal hotel—do they even have normal hotels in Tibet?—and she should have known those Tibetans wouldn't speak English, and she should have known it's hard to get out of bed in the middle of the night to answer the phone when the Chinese have chopped down all the trees in your country and the only thing you have to heat your house with is a little yak dung.

She probably wishes even more that Daniel hadn't called Rae to have it out with her *man to man* in the middle of Rae's New Year's dinner party when she had all her theater friends from Denver up to the ranch. She probably wishes she hadn't told her all the things John Candy's ghost said when he came to her house, or all the stuff about her and Rae being married in a past life, and about how tenderly Rae, back when she was a he, buried Mona's body beside the Green River.

She probably wishes she hadn't given Rae the Hello Kitty glitter gel, in February when Rae was on that speaking tour with Jonathan, and that she hadn't given Jonathan the spray to help ease throat pain, when she had never met him and it was clear her name had never come up between them and for all she knew that was the way he always talked and maybe his throat was just fine. She also probably wishes she hadn't seen a jar of Hello Kitty glitter gel later that night, sitting next to the trash can at the Starbucks around the corner from the theater, and when she thought about it, she probably wished she hadn't supposed it was a good sign that Rae hadn't put the jar all the way into the trash.

I bet she really really wishes that she hadn't sent Rae and Howard fifty-seven pounds of Easter candy when they became engaged, wishes she hadn't labeled one huge solid milk chocolate bunny with his name, and wishes above all else that she hadn't spent almost a hundred dollars to send all that chocolate by Federal Express. She probably wishes that she hadn't called Rae from the Pepsi Center women's bath-room, bawling her eyes out during the fifth game of the Stanley Cup Finals, because one time Rae had taken her to a hockey game there and she had got this idea that it was the happiest night of her life.

As I look back on Mona's "wish list" I realize I could sub-title it, *All the Reasons Not to Bother with Love,* not that I don't have plenty of examples from my own life. I'd cauterize my G spot with our crème brûlée torch before I'd go through any of that shit again.

Stanley #1:

I'm going to try to overlook the fact that my opinion was solicited so late in the game. Creatures of the feline persuasion are used to such treatment. However, you've done your project an injustice by not coming to me sooner.

Writers, it is said, all carry a chip of ice in their hearts, and the same can be said of cats. If you want to make all the kiddies laugh and the old ladies tear up, then go ahead and trot out your veterinarian with the heart of gold and your three-legged wolfhound. If you want the unsentimental truth of the matter, always ask a cat.

I'd like it also to be clear that the dogs and I have an understanding. That's how I like to think of it, *an understanding*. Rose likes to use me as a chew toy from time to time, and I'll allow it, as long as she doesn't have any little friends over who think the sky's the limit, and as long as when I make the move to the cabin roof Rose understands that's enough for one day. She's got a lovely soft mouth, and it feels good, for a while, to be massaged in such a manner.

Dante is another matter. He likes me a bit too much—if you'll excuse me saying so—he seems to have a kind of Socratic sexuality if you know what I mean, practically ignoring Rose even in the days when she used to go into heat, and getting his short hairs in a knot over buff little boy dogs, little hounds especially, fox hounds and Chesapeakes, and shockingly, from time to time, even me.

I suppose it's to be expected, given his overclose relationship with his mother, and neither of them is to be blamed for that considering all they've been through together. Who's to say Socrates and his friends didn't have the right idea all along?

I wouldn't know much about any of that, had my balls chopped off back in '92. Sure I get a little thrill when Rose chews on me, but that's kind of a size thing. That girl outweighs me by almost a hundred and thirty-five pounds.

There are Francophiles and there are Anglophiles, there are cooks and there are bakers, and there are dog people and there are cat people and when anyone claims to be both, well, I have to be a bit suspicious. Rae falls squarely into the A list in all three categories, which may explain her sloppy personal life, but Rae and I, too, have an understanding.

She allows me to live in her house rent-free in exchange for keeping the mouse population in check to the point where she doesn't find little red wriggly babies in her underwear drawer. She's not required to pet me or talk to me or make nice with me in any spurious display, but I am appreciative when she turns a blind eye to how much I enjoy

sleeping on her writing chair between ten and twelve in the
A.M. when the sun hits it in a very particular way, and when
she lets it slide if she finds me sucking and kneading on her
blue fleece robe with the grizzly bears on it. A cat's got to
exercise his instincts from time to time after all, even a cat
who has lost his balls.

I'd like to go on record as saying that I like Howard too.
That I am willing to overlook all the unpleasantries involv-
ing the squirt bottle, that I now understand he was new to
the house and not fully cognizant of the power structures in
place. That he believed Rae when she said she was allergic,
and he didn't understand, as we all have come to, that she's
actually talking about an allergy of the spirit, and if I do happen to sleep on her pillow between two-thirty and four-
thirty when the afternoon sun comes in their bedroom
window, he now knows that it is hardly going to send her
into anaphylactic shock.

I'm aware that there was some confusion about the interpretation of my response to the squirt bottle—ten little
mouse heads, all lined up in the mudroom, all facing the
door—and I want to clarify that there was no threat intended
whatsoever.

I was sending one message and one message only and that
was just a note to the front office about how consistently and
effectively I do my job around here. Don't think I'm not as
capable as the next cat of spelling out REDRUM in the body
parts of small furry creatures. If I want to send a threatening
message, they'll be the first to know.

That aside, Howard's a good egg. When you've lived as
long as I have in a house with two women who are mad at

their fathers, a hundred-and-sixty-pound girl dog and a three-legged mama's boy who's as queer as a two-dollar bill, you'd be happy anytime an extra Y chromosome showed up.

And while he's a far cry from what I'd call a man's man, Howard has learned how to use the fencing tool since he's been here, he fires up the barbeque of a summer evening, he's officially in charge of disposing of the rabbits I chase into the basement, corner and eventually kill, and he never fails to say, "Jesus, Stanley, this one's more than half your size," and I'll admit this old cat chest puffs up a little.

And let's face it. This ranch is the Morrison's Cafeteria of Catly Delights. You've got your field mice by the hundreds, your pack rats out in the barn, the swallows that build their nests in the eaves, the rock marmots who live in the culvert, and the jackrabbits that taste like shit but have got game like you cannot believe. That and the reducing diet cat food Darlene and the vet have suddenly decided I need. I say, *Sure thing sister, give me a little RD snack just before I go out and hit the north forty serve-your-self mouse-o-rama.*

But I've wandered from the subject again. I'm not a young cat anymore, though you'd never know it to watch me take a ptarmigan down. If I have any real opinion about Howard, I suppose it would be, Better Rae than Darlene.

And don't go mistaking that for anything it isn't. There is a reason Darlene and I get along so well, and it is not because I spend several hours of my day fretting over her emotional well-being. I don't waste my time having an opinion about whether or not Darlene will ever want to share her life with one of her own kind, or whether when and if she does make that decision, she will choose one that we all can live with, and I assure you she doesn't waste any of her time wondering the same kinds of things about me.

I'm a cat, for chrissake, and I have my own interests to consider. It's bad enough when Rae goes away on an airplane and I have to share Darlene's bed with that unwieldy, leggy hound. I have lived too long and come too far to share my bed with any man who comes down the pike. If he drives a milk truck for a living, or maybe raises wild coho salmon in his spare time, maybe we can talk. In the meantime, I've got everybody under control around here, and that's the way I like it.

Rae #3:

When I was nine years old my friend Victoria invited me for a sleepover and I wanted very much to go, but my mother wouldn't take me. Victoria was my best friend, and even though we were only in fifth grade at the time, we felt much older than that.

We had spent the fall campaigning for George McGovern together. We had knocked on a total of 415 doors that October, and people told us we were the youngest activists they had ever seen. When we were in fourth grade Victoria and I put on the Liza Minnelli version of *Cabaret* in her basement for her brother and her parents. She played all the female parts and I played all the male parts which I had to agree to because it was *her* parents who bothered to watch. I liked being Joel Grey best of all.

The more Victoria and I talked on the phone that day the more imperative it seemed to see each other, so I decided to walk, though it was too far for a girl my age—across busy intersections, through highway underpasses, across deserted cornfields and the enormous parking lots of an industrial park where anything at all might happen, but my mother said, *Go ahead and walk then*, so I did.

I packed my Barbie suitcase, and made it to Victoria's just fine, but on the long trip through the cornfields I made up a story about two police officers who passed me on the County Line Road and asked where I was headed. They searched my suitcase, I told Victoria, and said I was much too young to be out on my own. The officers made me sit in the car, I said, while they called in my description to see if anyone had reported me missing. I convinced them, I said, that I was young but competent, that my mother had approved of my initiative, and they wished me good luck and let me go on my way.

We had a much-too-cheesy frozen casserole for dinner (Victoria's mother was a feminist who didn't believe in cooking), and then her parents took us to see the junior high school production of *Man of La Mancha* because they believed deeply in supporting the arts. When we got home there were two police cars waiting for us in the driveway.

In an instant I knew that Victoria had told her mother my story, and that her mother (whom my father called the last of the great bleeding hearts) had called the cops. For the first, but by no means the last, time in my life I decided to stick to my story, and I did, while each of the cops asked me the same set of questions.

What did the headlights look like? What did the engine sound like? Was there one radio in the cab, or two?

One of the cops was short and round, a Weeble brought to life in a police hat and badge. The other was tall and muscular with a handlebar mustache that he twirled with his tongue while he listened. They thanked me for my time, thanked Victoria's parents for their time, and then they drove away.

No one ever said another word to me about the cops' visit, but years later, in high school, when we were on a French Club field trip to Quebec, and Victoria and I were in an off-again period in our cycle of friendship, she got herself picked up by a French sailor on the ferryboat crossing of the St. Lawrence River to the Place-Royale.

She was one of four girls sharing our room, and though I tried my best to convince Mr. McArthur, our kind and sad French teacher, that Victoria was *really* still in the shower, he finally went and banged on the bathroom door, and there was nothing left to do but tell him the truth. When he called Victoria's mother and said Victoria was missing, the first thing she asked was if I was along, the first thing she said was that she wanted to talk to me.

Yes, I said, I had seen Victoria speaking with the gentleman, and no, I said, she had not asked for my advice, nor had I given her any. This was the truth. We had all been watching Victoria talk to the man in uniform who, in fact, did not look so gentle at all, but we had gotten distracted by the little white Christmas lights that outlined all of the old buildings on the Quebec City Quay, and when we turned our attention back to Victoria, she and her sailor were gone.

It was 1977, we were sophomores in high school, and none of us had been raised to believe that going off with a full-grown French-speaking man in uniform could be regarded as any small thing. Once the goal was no longer to keep the truth from Mr. McArthur, we started to worry about Victoria, and the three of us hunkered down in one hotel bed during the wee hours of the night conjuring up Victoria's horrible, unspeakable demise.

She showed up just after six A.M., with a smile on her face like the cat who ate the cream cheese. When she found out that her mother had called out the National Guard, she asked politely if the three of us would give her a little privacy so she could call home. We went to the coffee shop, our imaginations turning to the thousand and one ways our parents would kill each of us had it been they who got Mr. McArthur's call.

"She's fine," Victoria said later, a bit mysteriously, "relieved of course."

When Mr. McArthur excused Victoria from the day's sight-seeing she said that she wouldn't think of missing it. The smile stayed on her face for weeks after we got back to New Jersey.

Ten years after Victoria's night out in Quebec I was back in Trenton visiting my mother for what would turn out to be one of the last times. I was already calling Colorado my home in those days, working on my MFA in playwriting at the University of Denver. Victoria had quit college after three and a half years and launched herself into a moderately successful acting career—at that point she was living in Hoboken—and my mother would send me her notices and reviews. *Sure wish this had been you*, my mother wrote in her curly cursive in thick black Magic Marker at the top of each article. My mother was writing letters directly to Victoria in those days too, asking her if there wasn't a way she could talk me into wearing a little lipstick, if she couldn't get me to think about joining a Weight Watchers class.

In my mother's car that day, as we passed an endless series of New Jersey strip malls, I made the mistake of mentioning that I had started seeing a therapist. A several-minute silence ensued.

"This generation kills me," my mother finally said, and waited for me to ask her why.

"Do you know what my generation did when we were so-called depressed?" she asked.

"Drank?" I said.

"We lived with it," she said, "until it passed."

At the store she came into the dressing room with me, crinkled her brow at my selection of twelves and fourteens, tucked things in that I would have left out, her arthritic knuckles and serpent's-head ring bruising the soft flesh of my belly.

Outside, summer was giving way to autumn and the air smelled like every day of my childhood, and I said a little prayer for Esther Robinson who was at that point three years in the ground.

"Do you remember," my mother said, as we were walking to the car, "when you were nine years old and you told Victoria that story about those cops pulling you over and searching your little bag?"

"Yes," I said.

She paused and turned for dramatic effect. "Everyone knew you were lying."

In my theory of drama class we had been learning that the storyteller is nothing more than a textual construction, a perpetual work in progress that gets created anew in the mind of each new audience member, but I didn't think that would make any difference to my mother.

"Not everyone," I said, hearing something very different from remorse in my voice. "At least not right away."

Howard #2:

Rae says there are only two good things that ever came out of Columbus, Ohio, and one of them is this pasta dish she had when she was driving across the country on Highway 70 back in 1984 and decided she couldn't take any more gas-station food.

Red pepper linguine with corn, red onions, jalapeños, fresh rosemary off the stalk, olive oil and heavy cream. She makes her own version of it now and always calls it the *Only Good Thing That Ever Came Out of Columbus, Ohio*, until she met me, and then I became the second good thing.

Victoria takes credit for introducing Rae and me at the Denver Center, which is fine with me even though it happens not to be true. Rae is a playwright, and Victoria has directed several of her plays. Rae was at the theater that night as a favor to Victoria, holding a conversation on stage with a younger playwright, a special treat for the donors.

Victoria casts me in a show from time to time, albeit not lately. Several years ago we did *I Hate Hamlet*—I played Gary, the agent—to unadulterated raves.

Rae and Victoria have been playing achievement leapfrog ever since Victoria edged Rae out for president of their third-grade class, or, to hear Victoria tell it, ever since she stole little Rusty McCormick's affection from Rae in the summer between first and second grade. They were both straight A students, both AP Honors everything. When Victoria was president of the Glee Club, Rae served as secretary. When Rae was president of the French Club, Victoria served her back.

In Mr. Lescanic's seventh-grade social studies class they signed up to do a report on César Chávez together. A nice story, but a little dry, so Rae's mother—the *Broadway* actress—suggested they add costumes to make the presentation more of a hit. They dressed up as heads of iceberg lettuce, which they feared at the last minute were unconvincing, and so they made little signs that said LETTUCE and hung them around their necks.

So they're up there in front of the classroom. Victoria is reading from Rae's index cards over Rae's shoulder while Rae reads out loud, and when they get to this quote where César Chávez says, "I don't know what the hell they thought they were doing . . ." Rae chickens out and says "heck" instead, which strikes them both as terribly funny. They try to hold it back, but eventually they are laughing so hard and so quietly that they are shaking up there, these two round green blobs just heaving and shaking, until Mr. Lescanic finally tells them that they can take their seats.

Later that year, Victoria got to play Birdie's sexy girlfriend, Kim McAfee, in *Bye Bye Birdie* and Rae had to play his mother who spends the whole first act wearing a trash can on her head, and in eighth grade Victoria got to play Daisy Mae in *Li'l Abner* and Rae had to play Mammy Yokum. In ninth grade they did *Godspell*, and Rae played the piano, which is pretty cool, but Victoria got to be the one to sing "Where Are You Going," which is cooler still. Rae graduated fifth in her high school class; Victoria was somewhere down in the twenties. After college Victoria got her name in lights all over the tri-state area and Rae went out west to start writing for a living, first a bunch of articles, and eventually the play that gave her a name. She was always telling Victoria about the mountains, how good it would be for her to get off the East Coast, to see the Denver Center theater complex that was bigger than anything of its kind back east. Victoria was living in Hoboken at the time with a history Ph.D. who made Victoria move out for a week every six months when his Catholic mother came to visit. He called himself a male feminist and said he wouldn't marry Victoria because of all the ways the institution of marriage had repressed women for centuries. Eventually Victoria decided to try her luck out west.

What happened—in fact—on the evening of Carmen's opening at the Denver Center, was that Rae came over to congratulate Carmen, and Carmen was hanging all over me the way she tended to whenever Duke wasn't around, and soon I found myself introduced to Rae.

I had heard of her, of course. But I have to admit I hadn't seen or read any of her plays. I have been told on more than one occasion that I don't have a grand ambition for the theater, and while that may be true, it is also true that I have more ambition for the theater than I have for anything else. I get off book faster than any actor I know, and if given the right supporting role I can make or break a show. Do I study the masters? Do I take classes when I'm between shows? Do I read widely in the canonized literature? I rent movies, and I work just enough to pay my bills, which I have managed, all my life, to keep to the barest minimum.

My mother always said, if you don't know what to say in a social situation just smile really big, and so that's what I did. I smiled and worked my expressive eyebrows up and down and didn't take off my cap. (It was, after all, February).

I made Rae laugh, she says now, though I hardly remember speaking, let alone saying anything funny. It was then, and only then, that Victoria approached, kissed me so sloppily she may as well have lifted her leg on me, and asked if I would make sure that Rae found her way back to the parking garage okay.

Now let me make it perfectly clear that if anybody ever wanted to find their way out of anywhere, I would be the last person they should ask for help.

Rae was wearing this very sexy black lace dress and these big square-heeled velvet boots which sounds like an odd combination, but it was really working for her at the reception. I guess the boots must have been uncomfortable, because before we left the theater she changed into her tennis shoes, and the tennis shoes with all that black lace made me feel sweet and sad.

We got to her car (as it turned out *she* led *me* to the parking garage), and these two enormous dogs leapt out of the hatchback. As if she had given some kind of command, the one with four legs ran right over to the drain and peed into it.

"This is Dante," she said, of the other dog, the three-legged one whose attention was so fixed on Rae it was as if he thought she might vanish into thin air at any second, "and this is Rose."

Rose winked at me, wiggled her butt, and trotted a large circle around our part of the garage.

"Rose isn't a very good listener," Rae said.

After we managed to corral Rose, and once the two dogs were reloaded into the 4-Runner I said,

"I'm glad I got to meet the dogs," and she said,

"Well yes, that's the important thing," and then we both got into our cars and drove away.

IN THOSE DAYS, checking my voice mail was often more than I could stand, but about three days later I got my nerve up and lo!, as they say at Shakespeare in the Park, there was a message from Rae Rutherford.

She started off with how nice it was to meet me, and then she apologized for driving out of the parking garage so abruptly—which she hadn't, by the way, I was the one who pulled out first—she said she was anticipating the pressure of the traffic she would find at the top of the ramp.

I liked that. It sounded like something I would think was too dumb to say. But then Rae said she heard I was going to Asia soon, and that she had been to Asia herself, several times, and if I ever wanted to talk about Asia, if I had any thoughts on Asia or questions about Asia, here were about thirteen different numbers where I could call her back.

Just so you know, I *am* one of those guys who needs to be hit over the head with a two-by-four, and that phone call, it had that solid wood quality, and for that I am truly grateful.

I held the phone away from my face and said to Duke and Carmen, "Check this out, you guys, Rae Rutherford, the playwright, is scoping me."

Carmen got one of those looks on her face, the old, *I'm really happy for you but you and I both know you don't have the emotional fortitude to get involved in anything like that* look. I closed my bedroom door and left Rae a message.

"This is Howard," I said. "I've actually already been to Asia, I went with my sister Connie, to Thailand and Vietnam recently, and it was wonderful and I'd love to trade stories sometime."

I paused then, a pause that felt so long in my own head that I couldn't believe the machine hadn't cut me off, and then I realized that it probably hadn't cut me off because I was making too much noise breathing, and then I thought, *That's okay I'll just wait to the end of the message until it asks me if I want to rerecord,* and then I thought, *But what if it's a machine and not voice mail and doesn't have that feature?,* so after what must have been about ten years of silence, I said, "I'm starting rehearsal on a new show this week, which means I'll have Fridays and Saturdays off for a while, and maybe we could get together and have lunch, or something."

I tried to suck the "or something" back into my mouth, but then the phone beeped and clicked and all I could do was console myself that although my message had been dweebie, it was nowhere near as dweebie as hers.

We made a date for two weeks from Friday.

Victoria said, "Howard, those dogs are her life. Make no mistake about it," on the same day she called Rae and said, "You know, Howard wears purple high tops, almost everywhere!"

Still, I was staying pretty calm right up until the Thursday night before.

"Here's the thing," I said on the phone when I finally got up the nerve to call her, too late, sometime after eleven, "I'm not really sure whether I want our relationship to go down the romantic path or the friendship path."

"Of course you aren't, Howard," she said, "we've only known each other for five minutes."

"Right, right," I said, "but I don't want you to have . . . unrealistic expectations."

"I'm sure," she said, "that I don't."

"Well, I'm glad to hear that," I said, "because I tend to be kind of a freak when things get complicated."

"Howard," she said, "it's only one date."

"That's just what I mean," I said. "I'm not sure whether or not we should call it that."

There was a long silence, and then a sigh.

"You know," she said, "I'm not going to be one of those girls who plays hard to get, because first, I'm too old for it, and second, I *am* hard to get, if simply by virtue of my schedule. I don't have time for the peek-a-boo part of a relationship, and if you could see how empty my expectation bucket is at present you would be truly amazed." She took a deep breath and waited for me to say something, but I didn't know what it might be.

"So," she finally said, "do you want to go out with me tomorrow night or not?"

When she put it that way, how could I refuse?

I guess you won't be surprised when I tell you that ours was not the run-of-the-mill first date. There was the reading of poetry, for instance, on her part, and there was my performance of *Freakus Discus,* the one-man show I wrote about the second coming of the God of Disco, and I did it up for her at her apartment as if it were a stage performance, the platform shoes, the 'fro and fake chest hair, the mirror ball I keep in my car for just such an occasion; she got the works. There was the trip to Boulder to see Madame Roslinka, the fortune-teller Rae first went to the morning after she met me, and Madame Roslinka told me there was a person who had been in my life for a very long time who would, as long as I let her, stand in the way of my happiness. And there was my decision, on the way back to the car from Madame Roslinka's, to shed all my clothes and climb a tree.

On the second date, on the way to dinner, I decided to lie down across Speer Boulevard during rush hour to express the intensity of the feelings I was starting to have for Rae. She was about to go off camping with her friend Mona for the week, and I didn't like the way it was making me feel.

But she just sat there, as calm as a post amid the blaring of horns and the screeching of brakes, so I got back into the car and tried to do the opposite of what I'm trained to do. I tried to convert action into speech.

When we finally got to the restaurant Rae looked across the table at me and said, "I want to make one thing perfectly clear, Howard, and that is that I know you are always acting."

All of a sudden it seemed a lot quieter in our section of the restaurant, and she said, "Like back there in the car, I mean that speech you made was maybe twenty, twenty-five minutes long, and there's no way the real Howard comes out for more than two or three minutes at a time."

I looked around and saw all these other people at all these other tables, eating their fish, eating the little piles of mashed potatoes and snow peas that the fish was sitting on, and I thought, *Yeah, but aren't they acting all the time too?*

And she said, "It's not that I think it's false, what you are saying; it's not that I don't believe you; it's just that there's Howard, and then there's the whole cycle of parts that Howard plays."

The waiter came over to ask if everything was okay, and I wanted to say, *But look, look at him, he's just acting like a waiter.* What I said instead was, "You're making me feel a little self-conscious here," and she said,

"I don't mean to. See, I'm always writing, and you, you're always acting. That's why we get along so well."

The last thing we said that night was that we weren't going to be like those ridiculous couples who call each other every five minutes, but the next day I woke up so charged up that I thought, if I wanted to, I could make electronic objects explode. TVs, stereos, the little refrigerator I kept take-out in next to my bed. This seemed like information worthy of a phone call, so I left the briefest message on her cell.

The day after that, *I* felt like the thing that was going to explode. I could picture it, on my way to rehearsal. The headline: *Beater Accord Hatchback Spotted on I-25 Being Driven by Beam of Pure Light.* How could I not call with news like that?

On the third day I was on my lunch break, sitting out-side the Market on Larimer Street having a green apple soda and my standard turkey salad sandwich, breezing through the entertainment section of the *Post*, when it hit me: I had met the woman with whom I wanted to spend the rest of my life. I must have been gasping or grunting or something at that point, because the two women at the table next to me collected their things and moved to a table inside.

I tore out a page from my notebook and began to write out my proposal. Rae and I had known each other at that point exactly one month to the day. We'd had three dates, two in Denver, one at her ranch, five phone calls where both of us were actually on the line simultaneously, and depending on what counts and what doesn't, sex somewhere between four and twenty-three times. I would seal my proposal in an envelope for exactly one year, and in twelve months to the day I would hand it to her, and she would know how long I'd been holding my breath.

I wrote out the proposal, looked around for a flower to seal in the envelope, but it was too early for flowers so I had to settle for a packet of Sweet'n Low and the parsley garnish that came with my sandwich, and licked the flap.

There was one other couple on the patio deeply engaged in conversation.

"Excuse me," I said, leaning toward their table.

"What?" the man said. His face looked as though it had been disfigured in a knife fight, and possibly his next victim would be me.

"I'm sorry to bother you," I said, "but I've just realized that I've met the woman I'm going to marry, and I can't tell her yet, so I'm telling you instead."

The man's face softened slightly.

"Why can't you tell her?" the girl wanted to know. She was a child, I realized, much too young for the man with the scar on his face, and yet clearly in love with him.

"It's too soon," I said, "but I've never been surer of anything in my life."

"How do you know she'll say yes?" the man said.

This was not a point I had considered. "That's why I have to wait," I said. "I'm going to wait one year from today to tell her"—I patted the envelope in my pocket—"or whenever I think the time is right."

The right time, as it turned out, came that Friday, three hours after Rae got back from her camping trip with Mona. We were sitting on the front porch of her Denver apartment. She was tanned from the desert, and her legs were extra ropy, extra strong.

"You and Mona—" I began.

"No," she said. "Once. And when I say once, I mean once. Not, you know, like once upon a time."

"Really," I said, trying like I always was with Rae to catch up to the conversation.

"We're in the trying-to-be-friends-anyway part," she said, "but to tell you the truth, I don't think we are going to make it."

Dante was lying quietly at Rae's feet, and he raised his head when three cairn terriers trotted past with their owner on the other side of the street.

"Girls can be mind-fuckers," I said.

"You can say that again."

Rose was inside, because she doesn't always listen, but she was standing right at the door and I could feel her hot breath on my leg through the screen.

"Well, I'm glad to hear that," I said, "because I've actually been doing some . . . well . . . I'm not sure we should call it, 'thinking about the future.'"

"Then what should we call it?" she said. She was massaging behind Dante's ears with her toes.

"I was thinking," I said, "that we could call it, 'checking in about the future.'"

"Checking in," she said.

"Yes," I said.

"Subtle difference," she said.

"Yes," I said.

"And if we were to 'check in' about the future," she said, stretching her long legs in front of her—there was something about the musculature that made her legs look longer than they actually were—"what would you say?"

"That when I think of the future," I began, "I find my thoughts running more and more often to the place where they involve you."

She nodded her head, didn't speak.

"I mean, please don't think that by bringing this up I'm expecting you to say anything back," I said. "That is absolutely not at all what I am asking for."

"Okay," she said.

She stretched her legs again and turned to the entertainment section of the *Post*. After what seemed like several minutes she said, "What kind of food were you thinking about for dinner?"

"Maybe I was wrong," I said. "Maybe I actually do need you to say just the slightest something."

"To check in," she said.

"Yes," I said.

"I don't have any problem with it," she said, and rose from her chair, signaling the end of the conversation.

In the morning Rae decided she wanted to drive up to Winter Park for what she calls the world's greatest breakfast at a restaurant called The Kitchen. We had been working on our first dog song ever, "No One Ever Gives Me Steak," sung to the tune of the old Howard Jones song "No One Ever Is to Blame."

"Hey," I said, as we left the interstate for U.S. 40 and its trip over Berthoud Pass, "let's you and I do a scene."

"I don't do scenes," she said.

"Come on," I said, "just one time, it will be fun." I waited her out while she stared at the rising snowdrifts on the side of the road.

"What's the scene?" she finally asked.

"Okay, you're the woman."

"Thanks."

"And you've decided you want to spend the rest of your life with me."

"I see," she said.

"And you are trying to tell me that, but I keep talking and won't let you get a word in edgewise."

I have to give her credit for trying, but between you and me and the fence post, it's a good thing she gave up acting to learn how to write. I poured sentences full of nonsense one on top of the other, and at last she managed to get the words out, "Howard, I want to spend the rest of my life with you," right as we reached the eleven-thousand-foot snow-covered top of Berthoud Pass.

"Pull over, pull over," I said.

There's not much at the top of Berthoud Pass, just a funky little ski area and the place where the plows turn around, but on a clear day you can see the Bear Claw to the north and all the way up into the Devil's Thumb country. "Come on," I said, "let's go sit in the snow."

We decided that there was too much traffic to let the dogs out, so we locked them in the car with the windows half open, and wandered over to a pile of snow that in a few months would turn out to be a picnic table, and that's when I invented Oprah Fantasy #2.

"In Oprah Fantasy #2," I said, "Oprah and I have become best buddies. She calls me up and we exchange recipes. She calls me 'Howard, my main male,' and I call her 'Oprah, my fine female,' but we're just kidding around of course because in reality, we're only good friends."

"In reality," Rae said, squinting up at the snowflakes.

"Right," I said. "Now remember the article you wrote in Oprah Fantasy #1?"

"The Most Amazing Motherfucker on the Planet?" she said.

"Yeah. Well, now you have expanded it into a three-act play."

"How clever of me," she said.

"And now Oprah wants you back on the show. But when I tell her I've decided that I want to spend the rest of my life with you, she comes up with this great idea. She says,

'Howard, my main male, how would you like to propose to Rae right here on the show?' And I say, 'Oh, wow, I'm going to have to think about that Oprah, and make sure it's what Rae would really want.' "

Rae was looking at me the way she does when I'm straying a bit from where she's willing to travel with me, so I pulled up for a minute.

"I mean, I *am* fully aware that the *real* Rae would not choose to be proposed to by the *real* Howard on the *real* Oprah show."

"And would likely never be given that choice . . ." she said.

"Right," I said, "but the fantasy Howard decides that the fantasy Rae would think it was a great idea."

"You are a strange, strange man," she said, which gave me the strength to continue.

"So Oprah flies Rae to Chicago to do the show and then she flies Howard to Chicago secretly."

"Is that the actual Chicago?" Rae asked. "Or another one?"

"The play has been a huge success, a big-dollar movie option, translation rights have been sold all over the world . . . you should hear it in the African languages with all the little clicks."

"Those are my teeth, Howard," she said. "I'm freezing to death."

"Oprah wants Rae to read from Act One, Scene Seven, which is the scene where the female character decides that she—"

"Wants to spend the rest of her life with the most amazing motherfucker—"

"Exactly," I said. "But the audience has seen the play so many times already that they have it memorized, and as Rae reads, the camera pans the audience and they are all mouthing the words along with her."

"Nice," she said.

"And Rae finishes the scene and everyone is clapping and weeping and Oprah wipes a tear from her eye and says, 'I don't want to change the subject, but I do have another guest we need to bring out right now, and that's Howard.' And I come out wearing purple—"

"And the audience goes wild."

"Well, yes, and Oprah says, 'Howard, how did you like that scene?' And I say, 'well I love that scene . . . I mean, Rae, I'm not a playwright, but I might make just the slightest change to the end of that scene.' And Rae says, 'Go ahead,' but she's got a slightly pissed-off look on her face, so I say quickly, 'In my version Howard says, "Rae, will you marry me?" ' and Rae says . . ."

I couldn't tell if the real Rae was frowning so much because she was cold or because she was mad, or because in Oprah Fantasy #2 I revealed a side of myself that is somehow unpalatable to her. I tried giving her the cue one more time.

"And Rae says . . ."

"Yes?" she said.

Cars with tightly packed ski racks were crawling up and down the pass toward Winter Park and a light snow had begun to fall. Rae was still frowning at me, and though part of me felt like I had just successfully pulled off the ultimate stealth proposal, another part of me sensed that something was very wrong.

"So what did you think of Oprah Fantasy #2?" I asked her.

"Howard," she said, "how many ways are you fucking with me right now?"

"Okay, okay," I said, "forget that." I looked around for a prop but there was nothing but snow on all sides of me. Back in the 4-Runner, Dante had his nose pushed out the half-open window into the air.

I got down on one knee, and extended one arm to the heavens. "In front of these magnificent mountains," I began, "in front of these perfect flakes of snow. In front of thousands of years of geological change. In front of my dead mother, and your dead mother—"

"Howard," she said, "cut it out."

"Will you marry me?" I said.

And she said, "Yes."

Four

·

The
Wedding

Dante #3:

She calls it the happy dance, though happiness is, in truth, only one component of it. I do it on the rare occasions when she leaves me at home . . . usually it's when we've gone to Denver, and she's going out for the evening and thinks better of parking me in some dank carbon-monoxide-filled downtown garage.

She'll say something like, "I'm sorry big man, but you are staying here. It will only be a couple of hours," and I'll give her one long look so she is clear that I would prefer it otherwise, and then turn and head for the bed—her bed—so she knows there are no hard feelings after all.

I'll spend the hours dozing, keeping one ear trained on the street, smelling her smells, dreaming of her return. There are other 4-Runners on our block, even one other '98, but I can tell the sound of hers for sure when she hits the corner of Ogden and Virginia.

By the time she turns her key in the lock I have my nose pressed against the door, and my tail thwacking whatever surface is most handy. She opens the door and I sprint down the three cement stairs and into the postage-stamp yard and spring, kangaroolike, in false charges and feints.

This is when she starts saying, "Oh we are happy dancing! Look at the handsome happy dancer!" and she starts leaping around as well, and the thing simply takes on its own momentum. We look like shadow boxers, I imagine, jumping around that piece of grass that's so small there's really more up and down than there is side to side.

If Rose has been sharing my vigil, though one could hardly call it that since she whiles away the hours eating or snoring on the *dog* bed, she runs out with me and pees. At that point the hierarchy demands, of course, that I have to go and pee where she pees. Sadly, the happy dance is interrupted.

Lao-tzu said, "Mastering others is strength, mastering oneself is true power," and I know that in peeing where Rose pees I fall down on at least one, if not both counts, so as soon as the peeing is accomplished, I'm back to happy dancing again.

I HAVE A PEN PAL. Her name is Sophie and she is a thirteen-year-old human. She has curly brown hair and warm brown eyes and a gentle manner that is very pleasing, and she is also one leg shy of a full set. I visited her in the hospital several times, but now she's back home and feeling better. She writes me twice a month and always includes a picture, and then my human and I write her back.

Sophie picked me out of a photograph album of dogs with osteosarcoma. She said it was because our histories of disease were so similar, but I think if she was being honest with herself she'd admit she fell in love with my face. I fell in love with her face too—a little—proof that even when one loves another more than life itself, it is possible, even pleasurable, to develop the occasional harmless crush. I am happy to share my human with Howard, and so far my human has been nothing but supportive of this dalliance with my new young friend.

"If you know the power of a generous heart," Buddha said, "you will not let a single meal pass without giving to others." That's one of my favorite sayings, one I like to meditate upon specifically when I am lying under the dinner table, waiting to see if a little lamb or pork or chicken might fall my way.

Another favorite, "For greater than all the joys of Heaven and Earth, greater still than dominion over all worlds is the joy of reaching the stream." This one seems particularly apt after a longish hike, and the two taken together seem like fairly incontrovertible evidence that the great teacher must have spent at least one lifetime as a dog. Or was just about to.

Dr. Evans, the man who stole these last two years from my cancer and gave them back to me, had, I believe, a generous heart. "Where can I find a man who has forgotten words," Buddha asked, "so that I can have a word with him?"

That is Dr. Evans. A man of few words and many Milk-Bones. He had a certain respect for my human that during the months of my most intense treatment turned into genuine affection. She fretted so about her middle-of-the-night phone calls to him when my infection flared up or about the times he had to meet her, halfway between the ranch and the hospital, no small ride for either of them, to change my bandage and assess the wound. But she would not have needed to fret. In a perfect world, each man's suffering would teach him to be kinder; in the one we inhabit, the truly kind tend to find each other in the end.

Two and a half years ago, when I was first diagnosed, my human sat down on the porch and cried. "If they have to cut off his leg," she said, "I'll never see the happy dance again." Little did she know I had a better happy dance in store for her, a three-legged gem of a happy dance so unique I know for a fact that she's never once missed the four-legged version.

Jonathan #2:

Rae says my problem is too much time on my hands. She says when you get to be our age there is nothing more satisfying than work, and I don't do nearly enough of it. And okay, it's true that I haven't had a play up since we did *Stop! Think!* at Teatro Spagnola, and what I have *not* been doing with my spare time is turning out sheets and sheets of new work. And while it is also true that Rae won't sign on to a project with me anymore after that year we got invited back to Sundance and I showed up three days late in a red Mustang convertible with a girl—and even then without the slightest idea in my head about what we might write there together—I'd like to say in my defense that sometimes I need more than time to make the writing thing happen.

For a while, coffee was the secret. Peet's Espresso Forte, don't spare the grinder, straight up, *serré*, as the French say, dense. When that stopped working I went to scotch. If it's good enough for so and so, et cetera. Scotch was a little pricey, and I noticed that quantity-wise it reached the point of diminishing returns faster than the Peet's, but I owe at least *The Guardian* and half of *Mortimer's Dream* to the well-aged oiliness of Loch Dhu and Talisker. I went through the typical crank phase in the nineties, knew a bad match when I saw it, and moved on with my savings account more or less intact. Then it was Italy. Rae was right; a new landscape was all I needed. I got Rae to go with me on more than one occasion by telling her that unlike the Americans, the Italians wanted theater to be imperfect and alive.

When I got tired of Italy I came home and moved to the Sierra foothills, told myself the formula for making writing happen was organic Scottish Highland beefsteaks for dinner and ESPN, very low in the background all the time. I learned so much about NHL hockey that year it gave Rae and me a whole new repertoire. Rae is a sports fanatic. It was the one point where she and her old man intersected, hockey games, baseball games, football games, but of all the games they went to, Rae loved hockey best. Irv's firm shared season tickets to the Philadelphia Flyers, good seats, right behind the home bench. All the trainers fell in love with little Rae, and why wouldn't they, this five-, six-, seven-year-old in pigtails and Keds, who knew the difference between a hook and a slash, between boarding and cross-checking, between a charge and a dive, who knew every starting player's plus/minus score, even the healthy scratches, who would stand up on her chair and scream in this tiny little voice, "Hey ref, is there somebody paying you off?"

She went home with a puck every week, usually from a trainer, but sometimes from a player and one time the great

Rick MacLeish himself—prettiest skater to ever grace the NHL—motioned her over when he'd come off the ice for the last time during the final minute of play in a 5–0 rout of the hated New York Rangers, and when no one was looking, he passed her his stick. She always wanted to get to the game in time to hear the National Anthem, and she'd get mad as a hornet at Irv when he'd insist they leave early to beat the bridge traffic if the game was in hand one way or the other.

When summer came it was the Phillies, and she knew all the position players' batting averages and all the pitchers' ERAs, starters and the bullpen. They sat on the first level, behind the away bench at the Vet, but she still managed to get her glove signed by Mike Schmidt, Greg Luzinski, Tug McGraw and a couple of the others, all those guys who would go on to win the pennant in a couple of years.

My personal favorite ESPN event is the World Series of Poker, all those pretenders losing all that dough, and the ones pretending to be pretenders . . . but that's the problem with a writing trick, inevitably the trick becomes more interesting than me.

Rae calls it the happy catch-22 of writing, that if we ever felt deserving we wouldn't do it anymore. She says what we have to live for are those moments when we are sitting in the theater, it might be the first read-through, it might be halfway into the rehearsal process, it might be opening night, and it might be halfway through the run. But somewhere in there is a moment when an actor takes the words we have written and transforms them into something alive, takes those flat black marks away from us, explodes them into something we had never, ever imagined, makes them bigger than we are and even bigger than the words themselves. That alchemical moment, Rae says, is worth the whole hill of beans.

And she might be right, but by the time that happens for me I don't care so much about that play anymore because I'm already on to feeling unworthy about the next one.

"All that unworthiness is just disguised grandiosity," Rae said, "and you should know that it doesn't fool me for a second."

Which I know really means, *Shut the fuck up, let's go get a burger.* Once you write with somebody long enough you can decode them that way. Sometimes after the first fifteen minutes of hanging out together Rae and I give up language completely and rely on gesture for a while.

It's hard not having Rae around much anymore. She had a way of brightening up my day somehow, even though she's always been one sad and tough little cookie. I'm glad she married a man who could make her laugh.

At the wedding Victoria kept shooting me these looks, like wasn't I so sorry it wasn't me after all these years, and I'm so suggestible—as Rae is constantly pointing out—that I wondered if the tingle I was feeling *was* regret, and not just a good old-fashioned altitude drunk setting in.

Rae had some fancy-pants caterer who came all the way from Denver. I don't know who was paying for that. Goat cheese and duck quesadillas and Cakebread Reserve chardonnay, elk loin and mashed potatoes with white truffle oil and a very fancy French cake, all done up with fresh columbines, white tablecloths and silver troughs to hold the flowers. A staff of eight for a wedding of forty. Wouldn't it just be the shits if we all found out Howard was secretly loaded on top of everything else?

His family didn't make it. I get the feeling either they weren't invited or they don't approve, but neither Rae nor Howard said a word about it. It's all part of this having-boundaries-as-a-couple thing they are doing, which frankly gets my goat. I mean, where were those boundaries when I was the only person she could reach on the phone when Adam finally left, or when Tucker was back in the drunk tank, or the day she came home from the grocery store to Peter's *Dear Jane* note.

Up her ass is where, I can tell you that.

Of course Howard's family wouldn't approve. I mean when the baby of the family, after staying almost immaculately single for thirty-two years, finally brings home his bride-to-be and it turns out to be Rae Rutherford?

I mean I love her. But let's face it. She's not exactly somebody you'd ever want to bring home to meet Mom. But Howard doesn't have a mom, and perhaps, Dr. Watson, we have solved the mystery at last.

I kept wishing all through the wedding that by some miracle that asshole Peter would happen by to pick up the expensive jackets he forgot. They were engaged, you know, not just living together. A big chunky sapphire ring that sat on her hand and that Rae recently had melted down and made into a necklace. The jeweler recovered so much platinum in the deal that Rae made a hundred dollars. All those plans and nothing but a three-line note left on the kitchen table. Not a word more, not a word even to this day.

Except one word that nobody knows about.

Victoria heard from Peter.

She didn't tell Rae. How could she? It was a couple months after he disappeared, return address from somewhere back east, maybe Virginia. Just a note to say hi. Just a note to say he hoped Victoria didn't take his picture down off of her refrigerator. Just a note to say that he thought they had an inexplicable connection, he felt it the night they walked around Aspen together and looked in all the windows of the shops.

Here's the punch line. Victoria's been to Aspen and Peter's been to Aspen but never at the same time. He has Victoria mixed up with Courtney, Rae's other very attractive, slightly older, and exceptionally thin friend.

That's what forty years of size three will get you. The likes of Peter sniffing around, never mind he can't keep her skinny ass straight from any other bimbo that comes along. I've never been sure whether Victoria is really a friend of Rae's, or just somebody she always felt she stacked up pretty well against. I don't trust Victoria, but then, there are a hell of a lot of people who don't trust me.

Rae spent half of her childhood over at Victoria's house, the other half with Esther Robinson. But Victoria spent a few nights in Rae's house too, checking out the stills Gloria had up all over the living room, black and whites of her and Sinatra, of her and Bob Hope. Gloria must have always been looking at Victoria a little hungrily too, the dress-up daughter she didn't get for herself. Victoria would barely enter the room before Gloria would whip out her little Le Sportsac bag to compare lipsticks.

"Come over here Rae and look at this color Victoria wears," Gloria used to say, "it would hardly show up at all" . . . and Rae would make a feeble gesture of acquiescence and the next thing you know Gloria would be drawing a bright little mouth in Holiday Coral over Rae's mouth, and Rae would endure it until her mother changed the subject and then she'd get rid of it with a swipe of her hand.

I've never had a problem finding somebody to have sex with—there was no shortage of easy targets at the wedding, and if I had wanted to put in any effort I'll bet I could have snuck Victoria away for a quickie as well—and I've already mentioned that marriage isn't part of my vocabulary. Rae was always my reality check, which is no small role, but not enough to ask somebody to put her own life on hold for. Howard's a hell of a guy, the first one who knows better than to try to get between Rae and that dog.

Rae's first word was *dog*, not *Dada*, not *Mama*, not even *Esther* (which was her second word), but *dog*. It was Esther Robinson's doing. Esther, the one good thing about Rae's childhood, a lonely old lady who had somehow become an expert on child-rearing even though the only marriage she'd ever had hadn't made it past the seventy-two-hour mark. Esther would come over to babysit and take Rae out in her stroller. She'd whistle once and these two big neighborhood dogs, German shepherd types, but mutts in their hearts, would show up before they got to the end of the driveway, like they'd been waiting all day for Esther and Rae to appear.

Rae would grab Salt with one fat little hand and Pepper with the other, and those dogs would walk along with that baby and the old lady just as long and as slow as they wanted to go.

A dog was the last thing Rae's old man wanted around. In four short years Irv had gone from being the most eligible bachelor in Trenton, New Jersey; from dating two virginal Catholic twins while keeping somebody named Isabelle—the one true love of his life—in the wings until he got good and ready; from filling his days with tennis and convertibles and just enough work to pay for his room at the old board-inghouse on the Delaware River and the kind of clothes that would fool everyone at the country club where he was more or less a permanent nonpaying guest because all those lawyers and surgeons were just aching for a chance to beat him out on the courts.

And then he met Gloria. She was in a show at the Bucks County Playhouse, *Happiest Millionaire*, with Walter Pidgeon coming out to New Hope to do the summer theater thing. She had great legs, shapely legs like Rae's that made her look tall on stage, much taller than she actually was. Irv went back again the very next night and had a dozen roses sent back-stage with his phone number. He took her out on Monday, the only night the theater was dark. He had a yellow Cadillac convertible and he picked her up with the top down in a powder-blue suit, a white Panama hat and a lavender hand-kerchief, daring her to resist him.

They went to Mary Marks, Irv's favorite Italian place in Trenton, and Gloria downed what in those days passed for some pretty classy gin in quantities Irv had never seen before in a woman, and then she got all weepy and confessed she was in love with her agent. He was a Catholic man who had married a Catholic girl, and while he and Gloria managed to see each other several times a year for a week or two at a time, the agent had been clear right from the beginning that he was far too invested in his religion to even contemplate leaving his wife.

She confessed that both Buddy Hackett and another actor whose name I don't remember but who I see from time to time on the tube doing those Pepperidge Farm commercials had proposed to her during the affair, but she hadn't found it in herself to say yes, if yes meant breaking things off with her agent.

Maybe it was the four cocktails, but Irv took that part as a challenge, and an hour later when he dropped her off at the summer theater housing, after she had thrown up all over the pale yellow leather seats of the third-best car he ever owned and didn't so much as apologize, he said to her, "You better get your shit together because we are going to get married," and six weeks later they were.

Everyone assumed that Irv and Gloria married because Gloria was pregnant, though it was just over a year before Rae came along. Irv couldn't have thought he would give up Isabelle. Perhaps he thought Gloria wouldn't really give up her agent and in that way they'd be perfectly matched. But she did give him up, exchanged him for a quiet and deadly rage that she directed at Irv and that Irv sent right back at her until she died and what Rae likes to call the Thirty Years War ended.

The first time I met Irv I told Rae that he wasn't the only soulless man I had ever met but perhaps he was the most convincing. Rae goes to see him once a year or flies him out to see her. She finds a way to take him to a ball game, swears he's mellowing with age, gets all hopeful after a phone conversation where they manage not to take each other's head off.

She says he'd probably like her a little better if she presented him with human—rather than canine—grandchildren.

It's fun to think about what Gloria would make of Howard, though she didn't care much for the men in Rae's life generally, so scared she was that Rae was going to settle down and start having babies and not become the *Next Big Thing*.

I'm not the type to go around telling people's secrets, but back when Rae was fresh out of grad school she got knocked up by that Russian choreographer who married her for the green card. Her first play had just come out to rather startling good reviews in Denver and when she finally broke down and called home in tears Gloria said, "Rae, you have a very special gift, a talent that many people envy. The second you decide to have that baby you become ordinary, exactly the same as everyone else."

"It seems to me," Rae has said to me on more than one occasion, "that having a baby requires an enormous amount of faith. More than I could ever imagine having." Her mother never said that having dogs would make her ordinary, which explains the current state of affairs.

You should have seen Dante back when he had four legs. I used to head up to the ranch on the weekends with them sometimes, back before Italy, when we were working together at the Denver Center. I'd take him walking with me first thing in the morning, when the dirt on the sides of the gravel road was standing up tall in response to the dew and he'd tear off after a rabbit or a rock marmot, or sometimes just for the sheer pleasure of running, and I would measure my stride against his and the count was exactly ten to one.

One time one of the cows from the neighboring ranch got over on Rae's land somehow, and Dante went out after her like a thing possessed. The cow's eyes rolled back in her head and she went over that barbed wire as if it were a pole vault and landed flat on her back on the other side. Rae made a sad sound and Dante looked worried until Bessie got up, shook herself down, and trotted off to join her bovine friends.

When Dante was diagnosed I told Rae, "No," which is not the kind of thing one says to her casually. "Quality of life," I said. "You can't know the mind of a dog, Rae, and no dog in his right mind wants to have chemotherapy." Which is not even to mention how he loved to run, which is not even to mention one leg shy of a full set, which is not even to mention that they were talking about getting him another year at the outside, if everything went great.

"If I don't know that dog's mind," Rae said, "I don't know fuck-all about anything."

Which I correctly assumed was the end of the conversation. And while it is true that he could run like something shot from God's own cannon, Dante was never what you'd call lighthearted or free. Even as a puppy he would worry about his toys; when they squeaked or rattled he seemed to think they were in some kind of pain, and he would bring them all onto his bagel bed, stare over them with those eyebrows of his going up and down, and nuzzle but never chew them.

He kept his eye on Rae like that too, as though if he lost attention for even a minute, some terrible thing would come along and get her. He liked to walk right behind her, his head slung down between those powerful shoulders, his wet nose every now and then brushing the crease behind her knee, his expression always drifting somewhere between wise and worried, his tail, long and strong beyond all reason, keeping time with both of their steps.

Shit. If I knew anything about that kind of love I might take on more than a houseplant, which by the way I don't have any of either. Rae never quite trusted me after I told her to let that dog die, though in my heart I was only trying to spare her.

"That's your problem," she said. "How good you are at sparing everybody."

Nobody's ever going to accuse Rae of killing anybody with kindness, but I'll say this about her, a person always knows where he stands. My reality check, like I told you. She said, "Jonathan, you ought to drag your ass back to the computer because what you make there is the only thing about you that doesn't suck," and I know what she was really saying is that I'm a little bit of a genius, and that she loves me, and that I basically rock.

Rae #4:

On the morning of the wedding we went to town to meet the mayor, who had agreed to do the deed. Howard said he wanted to write our vows and I thought, more power to him. I don't do crossword puzzles and I don't like Scrabble and the thing I maybe hate more than anything else on earth is refrigerator magnet poetry. When the mayor asked to hear the vows, it was my first time hearing them as well.

"I love Rae Rutherford," Howard began, his voice big and resonant, "I want to take care of her, raise dogs with her, strive to understand her, and build with her a happy life. I want to—"

"Howard," the mayor said, "those words are lovely, but it is usually the custom at a wedding to address your future partner rather than the audience."

I loved him so much in that moment, my Howard, always playing to the crowd.

It was right after we shook the mayor's hand and said we'd see her in a couple of hours that I started to feel a bad little buzz between my temples. I probably shouldn't have had the fifth latte. I probably should have tried to do a little better, that week, with sleep. But on the way back to the ranch from town, the impossibility that any of this could turn out well hit me like a bucket of cold water.

"Howard," I said, right after we hit the gravel road, "I can't marry you. I mean, no offense, but I don't really know you at all."

SO FAR IN MY life I've been the queen of the fake marriages. One time standing in a field with twenty-five other couples all dressed in leather and astride Harley-Davidsons (it was brief, my biker chick phase, but potent) and the next time in a civil court of law in pursuit of a United States green card. I married Mack because I was in town the day that everybody decided to do it, and I married Sergei because if I didn't, the government would have sent him back to Vladivostok. I loved both Mack and Sergei in my way at the time, which was not particularly well, but together they don't count as one whole marriage, and if they had I probably never would have gone through with either of them. Then came the years of Tucker, Adam, and Peter, the Dante years, the years of waking up.

This time, I was committed to the idea of getting married for real. I'd even gotten a big white fluffy dress with a train and a veil. Nobody needed to know I bought it for three hundred dollars at the Costco of wedding stores, six-thousand-plus dresses on the rack and then some. I was in and out of there in forty-five minutes, and I would have been faster if I hadn't had to keep telling the saleswoman to stop calling me sweetie-pie.

"I am many things," I told her. "But sweet isn't one of them."

All of the wedding preparations had felt so much like I was doing a series of impersonations: now I'm impersonating a woman picking out her engagement-ring setting, now I'm impersonating a woman who's talking to her wedding planner on the phone. But Howard and I said we were going to do it real and right and all that realness and rightness caught up with me after no sleep and five lattes and I told him so in the car, about six miles of gravel road from the ranch that was swarming with caterers and flowers and our Denver friends out in the yard building a temporary dance floor, Dante, already in his bow tie, and the Anders Brothers, all the way from Montrose, our very own three-piece cowboy band.

Howard stayed calm. I'll give him credit for that. Looking back now it may have been the first time I saw the real Howard, the Howard who, as it turns out, is a little more sane than anyone else you can think of on the planet.

"I don't know what I was thinking," I said. "Marriage. Oh my God. When I said *yes* I must have had a reason. Do you have any idea what it was?"

"I hired a pedicurist," Howard said, speaking slowly, driving even more slowly, the way we did when there was a thunderstorm right above the ranch and we wanted it to pass before we had to unload the groceries. "I think you should commit," he said, "only to the pedicure. See how you feel after that."

It was, it turned out, a brilliant suggestion.

"I can't believe how much better I feel," I kept saying to the pedicurist.

"Of course you do honey," she said, "you are having your feet rubbed," and sometimes life is as simple as that.

I HAD TO WRITE the vows on my hand in ink so I wouldn't screw up the wedding. I had awakened that morning with a big old cold sore on my lip that Alanis Morissette would probably call irony, but I just called it bad luck. I got into my fluffy white dress and my white beaded flip-flops that were designed, I knew, for beach weddings, but would be better for navigating the pasture than any kind of ridiculous frou-frou shoes. The woman who'd painted my toes had put my hair up in some kind of fancy French twist and Victoria lent me her pearls, and what I really wish I had photos of is when she and Darlene snuck down the hall and into my bedroom to see me all done up like that, shock on their faces so intense it bordered on noncomprehension.

Dante walked me down the aisle, of course. Or, since there was no aisle, he walked me across the pasture to where Howard was standing, and lay down at my feet until it was time to exchange the vows. At that point he stood and hopped off and took his place in the crowd. Victoria and Jonathan acted out part of the wedding scene from *Our Town* and in the middle of it I realized that at some point he must have slept with her too. Darlene got so drunk I think she went home with all three of the country-western brothers and the promise of a hot tub.

After a *real* wedding, it turns out, you are way too tired to have sex. Howard was asleep before his head hit the pillow and I would have been too if not for all the caffeine still coursing through my veins.

I lay in bed looking up at the stars I have pasted on my ceiling, wedged in the way I like to be between Howard and Dante, and wondered about that lie I told Victoria all those years ago about me and the cops, and all the other lies I'd told after that, which weren't as many as a lot of people maybe, but still quite a few. And I thought how every one of those lies had truth in them, and how each of them was just a different way of asking to be loved, or noticed, at least, seen and heard, the way you are on a stage, and also—I hoped—in a marriage.

Howard planted our wedding columbines in the front yard, in the shade of the deck. He built bookcases out of our temporary dance floor, lacquered the good-luck papers Jonathan brought us from Chinatown onto the sides of the shelves, and wore his wedding suit on stage the next winter in a play called *Three Viewings*. I zipped my white dress into its plastic bag and stuffed it into the back of my closet. I watched the sun glint off Howard's mother's diamond that now rested on my hand.

Howard #3:

So that's it, right? We're married. And in spite of Rae's anxiety trying to decide whether it was a good idea or not, she wound up having a very good time at the reception.

That morning she had said, "It's my wedding day, and I can have as many lattes as I want to," which seemed right to me, a person who has been known to indulge to the point of excess. I say, if five lattes is what you need to get the job done, then go for it.

Rae works too hard, and when she's nervous or sad about something, she works even harder. When I'm depressed or anxious it would take God's own army to drag me out of bed and send me to work, but not Rae. The bigger the worry the harder the work, no sleep, crap food, right up until she faints—down a flight of stairs, onto a baggage claim carousel, behind the wheel of her car, right into her appetizer.

If you had asked me when I met her, even when I proposed to her, in what ways Rae resembled my mother I would have told you no way at all, but the first time I saw her legs buckle underneath her right outside the Tattered Cover Bookstore on the corner of Wynkoop and 16th downtown, I thought, Holy Moses, if I haven't been in this very spot all my life.

I've been trying my damnedest to get her to sleep and eat and take some time off. I have a way of rubbing her feet that puts her out nearly every time, and I'm getting pretty good at the cooking. But on those days leading up to the wedding she agreed to take on one thing after another; she taught a playwriting workshop, she wrote theater reviews, she even did a rewrite for some Hollywood producer, something she had said she would never do again. She worked nearly around the clock the entire week before.

Dante, man; he stays awake right with her. That's how I get her to knock off every once in while, by telling her that a dog who is fighting cancer should get some shut-eye, even if she won't. No wonder she was so strung out the morning of the wedding. Then with the five lattes and the party and the early flight to Bali. By the time we left for the airport it had been a week since Rae had had a real night's sleep.

She did pretty well on the long drive to Denver, the first hour of which we devoted to what is perhaps our finest dog song to date, "All the Bags, and Dante and Me," sung to the tune of "Me and Bobbie McGee." She hung in there right up until the lady at the United counter told her that we hadn't gotten the business-class upgrade Rae had been counting on.

"It's Monday morning," the lady said, "and your plane stops in Tokyo. Businessman's special, you know."

But Rae wasn't listening. Her eyes had glazed over and she was leaning away from the counter and as the lady called her congratulations after us—"Don't be surprised if someone comes up and offers you a bottle of champagne!"—Rae had already started her walk of death.

She sat down on a bench. "Go see if the Jamba Juice is open," she said. "Get me something with every healthy thing you can find." I raced over to the Jamba Juice, but it was still too early. I came back empty-handed and that was the last straw.

"That's it," she said, matter-of-fact. "We're not going to Bali."

Before our courtship disrupted Rae's schedule, she'd been planning a trip to Mongolia. She had always been fascinated with Genghis Khan, and she'd won a grant from the NEA to go over and ride Mongolian ponies through the forests where Genghis Khan spent his youth. It was Victoria who convinced her that a yurt was not an ideal place to spend a honeymoon, especially if you shared it with ten or twelve Mongolian horsemen. We had decided on Bali because it was the most exotic place she could think of that catered especially to honeymooners. We'd have frangipani blossoms floating in our bathtub and rose petals strewn across the sheets, and still feel like we'd been somewhere. I was excited beyond all reason and knew this was not the time to speak irrationally. "Honey," I said, "I think you'll feel much better when—"

"When what? When I've sat upright in a coach seat for twenty-four hours listening to you snore? Howard, I don't have twenty-four more hours in me."

I have to admit, I was pretty excited. Here we were, a married couple, having our first fight at the airport.

"Maybe there's still a chance we'll get the upgrade," I said. "That woman only said it didn't look good."

"I didn't want to tell you this, Howard," Rae said, "but I haven't been feeling very good lately. I'm pretty sure I have cancer, or lupus, or both."

I had heard that people who are severely sleep-deprived will sometimes go crazy before they pass out. I got her up and walking toward the security checkpoint. If I got her through the metal detector I was pretty sure I could get her at least as far as LA.

"You don't have cancer and lupus, honey," I said. "Let's go to LA and see if we get the upgrade. If we don't, we can stay there for a day, and then decide what we want to do."

She followed me, stiff-legged, onto the plane bound for Los Angeles and we took our places in coach.

"You know what the refund policy is at Amandari?" she asked.

Of course I didn't. I had never stayed at a hotel with a refund policy in all my life.

"They keep it all," she said. "Every bit." It was a lot. It was more than my 2000 income. She looked at her watch. "We are leaving Denver twelve minutes late already; that only gives us thirty-seven minutes to make the connection. We are not going to have time to shop around for a better flight."

She might have cancer and lupus, but she was a machine when it came to travel plans. "Maybe," I said, "we could stay in LA for a couple days, get some rest, get some sushi, fly some other day when there's plenty of room in business class."

She said, "I'm sure the kind people at United will be happy to let us go whenever it strikes our fancy."

"How are the newlyweds doing?" The flight attendant approached with a corked bottle wrapped in a white towel like a baby. An animal growl came out of Rae, half dog, half she-bear.

"We should go home," she said, "pick up the dogs, go to that dog-friendly spa in Telluride." When we had left the house at three A.M., I remembered, Dante had refused to look at her.

"Sweetheart," I said, "I think Dante wants us to go to Bali and have a good time."

"Stop petting me," she said, yanking her arm away, and I realized I had been rubbing her shoulder for several minutes. "Why don't you go to sleep," she said, "since we know that's what you are going to do."

I tried to look serious but I couldn't keep the smile off my face. This then, I thought, is marriage. The place where you take a turn at being crazy, and then you take a turn at being sane.

I woke up to the sound of airplane brakes and the most polluted day in Los Angeles that I had ever seen.

"We're not staying here," Rae growled, and I could see by the look on her face that she had not slept at all.

She was right, of course. There was no time between flights to make any decisions, but as we got off the Denver airplane we both heard an Asian flight attendant butchering my last name over the loudspeaker.

"Run!" Rae shouted, and I did, three gates down, to where he held two business class boarding passes like Willy Wonka's golden tickets high above his head.

Cancer was vanquished, lupus eradicated. Just as Rae snuggled into her auto massage business class seat for what would be a solid twenty-four-hour sleep (I steered her through the

Narita airport for the connection at the ten-hour mark but she swears she doesn't remember it), she said, "I'm sorry I was such a bitch, Howard, but now you get to have all my cashews."

I watched movies all the way to Tokyo, and watched over Rae while she slept.

Sophie #1:

He was the obvious choice in so many ways. First off, he's so big, and I'm so little. No one even thinks I'm thirteen. Nurse Ann says it's good to look younger than you really are. She says I look twelve, but let's face it, I really look eight.

It's all the chemo drugs that have kept me from growing. Carboplatin, Adriamycin, and a whole boatload of others. One of them—I think it's doxorubicin—they scrape off the inside of a nuclear reactor, so its hard to understand how it can be very good for you.

My mom gets on a roll about that, and let me tell you, she can talk a blue streak about chemo drugs and cancer medicine, but it always ends up the same way. A big hug and a sniffle and a "but they must be doing something right because I still have you."

That was another reason I picked Dante. He had the same chemo drugs that I did, and we went through chemo at almost exactly the same time. We were diagnosed the same month, we started chemo the same month, we had limb-spare the same month, and limb-spare failure within a couple of months of each other. They cut his leg off about six months before they cut off mine, and it took me a lot longer than him to learn to walk without it, but it's not really a fair comparison because he has three legs after all, and I only have the one.

The first time I met Dante it was kind of strange because we were the first dog and the first kid in the Denver YAPS program. That's Youth and Pet Survivors, of cancer, sometimes osteosarcoma, sometimes Hodgkin's, sometimes Burkitt's lymphoma, sometimes Ewing's sarcoma, sometimes leukemia which is sometimes A.L.L. and sometimes A.M.L. If you are going to have leukemia, it's A.L.L. you want to have.

I'm pretty used to the media by now. I've been the poster child for osteosarcoma in this state practically since I was diagnosed. But the day I met Dante, I was sick of the TV cameras and all those ladies with the frozen hair that smile at you so sweetly, but inside they are saying, *Oh thank God, thank God it isn't my kid.*

Sometimes dogs are way better than people to talk to. They listen better, and they always know the right moment to rest their head on your knee. People are always trying to touch you when you don't want to be touched, like it's a thing they do to make themselves feel better.

I could tell Dante was cool right from the beginning because he waited for me to come to him. He didn't mind that I couldn't get around all that fast on my prosthetic leg— I had only had it for a couple of months at the time—and after we'd gotten to know each other better he leaned over and licked it, right on the knee hinge. And it wasn't for the TV camera or anything. It was his own idea and he did it when the only one who saw it was me.

After I met Dante I wanted a dog of my own so bad, and my mom and dad said when I came home from the hospital I could get one, and now I have Scruffy. They didn't really want a dog, but as Dante could probably tell you, when you have cancer you pretty much get everything you want, which isn't as good a trade as you might think it is, but every now and then it has its moments, and Scruffy was definitely one of those.

He's not nearly as well behaved as Dante, not wise and mellow and quiet. He pulls pretty hard on his leash and barks at just about everything, but he's the perfect dog for me, and whenever my mom gets fed up with him I remind her what Nurse Ann said about a dog being a reason to live.

My cancer came when I was ten, and then they thought it went away but really, it hadn't, and then it did, and now it's been gone for two years. There are lots of kids and dogs in the YAPS plan now, and sometimes the dogs die first and sometimes the kids do.

When I tell people that Dante is my pen pal they get a funny look on their faces wondering how the dog writes letters. I explain that Dante tells his mom what to say and she writes it down for him. He sends me presents too, little pencils and stuffed dogs and picture frame magnets to put on my refrigerator.

Then they get another funny look and I know they are thinking, *What if the dog dies first? How will that be for Sophie?*

and I want to say, *Yeah, I know I'm a kid and everything, but what do you think I don't know about death at this point?*

I may look eight, but I'm going to be fourteen next month, I've spent five full months in the cancer ward at Children's, I can list survival rates of more than twenty cancers—with and without treatment—before and after metastatic growth—the way most of the girls I go to school with can list the former boyfriends of Britney Spears, and more than half the kids who were on the ward with me are no longer with us.

If Dante dies first, I'll be sad for him, but it will also mean I'm still alive, and that is the thing I've been fighting for.

A lot of times when kids get diagnosed with cancer, they are more afraid of the treatment than they are of death. If you're lucky, when you are ten years old, death is a pretty abstract idea. At first, the worst news is that your hair is going to fall out, and then when you start throwing up all the time, the hair doesn't seem like such a big deal.

You lose your friends. That's one thing I wish they'd told me. They come and visit you while you still look normal, to talk about school and tests and dances. A few of them even come when you are bald. But when you start getting the dark rings around your eyes, when you lose a ton of weight and start looking like you are shrinking from the inside out, like you're being sucked, somehow, into your own center, that's when they stop visiting altogether.

I wanted to be strong for the other kids on the ward. The kids with A.L.L. have the best survival rate: fifty percent after five years. The kids with the brain tumors, in general, have it

the worst, because so many of those are inoperable. Osteosarcoma falls somewhere in the middle, but I figured if I
could get through the chemo and show the other kids that
you could survive, then maybe they could take some of my
strength and make it their own.

I was lucky because of how my mom and dad and my
brother and sister hung in there. At least one of them was in
the hospital with me every single day. A lot of kids didn't have
that. A lot of kids' mothers were too scared to show up too
often. The mother of this kid named Patrick ran out of money,
and she just packed up the car and drove someplace two days
before his surgery, and nobody ever heard from her again.

My mom might drive me crazy sometimes, making me go
to karate or something when I really don't feel like it, but
she's made my fight her fight, and just like Scruffy, I wouldn't
trade her for the world. Before cancer I was pretty good at
skiing, and at first I was afraid to go back and try. Then my
mom told me to remember how Dante would run across the
hospital lawn to his mom when she'd come back to
Children's to get him after our visits. He looked graceful,
only different, and I decided with my one big ski and the two
little skis that went under my poles I could look graceful and
different like him.

When you are in the hospital for five months you have a
lot of time to think. You start out feeling pretty sorry for
yourself, but then that gets boring and so you start to ask
questions like *Why me?* which is a kind of feeling sorry for
yourself, but at least it is phrased in a question. At some point
though, it stops coming out in a whiny tone of voice and
that's when you start coming up with some answers.

The first answers are things like, because I told on my brother for not cleaning the fish tank, or because of that B-minus I got in math in fifth grade, but when you think about it more you realize you haven't really lived long enough to do anything bad enough that God's going to punish you with cancer, and then you start to think, maybe it isn't a punishment; maybe it feels like a punishment, but maybe it isn't at all. Maybe you were chosen because you are so strong and brave and cool; maybe God chose you because He had a plan and you were the best one He could find to carry it out. Maybe the plan is that you were put on earth and given cancer so that you could tell everyone you meet how important it is to pay attention to the world every single day, and that maybe since the longer you stay alive the more and more people you seem to meet, maybe He's going to keep you around. Maybe He wants you to say, yes, I had cancer, and yes, I'm a little small for my age, but I'm alive now, and I've won three ski races and earned a green belt in karate and it has been almost two years since I had to spend a whole night in the hospital and I love my family and I love my life, especially now that we got Scruffy.

Five

·

**The
Fires**

Rae #5:

It was Memorial Day weekend, and we had driven out to visit Jonathan in Placer City, California, and I was ready to go for a hike. Jonathan had come home from Italy and built a cabin in a county documented as having more ex-cons than any other in America, and by the looks of the half-inhabited mine claims with black paint all over the windows, I was guessing it had more crystal meth manufacturers than any county in America too.

Jonathan said the weirdest thing about living in crystal meth country was the way that after a lab got discovered, the government guys would come in wearing HazMat suits and driving bulldozers and take the whole thing away. Not just the drugs and the waste and the equipment, not just the buildings, but the trees and the bushes, a big chunk of earth maybe fifty yards square and ten feet deep. He said after about a year the vegetation took over but for a while an evacuated site looked like a massive grave.

That's just the kind of thing Jonathan *would* think about, which is another reason we don't write plays together anymore. If it were me, I'd be thinking about the groundwater and what kind of diseases I was going to get from it. You see one of those guys in a HazMat suit and you can be pretty sure that's not the kind of shit you want to live around.

Sophie's mom gets on a roll sometimes about carcinogens in cleaning products and the fact that Denver broke the ozone limit twenty-four days in a row last summer, which confused me because I always thought ozone was a good thing, but I've got to believe living next door to seven thousand pounds of crystal meth waste is a hell of a lot worse than anything we've got in Colorado.

Jonathan gets madder than shit if I don't visit him at least once a year, even more this past year since I got married to Howard. Like everyone else in my life, Jonathan likes Howard better than me. I can't say I blame him because even though I am working on it, Howard is still a much better person than I am. So we all—dogs and humans—took a week over Memorial Day and drove across Utah and Nevada.

Jonathan had asked me to read from my new play as a benefit for his local library and he introduced me to the decent-sized crowd by way of a letter he'd written about me to the singer Jackson Browne, and the letter was in the form of a poem. One line in the poem was, *You'd love her, Jackson, she's a blonde with a brain* and another verse went, *Back in the day, Jackson, Rae would have been down on the beach with us on Friday nights, irresponsibly huge bonfires and Martin guitars. She would have taken her bikini off and let the ocean take her, strong legs kicking, teats pointed skyward.* To my knowledge it was the only time the word teats had ever been used in public, in conjunction with me.

The morning after the reading we all set off in the car together, Dante, Rose, Jonathan, Howard, and I. Jonathan couldn't really get into it when Howard made up his dog song of the day, "The Meat Heat's On," sung to the tune of "The Heat Is On," but I figured that was his problem.

We chose a trail that had a nice place to sit within the first quarter mile so Dante could feel like he was participating, then all the boys would sit down by the river and Rose and I would continue on for a two-hour power walk. It was one of the few things Rose and I had in common, the ongoing need to drop twenty pounds. Without her company I'd be far less likely to push forward, without my company she'd just as soon lie around all day with her face in a big bowl of food.

The trail was along the north fork of the Yuba River, with a picnic area in the first half mile, and then a deep blue swimming hole three miles later at trail's end. Before we left the house I'd told Howard the holiday would bring all the freaks in the county out to the woods and it would be a miracle if I didn't get gang-raped.

"You know the difference between Colorado and California?" I said. "If you are a woman hiking alone in Colorado, one out of every hundred other hikers you meet gives you a creepy feeling; in California, it's more like one out of three."

The river was high and looked dangerous as we rumbled along the Forest Service road to the trailhead. There was an overturned truck, a newer model, yawning up at us from the short slope between the road and the river. We'd passed about a thousand guys on Harleys in the tiny town of Washington, but the picnic area was empty when we got there, and except for the roar of the river, quiet. I turned away from Dante's plaintive eyes while Howard petted and spoke softly to him, and Rose and I slipped away.

The first thing I found was the plastic fish head. It was lying in the middle of the road, small and brightly painted, looking like the top to something, though I couldn't figure out what. I put it in my pocket to take back to Howard, who likes presents, especially mysterious ones.

A half a mile or so farther I found the dead hummingbird, and even though the head and legs were smashed in and starting to decay, its feathers were still iridescent, red and blue in sequence, like the scales of a Florida grouper moments after you catch it, and I put it in my pocket too.

There *were* a lot of people in the woods that day. I could hear them off in the distance, pictured them sitting around the shacks that stood on their mine claims, popping a beer, frying some burgers. I didn't pass anybody on the trail until I got close to a big messy claim with a couple of buildings and a bunch of rusted machinery out front, the kind of place that looked like the owners might still be mining, or had been, not very long ago.

I was relieved that there were women and children present among the big-gutted men with sideburns and ponytails. The man closest to the trail wore black jeans, black high-top sneakers, and a wife beater with a ZZ Top logo that had been washed so many times it was no more than a tiny rectangle hanging from a couple of spaghetti straps, covering only about ten percent of his hairy chest and gut.

A couple of the guys shouted something at me, but the river was behind them and I couldn't hear what they were saying over its roar. Rose trotted over to them and I sped up and called her back to me, and she took her own sweet time, as usual, to listen.

I made deliberate eye contact with one of the women who sat near a fire with a couple of small children at her feet. Rose finally caught up to me, and I started to trot to the end of the trail, the swimming hole in the river.

I had been to that pool the last time we'd visited Jonathan, on a week day back in October when there hadn't been anyone around, and I had taken all my clothes off and jumped into the cold river for a second, then sat on a warm rock till I was dry enough to dress and head back home. Now the river looked way too ferocious, even in the place where the shiny granite formed spillways into the deepest of the glacier-blue pools.

Rose was thirsty, so I decided we could climb down the granite slope into the river, and find a little eddy in the river-bank rock garden where she could get a drink and I could chill my Teva-weary feet.

We had just gotten down there, just committed to a bath-tub-sized pool near the end of a long skinny rock, but safely away from the current, when I saw Mr. Spaghetti Straps making his way down the granite slope toward me.

"Can I ask you a question?" he said.

I looked up and so did Rose.

"Sure," I said. I stood while I said it. He was at the other end of the long skinny rock we'd used as a bridge between two small braids of the river. My options were to head right for him, or stay where I was.

"Did you see anybody swimming when you got here?"

I looked at the swirling current behind me. "Nobody in their right mind is going to go swimming in that," I said.

"Wait, I can't hear you," he said, and took one step out onto the skinny rock.

He certainly could hear me.

"There's nobody swimming in that," I said again. "Did you lose somebody?"

He had reached my little pool and he jumped into it with me, knocking his shoulder into mine rather forcefully and laughing as if he were stoned. I pushed past him and climbed up onto the rock in my wet Tevas. I didn't look back as I moved carefully between the two swift-moving channels. For once, Rose came without being called.

I was at the end of the rock, the bottom of the trailside slope, when he boomed, "HEY!"

Rose and I both turned around. He was wobbling on the other end of the skinny rock, buck naked. He had his little dick in his hand and was waving it at us. I turned and started climbing, using all fours when necessary, straight up the slope that led to the trail.

Before Jonathan started writing plays he wrote a series of terrible short novels in what I always called his own special genre—environmentally conscious bi-friendly erotica—and as I climbed the slope my favorite line from one of his early stories came back to me. The protagonist had been lured by an androgynous eagle woman back to her beach house lair. On the next several pages she would morph slowly into a man and then back again to a woman, but right before all of that began the narrator exclaims, "She grabbed my cock, and stepped west."

"HEY!" The naked man called again, and this time I didn't look and kept moving steadily upward. My prevailing emotion was not fear but irritation. Wasn't there some age or weight or level of unattractiveness one could arrive at where this kind of thing stopped happening? *I'm lucky he's such a dumb shit,* I thought, *or he might have left on his shoes.*

"HEY!" I could tell by his voice that he was gaining on me. I turned around, and Rose turned with me. He was making progress up the rocky slope in spite of his bare feet.

"My dog will kill you," I said. And somehow managed not to double over laughing.

Rose may look like a Muppet, but there are still a hundred and sixty pounds of her, and when the sun lights up her golden eyes and she moves toward you throwing her big hips from side to side, she's enough to give a naked stoner pause.

This one did, just long enough for me to reach the trail, which I was happy to see was rockier at that point even than the slope. Too proud to run, I launched into the world's fastest power walk. A couple more "Heys!" followed me down the trail.

As I approached the mine claim I turned it up another notch. Who knew what plans this guy had made with his tank-topped buddies, who knew if they'd watched the whole scene at the river and would decide not to let me pass. I could see an old jeep that looked in running order parked alongside two shiny four-wheelers.

There was no amount of distance they couldn't recover with those. I flew past the mining claim to the sound of more hoots and catcalls. When I got around the next bend I started to flat-out run.

Rose was excited. She liked running, especially downhill. I kept one eye over my shoulder on the trail, one eye on what I could see of the river, one ear out for the sound of foot-steps, or motors, coming down the trail.

We were making good time, were more than halfway back to Howard when we reached a section of the trail that had been flooded and had a slick clayey bottom, and for the first time since passing the mine claim, I slowed my pace way down.

I stepped into the puddle carefully, looking down to pick my way across. My head snapped back up at a noise in front of me. On the other side of the puddle, about thirty yards far-ther down the trail, the biggest mountain lion I had ever seen had sprung onto the trail to face me. She was backlit, and tip to tail she was a few inches higher, and at least a foot longer, than Rose.

For the first five seconds, nobody breathed, not the lion, not me, and not even Rose, who is famous for wiggling up to anybody and anything, so steadfast is her belief that the world is her playmate. Then the lion broke eye contact, and leapt again into the small stand of bushes between the river and the trail.

"She's not going to like it over there," I whispered to Rose. "She'll feel trapped between the exposed trail and the river. Let's give her a minute to change her mind."

And it was a minute, maybe a full minute later, when she bounded back across the trail, not stopping this time, and back up into the forest that extended into forever on the other side of the trail.

Rose looked back at me, large-eyed. "Stanley's cousin," I said. "Kitty, kitty, kitty." And we were across the puddle and off and running toward Howard again.

One river bend later I came upon a man in a one-piece bright orange suit.

"Hey wait a minute!" he called, taking a few drunken steps down the trail toward me. "What's your name?"

"You've got to be kidding," is what I said over my shoulder, and didn't stop running till I could see the buck-and-rail fence that marked the edge of the picnic area.

I took the hummingbird out of my pocket and handed it to Howard. My running hadn't done its structural integrity any good, but its feathers were still gleaming in the afternoon light.

"Anything interesting happen here?" I asked the boys.

"Oh," Jonathan said, "we sat near the river for a while, and then some mosquitoes came out. And you?"

Jonathan told me in his best I-live-in-the-woods voice that the lion had been a much greater danger to me than the naked man. Surely I'd read the stories of people attacked by mountain lions while they were out jogging. Once you run, he said, the lion assumes you are prey.

But I knew the lion had come *for* me, that she had come— that is to say—on my behalf. I knew she wouldn't hurt me, nor Rose for that matter, and that she had come, not to protect me from the naked man so much as to make amends for him. As I write these lines now I wonder if the lion is the reason I am alive today, and the reason Jonathan is not.

"How do you even know it was a female?" Jonathan said.

"I just do," I said, and I did.

Howard #4:

Rae said that Jonathan had blackened with age, had never been blacker than that Memorial weekend, and it was hard for me to figure how he might ever get from there back into the light.

On Friday morning, the day after we'd first showed up, Jonathan asked Rae to ride with him down the valley nearly to Sacramento, to his favorite organic grocery store to stock up for the weekend, and she gave me a look that said it was important that I come too. Those foothills have grown up even more than the ones in Colorado, all fast food and strip malls, and we were in a long line of traffic, in what felt like an endless series of lights.

We were in Jonathan's Subaru Outback, Rae riding shotgun, me in the back, right behind a big black Dodge Ram, one of those trucks with the wide hips and the hemi under the hood. The license plate said VETERANS OF FOREIGN WARS, and there was a sticker on the back of the cab with a big red white and blue heart that said AMERICA, LOVE IT OR LEAVE IT. The guy driving had a buzz cut and ears that stuck out nearly two inches on either side.

The light changed and Jonathan shot into the other lane, gunned the engine and tucked back in, right in front of the Dodge, just before we reached the next red light.

The guy in the Dodge leaned on his horn, and Jonathan shot him the finger.

At the next red light I heard the beating of the hemi sidling up beside us, and sure enough, there in the left-turn-only lane was the Dodge, and though his door was higher than Jonathan's entire car, when I ducked down and looked up I could see that the guy was leaning across his passenger seat, rolling down the window.

"What's this shit!" Jonathan said.

"Road rage," Rae said. "Drive-by shooting." She snaked her hand around along the passenger door into the back seat and I took it in mine.

Jonathan rolled down his window. The guy with the crew cut had a slightly strained smile on his face. "Excuse me sir," he said, "but do you think I could ask you to drive a little more safely?"

"Sure," said Jonathan, "do you think I could ask you to stop being a member of the fucking Gestapo?"

Bang, I thought, *you're dead.*

But the man rolled up his window and I heard the noise of the hemi fading, tucking back behind us in the long line of lights.

Five minutes after we got onto I-80 I saw the lights of the cruiser.

"What's this shit!" Jonathan said again.

"This is a public service announcement," the coolest lady cop in California said when she reached Jonathan's window. "I'm not going to give you a ticket, but I want you to know that road rage is a very serious problem in this state, and if you keep acting like that you are going to get yourself killed."

Rae had said that Jonathan was in total denial about the existence of cell phones, and he was having a hard time figuring out how the lady cop knew what went on back at the stoplights. The day before we had pulled up to a light next to a woman on her cell phone, and through her window and his window, Jonathan had mouthed *Hang up your phone, hang up your phone,* while gesturing frantically from his ear to his lap.

"I can't believe," Jonathan said to the cop, "that you are going to take that asshole's word over mine."

"I don't have to," said the cop. "I've been following you since you got on the freeway. You are going eleven miles over the speed limit and you've changed lanes seventeen times without using your turn signal. But as I've said, I'm not going to give you a ticket. I'm just asking that you treat your fellow drivers with a little more respect. I'm going to run your license, and if you check out you can be on your way."

She went back to her car. I could feel Jonathan boiling in the seat in front of me, getting ready to blow.

Suddenly he threw the door open and ran back toward the cruiser.

Bang, I thought, *that's twice in ten minutes.*

But the cop didn't shoot, and I watched her nodding her head patiently, while Jonathan waved his arms.

"Your friend," I said to Rae, "seems a little high-strung."

Rae threw herself out the passenger door, walked back to where Jonathan was still arguing, took his arm with some force and led him back to the car.

Rose #2:

I don't care much for California. The woods are full of ticks and bad-smelling men and this great big cat that came right out of a nightmare I had one time after I knocked a huge pot of spaghetti sauce off the stove while my mom was in the shower and ate every bit off the floor.

Jonathan rubs my shoulders in that way that makes my lips go limp and droolly, and I enjoy it even though we all know he is doing it only to show Rae what a better dog dad he'd be than Howard. Yeah, as if.

Jonathan took me on a walk while Rae and Howard were packing the car to head back to Colorado. He tried to take both Dante and me on a walk but there was no way Dante was going anywhere while there was activity that involved suitcases and vehicles, so Jonathan said, "Let's just you and me go then, Rose," and so off we went.

It's not like I didn't stay in earshot. I mean this was the *woods* after all. There were scent trails to follow. But I wasn't out of his line of vision for ten seconds before he starts hollering *RO-OSE, RO-OSE*, and there was not a welcoming tone to his voice. I had happened upon a muskrat hole and was just doing a little preliminary reconnaissance before I started digging in earnest, and then came Jonathan's voice again, *ROSE! ROSE!*, this time even more agitated than before.

What I cannot understand is why the humans think any dog in her right mind would respond to a request delivered in such a tone of voice. If a human were to say, "Sweet Rose, why don't you come get a cookie?" wouldn't the odds of compliance improve?

"ROSE GODDAMMIT!" Jonathan's voice assaulted me from over a small hill, and it was at that point I decided that no matter what happened, we would not return to the cabin together. He crested the top of the hill, and I trotted over the next one. He started to run after me and I picked up my pace and circled back the way we had come.

"ROSE!" he said, and this time there was something in his voice that resembled a sob, something that made me hesitate. I wanted to say, *Whoa, dude, you've got way too much invested here.* But then a grey squirrel crossed my line of vision and I lost my train of thought entirely. I treed the little sucker a couple of hundred yards farther into the woods, and when I got tired of listening to him chatter at me I trotted back toward Jonathan's cabin.

He wouldn't look up at me when I arrived, but Howard gave me one of those looks where he tries to be all stern, and said, "Rose, did you put a move on Jonathan?"

Rae turned back to the house to keep from laughing. I winked at Howard, and I'm almost positive he winked back.

Jonathan #3:

Rae says I'm one of the people she worries about, one of the people who especially likes rooftop parties, who lingers too long over a bare razor blade found accidentally in the medicine chest of a friend, who drives too fast, who doesn't wear seat belts, who can't see—won't see, I think is what she actually said—all the reasons there are to be grateful for this life.

"Name one," I'd say to her, and she would look at me, exhausted, and say, "Jonathan, if you don't have enough imagination to see how much worse it could all be than this, then I wonder why I chose you as a writing partner."

At least she didn't talk to me about sunrises and barbequed oysters and the love of a good dog or any of that other shit. I'd say, "Honey, you should worry a little more about yourself, because one of these days your magic happiness dog is going to give up the ghost and then you better hope you are still laughing at all of Howard's meager attempts at humor."

Maybe it turns out I don't like Howard so much. Or maybe more to the point, I don't like Howard with her.

If I were the kind of person Rae has always believed I am deep down, I'd be doing handsprings on her behalf. Because she sleeps through the nights all of a sudden, because for the first time this year she didn't get depressed when the days began to get shorter, because there's some part of her brain that knows, even as she paces around her kitchen, that all of those Colorado wildfires gobbling up tens of thousands of acres only a few miles from her mountain hiding place have nothing personal against her.

"We'll rebuild," she said, her voice level as a plank, the first time she's called since Memorial Day. "It's not like the land won't still be here."

"Though it might look like nuclear fallout."

"I'm not going to call you anymore," she said, in that same even tone, "if you don't have anything positive to say." By which she meant, *You're scaring me, and there are too many things to be scared about, and maybe for once it is your turn to come to the aid of a friend.*

But here's who *I've* been thinking about every day since September 2001: the people who were trapped above the floors where the planes hit and who decided to jump. They stopped showing them on TV after the first couple of days to spare all those TV-watching children the trauma, but I remember the way the one guy's tie fluttered up and over his shoulder, the woman who was holding her shoes, the couple who jumped holding hands.

I'll admit, it's a little bit thrilling to think about their decision. You have to wonder, was smoke billowing into their offices, did they try all the stairwells first? Or were they some-how prescient, had they somehow seen the future at the moment of impact? Did they know that what might have looked like a hopeless, even insane, decision to those fortu-nate enough to be on the ground, would be the thing that later saved them—saved them?—from simply vaporizing when the towers collapsed?

Maybe I never was the person Rae believed in. Maybe I've always had everybody fooled, from all the women I sleep with to the few I call my friends. Maybe if I were on the hundred-and-twenty-first floor of the World Trade Center I would have seen my opportunity. It had to have been quite a feeling, once the decision had been made. How many sec-onds of free fall—and then shock, surely, just before impact.

What no one will ever say about those people is that they were cowards. What no one will ever say about those people is that they died of shame.

Rae #6:

We got back to Colorado just as the fires began, home to an autumn-brown pasture in early June, to thirsty trees, and low water pressure, wells drying up all over the county and stories of a hundred years ago when cowboys had to dig holes in the belly of the dry Rio Grande riverbed in hopes of getting their dehydrating, dying stock to drink. We came home to black skies and an orange sun, a creek that was barely more than a trickle, a hot howling wind that kicked up dust devils the size of tornadoes, and ash falling onto our hair and our cars and into our food when we were brave enough to try eating at the picnic table in the yard.

It was about six in the morning when I crossed Slumgullion Summit, the last pass between California and home. I was looking out my side window, trying not to obsess about the absence of snowpack, when I realized I was looking at a full-grown grizzly bear, in the heart of the San Juan Mountains, where they are thought to have been extinct for decades. I let the car roll to a stop and took in the blond tips on the ends of the rich brown coat, the flat mannish face, the hump, the casual two-legged stance. He didn't look like any black bear I'd ever seen, and I wondered what his appearance portended.

Bears always made me think of Jonathan, because I was camping with him, up in Wyoming, when I saw my first grizz. We were writing a screenplay together at the time, something called *Game*, a love story set in the Tetons, with what was supposed to be a minor suspense plot about bear poaching, and the illegal sale of the organs on the Asian sex market.

We both needed the money, and wanted the time together, so we headed up to Wyoming with a couple of sleeping bags and a bunch of freeze-dried chicken stew, and on our first night in camp, not two miles from the trailhead, a big old grizz invited himself to dinner.

We joked later that the bear was trying to tell us what we probably knew all along, that the producers would want the suspense plot to edge out the love story, that they had therefore hired the entirely wrong duo to write the thing, and that the script would be taken unceremoniously from us and given to some studio hack that had read the book that tells you on which page to put all of your plot turns.

But Jonathan waltzed that bear right out of camp with two trout he'd caught that morning—which is where we got our opening scene for the script. It didn't matter to us that the producers didn't get it. We got our checks, our bear, and a week in the Tetons together.

I had the good sense not to sleep with Jonathan on that trip, nor in fact at any other time, and in at least half a lifetime filled with bad decisions, I feel pretty good about that one. It was more tempting in those days when he was lighter of spirit, and when there was nothing that ailed him that a good trip to the mountains and an ounce of hallucinogenic mushrooms wouldn't cure.

Now whatever ailed Jonathan felt incurable, and back home in Colorado, the mountains weren't so friendly anymore. The creek was so low the horses had to pick their spot just to get their fat lips under the surface. We'd had to throw hay for them all spring because the snowpack was so piss-poor and it didn't precipitate one time from the first of March forward, and now the pasture sat dormant as if it still were March or maybe November. Darlene said it was so dry down in the San Luis Valley that even the irrigated farmers might not get a first cutting; that some people were buying their hay from Texas and having it hauled up here. Every time a front came through it came as wind, which dried the ground out even more and sent up clouds of dust and smoke from new, smaller fires that were cropping up all over the state.

A week after we got home a fire started less than thirty miles to the west of us, eating up ten thousand acres of national forest a day as it raced in our direction, and over the next three weeks it continued to walk steadily toward our ranch. As it closed the gap between us and it, another, smaller fire began burning acreage and houses twelve miles to the southeast of us, and that fire was heading due north.

The first fire, the Missionary Ridge as they called it, had been started with one cigarette, and the Million Fire, to the south, started when somebody illegally dumped a load of fertilizer that spontaneously combusted on the ground. A fire a hundred miles to the north of us started with a spark from a tailpipe of a ten-year-old car.

The Forest Service closed every bit of the backcountry, first to campfires, then to cookstoves, then to backpacking of any kind, and eventually altogether. The Texans came up anyway, of course, with their leaky gas cans and their illegal fireworks, and politely moved the barricades out of the way because they've always thought this whole state existed just so they'd have a place to get out of the summer heat.

At one point the State Police had Highway 149—the only road in and out of this county—blocked in both directions, a two-day period that fell right in the middle of the three solid weeks that our local sheriff had put us on standby for evacuation, and everybody in town was talking about whether, when it came right down to it, we would break the law and stay with our houses, or break through the Stateys' barricades and go.

Howard and I made an evacuation list and hung it on the refrigerator. All the paintings first, then the photographs, then the theater books and paraphernalia, then the textiles from Bhutan and Mongolia, then the ceramic bowls I hand-carried back from France, then the All-Clad cookware, then the Wüsthof knives. Tax returns were on the list somewhere, and passports.

We backed my little boxy trailer up to the front door and waited. If everything happened fast, as it had for some people on the other side of the Divide, we would load up Dante and Rose in the truck and drive the trailer to the center of the gravel pit down the road and leave it there. Then we'd run back and lead the horses down there too, and stand with

them in the middle of the gravel pit in flame-retardant jackets till whatever the fire could make of our already singed
pasture burned off.

Howard had a plan that involved surrounding the house
with as many kiddie pools as it took to make a circle and filling them from the hose, assuming the well held out. When
the fire raced across what was left of the grass it would hit a
kiddie pool, melt the plastic, and douse itself. Everybody in
town laughed at his plan, but I didn't hear them coming up
with anything better.

I'd never felt the need to own a horse trailer, since we have
a hundred and twenty acres here for the horses to live on and
unlimited Forest Service trails right out the back. But all of a
sudden the national forest seemed like our worst enemy, not
counting the thirty-mile-an-hour winds that wouldn't quit
and the thunderclouds that wouldn't gather quite enough
energy to send down rain.

There wasn't going to be any pasture that summer, that
much was clear, so when Highway 149 reopened I drove my
old turquoise Ford F100 with the gearshift on the steering
column down to the valley where the Great Sand Dunes
were shimmering against the heat like a prophecy of things
to come. I begged thirty bales of hay from the farmers at the
Co-op who assured me (while loading it) that they had none
to give. That they'd used up a whole summer's irrigation just
trying to get a first cutting, and if I weren't so cute they'd be
saving every bale they had for their own stock.

I felt anything but cute with my scaly skin (I had stopped
using lotion in solidarity with the pasture) and my forty-
year-old laugh lines turning, that summer, into something

else entirely, and my dirty split hair (Howard and I had started taking showers every third day) and my dusty clothes (and stopped using the washing machine altogether). I had my feet stuffed into boots so the farmers couldn't see my thick green toenails to which I added a thin coat of Emerald Mist as a prayer every night we didn't get rain.

I'd thought at first that I might be able to trick the weather gods, by hanging laundry right at the peak of afternoon cloud development or by leaving the sunroof on the 4-Runner wide open, but nothing, including standing in the yard under the clouds and yelling *Please!* seemed to be having any effect.

I kept a close eye on the creek, which should have been thigh-high in June. I planted sticks to mark the width of the trickle which got thinner and thinner, and I kept waiting for it to dry up altogether or at least turn intermittent. But one day it just stopped getting smaller and it held its ground after that, and I figured if it could, maybe I could too.

I tried hiking in the mornings, before the wind started blowing and the blue sky turned porcelain, then grey, then black with smoke; before I could feel it in my lungs, sharp and burning, strong enough to decide I'd be doing my health a favor if I stayed inside, along with my cancer-prone dog. By evening everything inside the house smelled of smoke, and the Denver weatherman pissed me off every night by standing right in front of the part of the map that showed our county when he gave the fire updates and the weather forecast.

Denver had a fire of its own to worry about, the largest in Colorado history and twice the size of the one we had just to our west, which was the second largest in Colorado history, which were only two of the fifteen fires burning statewide on any given June day. It started to feel as if there wouldn't be anything left of the state by the time the biggest bunch of Texans arrived to celebrate the Fourth of July.

The woman who started the fire near Denver was a park ranger who got it in her head to burn a pile of letters from some ex-man in her life, and although she lied about that at first, and though hundreds of people's homes were destroyed, I never quite lost sympathy for her because it sounded so much like something I might once have done, and exactly the thing that would happen if I had. I had a little sympathy, too, for the firefighter in Arizona who started an even bigger fire than the Denver fire, in the hope that he could get some work, earn some money. And though I felt bad as all hell for what must have been the tens of thousands of animals that died in those fires, Theo said the fact that I felt something other than malice toward the people who were responsible for the fires was definitely a sign of positive change.

Theo had taught me how to recognize the feelings that cast me back to my powerless childhood state, so I knew what was happening when I stood at the window every morning before it got too smoky to see, and watched the Divide for smoke plumes or flames, believing that the fire had my name on it, that it was coming expressly for me.

Those teasing clouds would build up every afternoon and I would stand on the porch and will them to amount to something, some days crying because I was trying so hard, but Larry Green on Channel 4 said the humidity had been less than ten percent for over a month, and the dew point was so high that any moisture that tried to form inside the clouds would get sucked up into the ether before there was a chance for gravity to do its work.

We were the last house before the national forest wilderness area and there are rules about how you can't go in there with anything that could be called a machine. A couple of years ago there was a big debate over mountain bikes, and if they wouldn't let those in, I knew we could forget about four-wheelers and bulldozers and the planes they drop water from, not to mention those chemical retardant bombs which can't be very good for the groundwater or the trees. The national forest service guy would get on TV and explain over and over again why the forest needed to burn, and in theory I was all for it. But if a fire grows and grows until it's more than a hundred thousand acres, and yours is the first house directly downwind, I don't know who you'd have to be not to feel singled out.

Our well was in trouble and I knew it, but sometimes, when Howard was asleep, I'd get up in the middle of the night and turn the hose on and water just a thin ring of hope around the house. I swore the next morning that I could see a hint of green in the brown stalks.

During the last week of June I had to go sit in on the rehearsals of a new play I was having workshopped at the Denver Center. It was Howard's and my one-year anniversary that week, and he had planned on coming with me, but we were still on standby to evacuate, which meant that at any moment there could be a roadblock set up, and if you weren't home when they called you, you couldn't go back.

The play was one that Jonathan and I had conceived of together and that he had lost interest in and bequeathed to me when it came time for the writing. It took place on a cruise ship between Hong Kong and Singapore, an American father and daughter meet an insane German woman, and the actress doubles as the dead mother/wife.

Every night after rehearsal I thought I would call Jonathan, let him know how it was all turning out, and yet night after night I didn't. After the incident with the cop in California, Howard had asked him outright *what the fuck was up, anyway,* and he had sounded a lot like himself when he described all the ways his lifestyle wasn't fulfilling him, and I thought, *Okay then, no cause for alarm.*

I put four days in at rehearsal before I realized I was so sick with worry about the ranch that it wasn't doing the actors any good having me there. Halfway home from Denver I stopped near the Great Sand Dunes at a ranch called the Medano-Zapata. It was the first of July and the fields should have been covered with a sea of purple blossoms called bee plant, which in August would give way to yellow sunflowers, until mid-September, when the cottonwoods would start to change. This year there was nothing but parched earth and dust devils and the trees were so stressed the leaves were changing color already.

I had heard that there was an aquifer under that ranch that covered three hundred thousand acres, and no matter how much water the potato farmers downvalley pumped out of it, it still came back strong, year after year. I'd heard that if you walked in the shallow creek that ran across the ranch and let your feet sink down, deep in to the muck of the creek bed, you could feel the cool of the aquifer running along below, trying to bubble right up through the holes your toes had made. If this was true, it sounded like hope to me, and I wanted to feel it for myself. I would dig my green toenails down into that sand and muck until I felt the aquifer, and beg God or Gaia or Zeus or whoever was in charge of thunderstorms these days to actually bring one to life.

I tried to explain all that to the rancher, a crazy-looking white-haired guy with paint spattered all over his clothes bent over a tractor engine, and you can imagine the look he gave me. But luckily his wife Jodi came outside just as he was asking me if I had any idea how much free time a man might have who was trying to keep fifteen hundred head of free-range American bison alive on three hundred thousand acres in the worst drought since the Middle Ages, while still finding enough time to keep four Manhattan galleries in the postmodern surrealist paintings that financed the whole operation.

"Don't mind Hank," Jodi said, taking my arm and pulling me toward the farmhouse door. "You can take the man out of the city," she said, as we entered the biggest single-family kitchen I had ever seen in my life. She made me a cup of tea and showed me the quilts she was making.

"Did you take the man out of the city?" I asked as we settled down at an enormous bright yellow table.

"Two of them," she said, smiling. "Vegas, and before that New York."

"And he paints?" I said.

She shook her head. "He's a painter. A subtle distinction, but I've learned to live with it. He's a little bit famous, in carefully selected circles. Enough to pay for all of this." She indicated the big kitchen, the house, the land that surrounded her.

"I'm a little bit famous that way too," I said. "I write plays."

"That's cool," Jodi said. "I used to sing. But it never worked out for me. Then I found my true calling: bison-whisperer. The hours are longer, but there's a lot more room at the top."

"Fifteen hundred bison sounds like a lot."

"About a hundred and fifty thousand pounds, give or take. We've got five serious cowboys that do most of the work around here, but Hank usually leaves them out of his daily whine."

A half an hour later we were rolling along a two-track in Jodi's old Chevy pickup, scattering bison cows and calves in every direction. Her dog Misha, the unlikely visual combination of golden retriever and basset hound, had his butt on the seat between us, and his short stubby paws up on the dashboard. Jodi stopped abruptly in front of a lone female that wouldn't get out of the road.

"That's Amelia," she said. "She used to be our pet, but we are trying to reeducate her in the ways of the herd." Amelia scratched her butt against the pickup while I tried to fathom, out of the several hundred identical bison that surrounded us, how Jodi could tell that this one was Amelia. She picked up one of her dainty little hooves and began to scratch the back of her massive head with it, and Jodi reached up to help her. I had never been that close to a bison, and with their narrow butts, skinny little legs, and Mack truck head and shoulders, it seemed like a trick of physics that kept them from pitching over nose first.

I reached out to feel Amelia's curly brown coat.

"Slowly," Jodi said. "She's a pet, but she could put her horns right through your pancreas as fast as the rest of them."

Amelia was leaning her entire upper body into Jodi's finger-
nails, eyes closed, and it looked like my pancreas was the very
last thing on her mind.

We got back into the pickup and swung right onto a road
that took us back east, toward the sand dunes, with the Sangre
De Cristo Mountains behind. We could see orange-tinted fire
clouds at both extremes of the range, to the north, near Poncha
Pass, and to the south, beyond the New Mexico border.

"You can leave your shoes in the car," Jodi said. "It's pretty
marshy between here and the water."

We squished through mud laced with buffalo pies and
though the stench was overwhelming, I was happy to have
something under my feet for a change that wasn't dry, dusty
and cracked. The creek was only a couple of inches deep in
most places, and almost as warm as the July air. We turned and
walked upstream, toward the dunes.

"We've lost some calves to the drought already," Jodi said.
"About a hundred cows spontaneously aborted back in May
when the grass didn't come in. Like they knew what we were
in for."

"That's amazing," I said.

Jodi shrugged. "Nature's way," she said. "I worried so much
about fire, but now there is nothing to burn, at least. We can
keep feeding hay through the summer—we got a loan—but
if we lose the creek, we'll never find all the stock. They'll
dehydrate and die where they stand."

A great blue heron flew up from the creek a hundred yards
upstream, and Jodi pointed at a young great horned owl in
the limbs of a cottonwood on the right bank.

"I worry about those guys too," she said. "It's a lot farther between watering holes these days."

The water had gotten a little deeper all of a sudden, and the sand along the bottom had more give.

"Here we are," Jodi said. "This is a good place." She dug her feet in and did a kind of a twist to sink herself farther. I was about shin-deep in sand when I felt it, first a layer of sand that had to have been twenty-five degrees cooler than what was above it, then the bubbles of icy water bursting up through the sand against the bottoms of my feet.

"There it is," Jodi said, "the world's biggest beer cooler."

I looked around me, east to the dunes, north and south to the billowing smoke plumes, west across the vast dry valley, and imagined the water, rushing under all of it, rising to the surface to slake the thirst of the bison, the heron, the great horned owl. If a lake the size of metro Denver existed under there, what else? Mountains? Trolls? Another civilization where people valued the land and took care of it?

I thought of my midnight hose excursions and knew I was just as guilty as the potato farmers. I closed my eyes and said a prayer to the blank space where God should be, for the aquifer to stay strong and deep and healthy, and as I did every day, for rain. When I opened them again I saw that Jodi's face was covered with tears.

"It's enough to make you believe somebody's looking out for us," she said, and gave a small embarrassed laugh.

"It doesn't hurt anything to hope for that," I said, and we hauled our feet up out of the cool wetness, and headed back downstream.

Jodi #1:

We moved there because I was going to sing, okay? Not because we're tacky or because either one of us is a compulsive gambler or because we can't tell the difference between Vegas and a *real* city. We moved there because SoHo was getting too damn scary—in more ways than one—and Hank was getting too damn old, and the houses were cheap out in Vegas and the entertainment plentiful.

Oh sure, we did get married there, and there's a soft spot in any marriage for the one place you had the most sex. I wanted to get married somewhere really screwy, like underneath the glass-bottom white tiger cage at the MGM or maybe on whichever one of those pirate ships sinks every hour outside Treasure Island, but Hank said that would be a bad omen and I had to admit he was probably right.

He wanted to get married in front of Bellagio while the fountains danced to "Con Te Partiro," and I said we'd probably time it wrong and wind up with "Proud to Be an American," and besides which, every three months a knocked-up teenager with braces on her teeth from Jersey gets married out there. I barely escaped with my life from Kearney, Nebraska, at the age of eighteen, and I get pretty nervous anytime Hank momentarily loses touch with the irony I married him for.

We compromised by getting married behind the Flamingo Hotel right between the Bugsy Siegel statue and the live penguins. The only people in attendance were my folks and Hank's kids. The presiding official, whose name was Shark, found it hilarious that Hank was older than both of my parents and I was younger than both of Hank's kids.

"It's like one of those what's-wrong-with-this-picture pictures in *Highlights* magazine," Shark said.

"Perfect," Hank said, and then everybody signed the papers and we left.

Doesn't every twenty-three-year-old ex-Cornhusker head cheerleader and president of the Glee Club think she's going to marry a fifty-one-year-old surrealist painter from the Bronx? And ten years later, just when she finally gets used to SoHo, learns how to move inside its various levels of pretense, just when she's finally found a Reuben on dark rye with a real kosher pickle for under six bucks, just when she finally can say she owns the subway and all its grotesqueries, doesn't she imagine that she'll come home one day from her hot yoga class and say, just because she's feeling peckish, "I think if we moved to Vegas it would be easier for me to work," and her sixty-one-year-old husband who has never lived outside of the five boroughs in his entire life, who has never learned to drive a car and says he doesn't care to, will say, "Okay, honey, whatever you'd like?"

In New York there had been so many excuses. So much competition, younger, thinner, so much better trained. The gigs I got there were either short-lived, or they devolved into cat-fighting and general ugliness so fast I excused myself. A half a century ago a singing dancing comedienne in her early to mid-thirties would have had her choice of venues in New York, but it was no longer the case. It made me mad that I was born too late to do what I was good at, and born nearly too late to spend my life with Hank.

In Vegas there would be far more jobs and far less talent. Hank had supported me for ten years, and the mother of his children for twenty years before that. Not that he ever talked about retirement. Hank would paint until he couldn't raise a brush anymore but that wasn't the point. I would be a late-blooming desert flower and find a way to keep Hank in the manner to which he'd grown accustomed, whether he needed me to or not.

The only hitch was, once we got to Vegas, I didn't want to sing and dance anymore. My primary job for ten years in New York had been keeping the painter happy, and I hadn't realized how much I liked it until it was time to give it up. Like most artists, Hank's not good at the really simple things. What kind of espresso to order, for instance, can stymie him for ten to twenty minutes, or putting the Cuisinart back together when it comes out of the dishwasher, or getting money out of an ATM. He still can't fill out the FedEx forms by himself, and if there's anything around the house or the yard or the car that needs fixing, you might as well forget about that.

Hank kept saying that one day I would find something I really loved and go straight after it, that some people waste their greatness all at once when they are young and then they have nothing left for the end. He was talking about himself at those times, not me, because in his twenties you never heard his name in a sentence without the word *genius* attached to it, and lately you are more likely to hear *solid* or *consistent,* but Hank says he doesn't really give a shit about any of that as long as there keep being people who want to pay him money to put his art on their walls. When Hank said I was saving my greatness for later we both know he meant, *for all those years you'll live after I'm dead,* but he never said that and neither did I.

But then sometimes I would look at his sweet pink face, at the crazy tufts of white hair that rise in no particular order off his pink, pink scalp, at the Red Wing boots he insists on wearing every day, even in Vegas, even when it was a hundred and forty degrees and I would think, *No, Jodi, your greatness is right now, it's loving this man, this strange funny man who won't eat anything but clean eggs and cheeseburgers and who has a penchant for Russian pop music and who when we moved to Vegas, began to sign all his checks, inexplicably,* Regards from Mr. Tommy. *Taking care of that man is the greatest thing you'll ever do, and it would just be perverse of you not to revel in it.*

It was sometime in there when I decided I wanted a ranch. Cattle hooves were bad for the ground and horses don't earn enough back. The sheep we had in Nebraska were dumber than fence posts. Emus and ostriches will claw you half to death if you piss them off, and I didn't feel right putting fences around a herd of elk. Some Japanese conglomerate was selling a bison ranch on the Internet for what seemed like not enough money, so I talked Hank into loading our dog Misha into the car and heading for a place in Colorado called the San Luis Valley.

When we got there we saw the reason for the price. The Japanese executives had gotten their hands on the ranch somehow and tried to convert it into a resort. About halfway between laying sod on the new golf course and tripling the size of the kitchen they realized hardly anybody came to the San Luis Valley, and those who did come were more likely to want to go backpacking than to eat gourmet food and play golf. When Hank and I arrived on the scene the place had been abandoned for two years, and the golf course was being reclaimed by the prairie. All the carefully made humps and hummocks were overrun with sunflowers and bee balm, the sand traps full of tumbleweeds and goat heads, and rabbit-brush stalks tough as telephone cables pushed up the macadam of the little golf-cart paths leaving potholes and cracks. It was a sight out of some futuristic novel, this ghost of a golf course, the way the land will take over when the last human has blown himself off the face of the earth. The whole place gave me the creeps at first but it appealed to Hank's macabre sensibility.

"Think of the dinner parties we could have," he said, walk-ing around the thousand-square foot kitchen.

"We don't have any friends," I reminded him.

"We'll make some," he said. "Isn't that what people in the country do?"

But once I got here; once I felt my nostril hairs freeze all the way up inside of my brain on a twenty below morning; once I saw the steam rising from the backs of those big skinny-legged, curly-haired supermodels out there; once I saw the sky on a winter night—more stars than the world has ever known above me—the Milky Way stretching horizon to horizon like something in a children's book or a planetarium maybe, but never, never, in real life, I knew we'd lucked into the best possible place to make a new start.

I've learned many things in my ten-plus years with Hank and one of those is that when you spend all your time in the company of artists, you don't get many chances to talk about God. Or whatever you want to call it.

Religion is pretty much over for me. By the time I was fifteen it seemed like I'd been felt up by every man with a clerical collar in southwestern Nebraska, and I got sick of using the scepter and the chalice as weapons of self-defense. But then I start to think about all the things I'm grateful for, and I find it hard to let go of Him altogether. Hank, of course, and Misha, my mom and dad, though Lord knows they drive me crazy, and this piece of ground where I can sit at my oversized kitchen window and watch the golf course disappear into the earth. Now all of a sudden it looks like I might have found a friend.

Rae showed up here looking like she was on some kind of a pilgrimage to the land of the holy waters. That's the humor in all of this. The Japanese businessmen didn't stick around long enough to understand that the real value of this land is in the aquifer, the underground body of water that I'm dedicating the rest of my life to protecting from the real estate developers down in Colorado Springs. Rae's house was only eight miles from the Missionary Ridge fire, and it showed all over her face. She called home to her husband twice during her two-hour visit to see if the fire had jumped the Divide.

When I told Rae that Hank was twenty-eight years my senior, she didn't hesitate a moment before saying, "Oh, wow, that's a great idea, you'll get to have two chances at it without that whole mess of divorce."

I knew right then how much she and Hank would take to each other, peas in a pod, she and Hank, which must be a Tri-State Area thing.

"No disrespect, of course," she said. "I'm sure he's a lovely guy."

"No disrespect," I said. It was a phrase Mr. Tommy would have used himself.

When she got in her car to cross the two county lines that separated our ranches she said, "I don't think we're done with each other."

"No," I said, getting the right answer for at least the second time in my life.

Brooklyn #2:

Rae has a portrait on her kitchen wall of Dante, grey face, white beard, on a mottled green background. He's wearing a maroon hunting jacket, with a high white collar, open, but standing up underneath. Depending on the angle from which you look, he either resembles Sean Connery, James Taylor, or Stanley Tucci. A Florentine painter who had never met him painted the portrait from a series of photographs that Rae had brought to Italy. She caught not only his look but his mood, his countenance, that's how strong a presence he has; it leaps off the glossy emulsion, and off the thick brushstrokes as if he were in the room.

I saw the portrait when I drove down to pay a visit to Dante, on the two-year anniversary of his amputation. The Army had assigned me to a base in Pennsylvania, where I had worked quietly for nearly two years, but things were heating up in the Gulf again, and I was suddenly notified of six weeks' paid leave that I hadn't been expecting, reassignment to follow.

I came home to Walden, to less snowpack and pastures drier than I could ever remember, and a tension between my parents I couldn't absolutely identify, though they assured me things would ease when the monsoon finally came and it started to rain. I got in my car and headed south, through a landscape that resembled October far more than July. After about an hour I realized I was headed for Rae's ranch, to check on her and Dante.

"If he had known your car," Rae said, "he might have leapt the fence for you." I was gratified by Dante's enthusiasm, once I had stepped out of the car and identified myself.

"We still feed him with the fork," Rae said. "It's become our favorite ritual." I had started feeding Dante that way when he was confined to the hospital, on the days he seemed too much in pain or distracted to eat by himself. Now he stood tall, strong, regal, then he gave himself over to a happy dance, and we both applauded.

"People ask all the time if he was born this way," Rae said, and it was true he made it look easy, almost natural.

"The rare three-legged Irish wolfhound," I said. He came and leaned his strong shoulder against my hip.

"It's good to see you," Rae said. "Come in, and we'll get a drink."

Some of the vet students had said Dante looked like a wookie from Star Wars, others mentioned a creature from a film I've never seen called *The NeverEnding Story*. I've always thought he looked a bit like a camel, but a wise one; the camel with the oldest soul in the world.

In the first Gulf War I was stationed in the Euphrates River Valley, and there was a private zoo there that had fallen into disrepair. I made it my business to try and find out what had happened to the proprietors, if they had been killed, or driven out of town. Why they had abandoned the animals that I could see, by the expense that had gone into the original facility, they had once cared deeply about.

When I couldn't find out anything, I decided to give the animals what care I could during the brief time I was there, though in the case of the tigers, it may have been more humane to shoot them. Mobile Army units are stocked to the gills with medical supplies and food on the verge of expiration, and I grew up with enough husbandry to know in general which drugs might help the animals and what, of our rations, they could eat.

The cats were the biggest challenge. The zoo had three Siberian tigers, a male and two females, and it was the females you couldn't turn your back on. The males were aggressive, but they were aggressive like drunken frat boys, sitting around lethargically and occasionally letting out a deep roar. But the females were furious, furious at their treatment, furious at their captivity, and the two times I forgot to focus on that fact, I wound up disentangling their claws from my shoulder blades.

The camels were young and untrained, which was the only reason why nobody had come along to steal them, though I held out hope that somebody would. Their disposition was not unlike our horses in Walden, but they had a more complicated sense of humor (one of them loved to knock the hat off my head, another would try to unzip my jacket as I held the feed bag with both hands), and I imagined myself breaking them to saddle, and setting off across the vast desert that

I had never seen but that I knew stretched out into infinity beyond the oil fires to the west.

I found myself telling Rae about the camels and the cats. We fell back into the easy rhythm of conversation we'd always had on the hospital lawn. Dante was back at her feet, though this time without the cast and bandages, without the anxiety in his eye that we were approaching the moment when she would rise, reluctantly, and I would have to take him back to his cage.

He had always gone with me without complaint, but not without reservation. He always threw a couple of glances back over his shoulder, long enough to assure Rae he would prefer it otherwise, but short enough not to encourage her guilt.

By the time I left the Kuwaiti/Iraq border, I had found a young man who said he would care for and train the camels. When I told him that they both enjoyed any fruit that wasn't citrus, and loved to be rubbed with a curry comb everywhere, but especially at the base of their necks, he looked at me strangely, and I wondered if I was making a mistake.

"I think," he said, in near-perfect English, "that we have a different relationship with these animals than you do."

He was not, as I first thought, chastising me for pampering, even spoiling the camels. He was simply offering me a gentle reminder that the history of Kuwaitis and camels go back further than any notions of history I might have. *And when you are gone,* he might have said to me, *someone else will feed the tigers, or they will not, and you will have the luxury of not knowing.*

I shook his hand and watched as he led away the camels. I had no choice but to leave the tigers on their own.

Howard #5:

It started to rain on the Fourth of July, canceling the fireworks in town, which pissed some people off, which tells you a lot about some people. They'd been canceled in most towns between here and Denver, most towns whose population had half a lick of sense.

Rae and I stood on the ranch's wooden porch and watched the rain walk toward us from Red Mountain. I could see it coming down between us and the big forest that stretched up to the Divide and I could tell Rae was trying to keep her happiness in check just in case it rained itself out before it got to us. She said it would be okay if it did rain itself out, because it was already raining on the place our creek came down from, and our well water, and it was soaking what little space remained between us and the leading edge of the fire, but we both knew if we didn't get to feel it on our faces we would probably start to cry.

When I was sure I felt the first few drops (I didn't want to scare it away with my cockiness) I put a five-gallon bucket under the rainspout so we could water our still-leafless trees. Over the next few weeks that would become our measure of whether or not it really rained, if what ran off the roof filled a bucket.

I became fascinated by how the parched ground resisted the water at first, rolled it right off its surface like olive oil. The hummingbirds, who'd been hiding who knows where all summer, showed up within five minutes of the rain and circled my head on the way to the feeders that had been hanging pink and full, untouched all summer. They were mostly green, with ruby throats and gold iridescence on their backs, but there had been one short-necked red one the year before that I always called Jimmy Durante who liked to boss all the other hummingbirds around.

"This is my feeder, see?" I always said, which made Rae laugh every single time, and made me think, a good life is as simple as you let it be. A rainy afternoon, baseball murmuring low on television, a nap on a couch made of goose-down pillows.

This is a small town, and in general the townspeople don't care much for Rae. The repertory theater did one of her plays last summer and the local people who saw it said they didn't like the way she "used urban humor at the expense of the rural sensibility" and they found it offensive when her female characters occasionally used the word fuck. Rae got a cigar box full of hate mail over that play which was in reality about as controversial as *Our Town*, including one letter from the woman who owned the only bar in town, barring her from ever entering it.

"You think you're so famous, well you're not as famous as John Wayne," read one of the most memorable lines.

Jill, who owns the coffeehouse told me, wait a week, something else will happen, and sure enough, Molly Finnegan got a dog-at-large ticket for her Airedale, Curly, and brought him right down in front of the courthouse and shot him. Molly Finnegan is one of the people in town that we call "eccentric" and the rest of the world would call bipolar. Anyway, Jill was right, after that everybody did stop talking about Rae's play.

Rae comes from a long line of sun worshipers, and she has always been one herself, subject to Seasonal Affective Disorder symptoms when she finds herself in one or another winter-grey city, but when the smell of rain fell on our pasture and our porch and our cracked dusty skin for the first time that summer I believe she was cured of SAD forever.

Once it started to rain it rained for three days straight, and for the first time in two months Rae didn't wake up in the middle of the night sniffing for smoke coming over the Divide. I could see her whole body relax incrementally each time the rain fell. Maybe the fire hadn't been coming for her after all, maybe what Theo told her had been right, maybe sometimes the good things do happen.

It was on the third day of rain that Rae got the call about Jonathan. He had shot himself, straight through the heart in room 126 of a Reno Howard Johnson's.

What she told me about first was a night long ago in Utah when they had fed the fattest raccoon in the world a whole bag of Cool Ranch Doritos. What she told me about second was a conversation they'd had on the Saturday night of Memorial Day weekend. They were eating Thai food with a bunch of Jonathan's overeducated underemployed fishing buddies and I had volunteered to stay in the cabin with the dogs.

Jonathan had said, "The thing I find most frightening, is that we have no real system of beliefs to fall back on when things in our life go to hell."

"Sure we do," Rae said, though she wasn't sure what she meant by it. "I do," she said. "And you do too."

"No, I don't, and you don't either," he said. "The only person around here who has a system of beliefs he can rely on, is Gene."

Gene was a California Buddhist with bumper stickers on his car that said things like, IF GOING TO CHURCH MAKES YOU A CHRISTIAN, THEN DOES GOING TO THE GARAGE MAKE YOU A CAR? (*Mechanic*, I always wanted to say, would complete the analogy properly.) Gene had a rule about stopping and saying a prayer every time he passed roadkill, but like Jonathan, he drove so frenetically he was usually praying on the way back up the mountain for something he had smashed on the way down.

"You've got to be joking," Rae said.

"No," Jonathan said, "I've watched him. Gene has a way of rising above. . . ."

"And so do you," Rae said. "I've watched you. And so do I. It might not be as effective, as reliable as the next person's, as Gene's, if that's who you want to deify today. . . ."

Gene was at the table too, and Rae could see he liked that their argument had his name in it. Gene's wife was sleeping with three of Placer City's six volunteer firemen. All six of them currently had DUIs, and so whenever there was a fire they had to call over to the larger town of Pine Valley, and ask one of *their* guys to come drive the truck.

"You're wrong," Jonathan said, "and when something really bad happens to you, you'll see that."

"Is there something really bad that's happening to you?" Rae asked.

"I'm not having this conversation anymore," Jonathan said, and he got up and left the table.

Bang, it was so obvious. Rae would be mad for a while, I understood, before she started to think about all the things she might have done.

Six

•

The
Hockey
Player

Rose #3:

Do you ever get the feeling that your particular corner of the world has entered some kind of bad spell, and there just isn't any way through it, but through it?

I mean summer is supposed to be the happy-go-lucky time around here, when the horses have belly-high grass and a big bubbling creek to drink from. Stanley's out patrolling the garden with plenty of fat furry creatures to snack on. Rae's friends come to visit, full of pets for me and Dante, and everybody kicks back a little bit with a pitcher of lemonade on the redwood porch. There's music on the stereo, or a Rockies game on TV, fresh greens from the garden, and plenty of meat trimmings from the Denver Whole Foods that Rae always slides in our direction.

Howard's up making lattes every morning in the cute red Illy espresso machine that makes a heck of a noise, and sometimes he slides a couple of peanut butter cookies onto Rose's special plate while he is at it. There's plenty of shade on the back porch which is piled so high with dog beds I swear the ones on the bottom are starting to metamorphose into rock, and there are tons of flies to catch and eat on the mudroom window screens. There are rowdy after-dinner games of Two Truths and a Lie around the old pine table, sometimes a little dancing in the moonlight, sometimes the dogs, sometimes the humans, sometimes everybody piles on the goose-down couch for a midnight watching of *The Last Waltz* with the speakers turned up high.

The days are long and the nights smell sweet and Rae— and sometimes even Darlene—can let go of the things that haunt them, take a deep breath, and sing, though the singing is mostly on the inside. That's what summer is supposed to be around here.

This summer has been about cracked ground and military showers, fights between Rae and Darlene about excessive loads of laundry, shriveled-up baby lettuce leaves in the garden that no self-respecting rabbit would dig under a fence for. It's been about black skies and paws that won't get clean with any amount of licking and that hot wind that blows so hard and dusty it's hard to walk against, and so relentless it's hard not to think, for at least a minute, of some dark cookie-less hell. When it does rain the lightning comes with it, and it's enough to scare a Rosebeast half to death, cracking right down on the ground next to where she is sleeping.

This summer has been about hours and hours on the phone full of bad news and unanswered questions, about guns and funerals and sometimes even forgetting that a can of Lamb, Duck and Pasta is supposed to accompany the dry food in the big meal that is served at midday. Mostly this summer has been about waiting, for the fire to come over the ridge, for sand to show up in the well water, for the wind to stop, for the rain to start, for Rae to cry over Jonathan, for Dante's cancer to return.

There is no way through it, as I said, but through it. It's just making the Rosebeast a little nervous, is the point I'm trying to make. I just hope everybody is still standing when we reach the other side.

Darlene #3:

What is it with stalkers and Federal Express? I mean, it wasn't all that many months ago we stopped getting FedExed Easter bunnies from the little snowboarder, and now all of a sudden the square white truck starts to appear in the driveway again, every afternoon like clockwork, bearing boxes and boxes of sportswear that we apparently can't live without for one more day. With Jonathan gone and Mona out of the picture, it was only a matter of time before Rae invited some new stray dog to the ranch.

"Hey Fred," I always say to the driver, "can I get you a cup of coffee?"

"I'll take a rain check on that, Darlene," he says, jumping back in the truck, and why the hell wouldn't he? He'll be back this time tomorrow, sure as shit.

The difference between this one and the snowboarder? Eddie Kominsky has got a buck or two. He used to play hockey in the NHL. We don't even have a public gym in this county, so when I try to explain to people why everyone in our odd little family unit is suddenly all outfitted in brand-new Adidas running shoes and International soccer jerseys, I say, *Rae knows somebody with connections.* People are already too suspicious of her for me to say any more than that.

We first met Eddie at a hockey game, on a warm December night, in line to get Philly cheesesteaks. There's nothing like hockey to take Rae back to her New Jersey roots and that craving in no time winds up in her stomach.

Rae says there's nobody west of the King of Prussia Mall—wherever that is—who knows how to make a good cheese-steak, and they get it so wrong out here she's even seen a sign reading NEW YORK FILLY CHEESESTEAK, which she says sounds like a punch line to an old joke, I Left My Heart In Sam Clam's Disco, some crazy thing like that.

I've never been east of the Nebraska state line and I think the cheesesteaks at the Pepsi Center aren't half bad. Rae says the roll isn't chewy enough, but she also agrees that if you put enough horseradish and hot peppers on it and close your eyes, it's the closest you are going to get, this far from the land of Tasty Cakes and Taylor Pork Roll.

When Eddie said his full name we both did a triple-take. He has less hair now, and a rounder face, and the accent of an *NHL Tonight* commentator, born of too much time around Canadians and a mouth full of gleaming false teeth.

"Shouldn't you be in a private box or something?" Rae said.

"I was just heading there," he said. "I'd love it if you joined me."

The box came with its own waitress, and unlimited food and drink. Eddie used to play for the New Jersey Devils, then for the Colorado Avalanche in their inaugural season when they came down to Denver from Quebec. Seven concussions in a row that season aborted his debatably promising career. He holds one statistic still, most penalty minutes by any franchise player in a first-round playoff game. He was famous for knocking the crap out of anyone who looked at him sideways, broke more noses, liberated more front teeth in his four years in the NHL than anyone before or since.

"I do miss it, in fact," Eddie said, when we'd settled in. "Not the games as much as the simple motion of skating, the acceleration, the speed, the sound of my blades on the ice. It's the ice that makes hockey marvelous."

"It's true," Rae said. "I don't know how many times a game I stop and remind myself that all those stops and turns, all those shots and hip checks, they're all happening on a surface where I could barely stand."

"It's all about the architecture of the play, really," Eddie said. "You commit to your linemates, to the passes you've practiced, you commit to the architecture and you forget it's all resting on a quarter-inch blade."

Rae's had crushes on hockey players her entire life, and she'd always been grateful she hadn't met one, sure if they ever actually spoke to her they would reveal themselves as grunting misogynists, shattering the almost perfect pleasure she has always derived from the game.

I glanced at Howard, who had immersed himself to his elbows in a complimentary sashimi tray. Not a flicker of jealousy crossed his face as he faced down a maguro hand roll with nothing but his own good fortune on his mind. I saw

him pocket a little arc of hamachi sashimi wrapped in a cocktail napkin that I knew was earmarked for Dante and Rose.

"Of course," Eddie went on, "I still do quite a bit of skating. This and that event for charity, the golden oldies leagues
here in Denver, and I coach two co-ed teams and one boys'.
Girls are so much smarter about this game than the boys are,
it's really something to watch, the mental advantage isn't
everything, but it's a lot."

Even I had to try pretty hard not to be impressed, but
somehow I managed.

In the time we'd been in Eddie's box the Avs had scored
two more goals and were letting some of the new kids get ice
time. It was a beautiful view from the box, and the seats were
big and more comfortable, but I missed the feeling of being
back in our old seats where people were screaming and
punching and high-fiving each other. Being in the box was
too much like watching the game on TV.

The second time we came to Eddie's box he said, "It's a
pretty special kid that wants to play hockey, a certain kind of
overachiever, not always from the happiest family. I guess
you'd know something about that."

Rae raised her eyebrows at him.

"Come on," he said, quietly, "it's all over your face."

"Maybe," Rae said, watching Howard, who was watching
the game.

"We're the same, you and I," Eddie said, more quietly still,
"we've been down the same dark alleys."

"Probably not quite," Rae said.

Eddie was not the first person Rae had heard this from.
Therapists, students, actors, masseuses in particular, seemed

uncannily good at identifying her emotional history. They were always whispering in her ear, *I have a new technique I'd like to try if you are game for it.* Rae was pretty much always game for anything.

One masseuse tried to take a block out of Rae's heart chakra, another blew a baby deer into her chest. A third tried to *tone* the blackness out of her by singing loudly, her hands hovering above Rae's prone body, dragging the air upward with her open palms. A fourth simply stood behind her head, with one hand on either shoulder and screamed, "GET THE FUCK OUT OF RAE'S BODY, GET THE FUCK OUT OF RAE'S BODY," until Rae couldn't keep the laughter in anymore and the masseuse gave her a dirty look and left the room.

"I mean this in only the most self-deprecating way," Rae said, "but so far I haven't met anyone who is actually the same as I am."

"You have now," Eddie said.

And so it began.

And I'd just like to go on record as saying, I never trusted him. And yeah, I know, I don't trust anybody, but I trusted him even less than that. It's my feeling that when somebody says, "It feels like I've known you all my life," what they really mean is, "This dynamic we are creating here is similar to one in my unhappy childhood." Not to mention that Eddie's got God and all His avenging angels on *his* side. He tries to keep all the Holy Roller stuff toned down so he doesn't scare Rae, but he sneaks it in, throwing around words like miracle and savior and sin and redemption as if they were part of the common vernacular, which in this house, I can tell you, they are not. When I asked him which denomination was the church he attended, he hedged for a minute and then said, "Well, it's charismatic enough that we speak in tongues, but not so charismatic that we roll down the aisles."

They were bound up together for Eddie, ice hockey and God. The last time he got clobbered the team doc said if he wanted to be able to count to ten and feed himself at the age of fifty he ought to come up with some way to make a living that didn't involve using his head so often as a weapon. It was that same day, lying on the massage table in the weight room with ice packed all around him that God first spoke in his ear.

"Eddie," he said, "you're a pretty good hockey player, but there is more important work in the world than this."

"I believe that's true," Eddie said. "But I'd like to hang around long enough to get my name engraved on the cup that belonged to Lord Stanley."

God asked Eddie how much money he had saved and Eddie said not as much as he should have. He was making close to half a million dollars those last two years, a nice paycheck in those days for a young up-and-comer, especially one who was more talked about for his fists than he was his finesse. But there were too many girls and too many drugs and too many late nights at the Chop House. He fessed up to having only a couple of paychecks in the bank, plus the bonus he'd get if the Avs went all the way.

They will! God said, and then they did, and then He told Eddie how to invest his bonus and ten years later, to hear Eddie tell it, he could buy that team for cash. "It's so easy to see the path once you've lived through it," he said. "The first goal is the NHL. The second is the Stanley Cup. The third is the Holy Dove. After that it's all about helping the other guy get where you are."

You will not be surprised to hear that at this point in the conversation I was checking my distance from the exits and looking around for anything that I could use as a weapon, but Rae was smiling and nodding like she'd been waiting for somebody to come along and convert her her entire life.

When Eddie got up to use the rest room, she said, "I know what you are thinking, Darlene, but what if Jonathan sent him from the other side?"

I narrowed my eyes at her. "You don't think Jonathan would have done better by you than this?"

But she extended an open invitation to the ranch to Eddie, and before we could say Immaculate Conception, he came. Every time he visited he left another bottle of this Miracle II Holy Water in one cabinet or another. It's got a label on the back calling it a *spiritually revealed formulated product*, and a contents list including *electrically-engineered, eloptically-energized, stabilized oxygenated water*, whatever the fuck that is, *Ash of Dedecyl* (their caps, not mine), *and prayer.*

There's a little flap you can lift to read all these testimonials as to how it cures cancer and eczema and ulcers and plantar warts, and even one from some guy in Louisiana who dumped a gallon of the stuff into a one-acre crawfish pond saying how it made the crawfish grow to twice their normal size. I go to take a shower and there's some soap version of the shit in the bathroom. I can tell you where all the miracles are going to be happening next year, out at the Mineral County Dump.

Dante #4:

When Eddie suggested that we all take his jet on a tour of Canada, following the Colorado Avalanche to a series of away games in Vancouver, Calgary, Edmonton, and a few days later Ottawa and Montreal, Rae's face lit up like a seven-year-old's.

"Can we bring Dante?" she asked.

"That's the beauty of the jet," Eddie said, "and I'll call ahead and have my assistant make reservations in all the best dog-friendly hotels."

What was wonderful about Eddie was also what was most terrifying about him. The way he could anticipate Rae's fantasies and indulge them, and mine, and Howard's, and even Darlene's. When Darlene admitted that she'd rather stay home with Rose than spend all those days in several cities, Eddie called the Avalanche's general manager and had a signed Peter Forsberg sweater FedExed to the door by ten-thirty the next morning, and as she waved good-bye to us she was already wearing it, and she couldn't hide the smile on her face.

The trip was one indulgence after another. Hotels that offered not just Milk-Bones at checkout, not just water bowls in the lobby, but an entire canine room service menu, and spa services—shiatsu and reiki—for dogs and humans alike. We all had fun together, for at least five out of seven cities.

But such luxury never comes without a price, and I watched Rae watch Eddie to see when he would exact it. I watched Eddie watch Rae to see when all his generosity would make her want to pay up. The only one not watching was Howard, who dedicated himself to NHL hockey, French food and wine. He was friendly and appreciative with Eddie, devoted, as always, to Rae.

It was late at night and we were in the jet, somewhere between Ottawa and Winnipeg. Howard had eaten a plate of smoked salmon big enough for ten people and was sleeping contentedly on one leather sofa, and I was stretched out on the other. The northern lights were doing their ghostly dance out on the horizon, and at sunset a shooting star had shot right across the sky beside us.

"What more do you want Him to do?" Eddie asked Rae, but she just smiled at him, noncommittal. He had told her three times that day that she was failing to see the big picture, and I could feel her patience wearing thin.

"It takes the average person seven-point-six times hearing the Word before they get saved," Eddie said. "I might be your first time, and that is why you are so resistant."

"Well," Rae said, "I heard it takes the average person four-point-nine times hearing they need a shrink before they actually make an appointment."

"*God* is my confessor," Eddie said, after some time.

"Yeah, whatever," Rae said. "And I'm the cow who swallowed the moon."

"You should leave him," Eddie said suddenly, bending his head toward Howard. "As long as you stay together, neither of your souls can be free."

"I won't," she said. "Not in a million, trillion years."

"He's not enough for you," he said.

"And you, my friend, are far too much."

"That's not the point of this conversation," he said.

"And what is?"

"God," he said. "We were talking about God."

She got quiet and fumbled for the headphones that had fallen under her chair. Outside the northern lights were turning pink, then magenta.

"The night before your friend Jonathan shot himself," Eddie said, "I saw a puddle of blood on the floor of my room."

"Shut up," she said.

"I was going to call and warn you," he said, "but I couldn't be sure whose blood it was."

"Shut up!"

She turned her body so it was facing out the window, away from both Eddie and me.

"Dante's cancer is back," Eddie said.

Her head swung around, eyes narrowed, locked first on mine, and then on his.

"The doctors won't be able to see it for a couple of months," he said, "but it's there, tiny now, but growing."

"You son of a bitch," she said. Howard stirred in his sleep and then snored a little.

"When your soul is full of darkness," Eddie began, "these kinds of things are going to happen all around you."

"What kinds of things?"

"Death," he said, "suicide, terminal illness."

She stared at him.

"You could do the people you love a great favor if you'd let me perform a simple exorcism."

"Wait," she said, close to tears now. "My soul is the reason that everybody dies?"

"I've talked to your friends," he said. "They all agree."

"Eddie, I don't have any friends who would use the *word* exorcism."

"We could do it at the Brown Palace," he said, "with room service. It would take only four days. We'd leave a single candle burning. We've been speaking your language all along, but during these four days we'd speak only my language."

"You," she said, "are completely out of your mind." We heard the pilots exclaim over another shooting star.

"God told me when you are going to die," Eddie said, "It's not the kind of information I feel right about passing on, but I think you should know, you don't have all that much time to—"

"Fuck you."

"It's not me," he said. "God said I have to—"

"Then fuck Him too," she said.

I opened one eye and hung my head off the end of the couch so my nose could make contact with her toe. "When Dante's gone," Eddie said, "you'll see exactly how thin your life as Howard's surrogate mother actually is."

She turned back toward the window.

"He's the one who told me that you should leave Howard," Eddie said.

"God?" she said.

"Dante," he said.

"You are," she said, "such an unbelievable asshole."

She got up from her seat and came to sit at the foot of my couch. She took my head in her hands and kissed me hard, several times on my big black lips. She looked into my eyes as I measured the relative weight of true love and honesty. Whether it was God's word or just a lucky guess, we both knew that about one thing, Eddie Kominsky was right.

Howard #6:

We'd just come back from that crazy plane trip. And first, I want to say something that won't get said now that we've established what a sick dude this Eddie guy actually is, but he was very generous with his money, and in general, those are the kind of people I like. I mean I don't even know how much a jet costs, say to fly from one end of Canada to the other and back again, but I know gas is even more expensive up there than it is down here, and that little fucker must of burned the shit out of some fuel.

And here's another thing, the pilots on that plane, Bob and Steve, they were about the two nicest guys I've ever met. It must have been kind of fun for them, flying into a new city every day, a new country. Having to look it up in the book, Hey Steve, hey Bob, what does the runway look like *here*.

And the catering. Smoked salmon and sushi when we were on the coast, rare roast beef sandwiches and Caesar salads when we were inland, ice-cream sundaes one place with three kinds of topping. Snacks and snacks and snacks galore.

It's a dangerous thing, getting used to that lifestyle, getting used to having the limo pull right up to the jet and three big friendly guys asking what you need for the evening, what you'd like them to lock up on the plane. No I.D., no security, no lines, no filled-up overhead compartments, no babies kicking you in the ribs. Jet to limo, limo to the Mandarin, or the Hilton, or the Ritz, room service pregame, seats on the glass, a hearty dinner afterward with a retired player, some-times a current player. Shit, I didn't know anything about hockey a couple of years ago, and now I could practically write a book about the game. I mean, if I could write.

I REMEMBER WHEN Rae and I were first together and we went to a bar to watch the Avs in the playoffs and even though I hadn't watched a hockey game for Christ knows how many years, I was going to get into it for my baby. So I started yelling and cursing at the TV, acting like I think a sports fan is supposed to act, giving the refs the finger when the calls went against the Avs, going boohoohoo, boohoohoo, when one of the LA Kings players got called for high-sticking, till she put her hand on my arm and said, "Is this how you are going to be?" And I said, "No, absolutely not," and I decided to be a less obnoxious fan from then on.

But the next fall we went to see a live game for my first time. The Avs were playing the St. Louis Blues on Halloween, and Rae surprised me by saying she wanted us to go in cos-tume. We went to the Treasure Chest in Cherry Creek and I wound up with a Elvis/Wolfman mask that would color-coordinate really well with my Joe Sakic sweater and Rae bought a kind of jester's hat, lots of fuzzy points in different primary colors, and a little Mardi Gras eye mask in all the same colors as the hat.

She buys tickets one game at a time, so we don't always have seats that are right together, and on Halloween she was one row in front of me and about five seats over, and there was a guy in a St. Louis sweater right in front of her. The kid was a little asswipe, I could see that from where I was, with his turned-up ball cap and his dad's season tickets and his Chris Pronger sweater two sizes too big. He had a lot to say about our goalie Patrick Roy's mother, and he had a bad habit of standing up and screaming, "Roy Sucks!" every time the action heated up in front of our goal.

"SSSSIIDDOOWWNN!" It was loud, and like it had come from an animal, but an animal whose voice very closely resembled Rae's.

The young man turned around and glared at her, and behind the Mardi Gras mask, she glared right back.

"Forsberg sucks my cock," the boy yelled.

"Get a life," someone from the row behind me screamed.

"Get a Cup!" screamed someone behind them.

At the end of Rae's row a big guy in a Forsberg sweater stood up and started gesturing to the kid with his hand in front of his own crotch, "Hey Girly Man! Hey Girly Man. Bite Me, Girly Man, Bite Me."

The guy in the Pronger shirt turned to judge the distance between them, how a fight might be accomplished over the legs of the people that separated them, over the lap of my wife.

But the usher heard it too, and he was bigger than both the

hockey fans put together. He put his arm around the Avs fan, said something close to his ear.

The Blues fan started screaming, "He started it! He started it!"

"You started it asshole!" It was Rae again, with her Dan Hinote sweater and that ridiculous hat and her little carnival mask, her voice more resonant than any of the others.

I leaned across the people between us, touching my nose. "Honey," I said, "are you trying to start a fight?"

She'd broken her nose not two weeks before, not fighting, but catching her untied boot laces in the Denver apartment door, letting Dante out in the middle of a dark dark night, and falling forward down the three cement stairs so fast she didn't have time to lift her arms in front of her face. She came back to bed bleeding hard and laughing. "The saddest part," she said, laying an ice pack across her face, "is that you didn't get to see that."

Darlene said Eddie was too good to be true and even Rae said it a few times herself. She and I would be back in our fancy hotel room and Eddie would be off making plans so that the next day would be even more perfect than the last and she would look at me with her big blue eyes and say,

"Howard, do you think maybe it's just my turn for the treats?"

"Of course it is, honey," I'd say, and I'd think, *Why shouldn't it be? She works so hard to keep me in designer clothes and Darlene in carpentry projects and why shouldn't we live in a world where some millionaire with more money than sense would want to turn her into Cinderella?*

It was all a little unclear to me how Eddie made his money.

I mean hockey, sure, but not that much and not for all that long. I asked him one time and he said something about the big man upstairs, which at the time I thought meant *mafia,* but now I understand means God.

"You know, Howard," Rae said, "most men would be awfully jealous of Eddie right now."

"I'm not," I said, and it was true. There were things I would never be able to do for Rae, and that wasn't a secret I was keeping from myself. Maybe I was just lazy. Maybe I was saving all my greatness up for some important later date in my life. Maybe she did act too much like a mother, and maybe I acted too much like her kid, but if I knew one thing for sure it was that Rae Rutherford deserved to realize her childhood dream of seeing her team play hockey in every NHL rink in Canada, and if all I had to do to make that happen was not be jealous of Eddie Kominsky, then I figured it was the least I could do.

"I don't want to ruin this," she said, "just because of that same old thing about how I don't deserve it."

"Then go for it," I said, and gave her my biggest smile, the one that's always gotten me the parts.

She opened our suitcase and dumped it on the bed. We had only known Eddie a little over a month but every single thing in that bag was something he had given us. We had sweaters signed by the players of five different teams, we had matching NHL All-Star Game leather jackets, we had hockey boxer shorts and hockey pajama pants and hockey socks and T-shirts and shoe laces and fleece vests and ball caps and wool caps and scarves and mittens. With the signatures, I figured we had upward of ten thousand dollars' worth of hockey gear in one officially sanctioned NHL HOCKEY RULES! duffel bag.

"We've got a lot of cool shit," I said, and finally she was smiling.

"If he falls in love with me," she said, "it could get ugly."

"To say nothing of what will happen if he falls in love with me."

"He says he doesn't have the gene for that," she said.

"Butt-fucking?" I said.

"Romantic love," she said. "He says he wasn't given that gene."

The next day Eddie started talking to Rae about God, and I could tell things weren't going all that well between them. When all the catered food was gone I went to sleep on the plane because I figured they'd work it out better without me, but each time I woke up things seemed even worse than before.

We'd all be fine at the games, as long as we had the Avs to root for and the plays to talk about, but Rae stopped wanting to go out to eat afterward, and each morning, instead of jumping out of bed to see whatever new city we were in, she'd close herself up in the four-star bathroom and take a series of really big baths.

Eddie pretended not to notice her absence. I focused on the food and the fact that we'd be home in forty-eight hours. I have to admit that in spite of all his money, the look on his face made me feel a little sorry for the guy.

When the jet set us down back where the ten-day hockey odyssey had begun, at the little Forest Service airstrip not fifteen miles from the ranch gate, Eddie asked to come back with us to the house. Later that afternoon he stopped me on my way back from cleaning out the horse trough. I was peeling long rubber gloves off and a smell like the swamp thing was rising up from my shirtsleeves and I couldn't wait to get inside, into a hot shower, and wash seven days of accumulated horse slobber from my hands.

"Howard," he said, "can I bend your ear for a minute?" I stopped and held out my arms, half surrender, half complaint, a gesture I made often, and one he probably never did.

"I was hoping," he said, "that Rae would find a way to tell you this herself, but it's high time we all acknowledged that there's been a changing of the guard around here."

I watched his eyes, watched the way he pressed his hands together.

"Rae would never want to hurt you," he said, "and she made a promise to you that she takes very seriously."

I took a quick look back at the house and thought, despite the glare, that I could see Rae in the kitchen window, though it could have been a trick of the light. The word *mafia* came into my head again. How much money did you need before you could kill somebody and get away with it? How much did O.J. have? What about Robert Blake?

"There will be plenty of ways that she can honor that promise, and she's hoping you'll agree to stay on at the ranch after all the necessary paperwork is completed, in exchange for a more-than-generous stipend, of course."

Only in retrospect do I understand that this is the moment I should have hit Eddie Kominsky. Never mind all his penalty minutes. Never mind that he would have kicked my fucking ass.

"In the first place, Howard, you can't deny, surely, that I can offer Rae the kind of life that you can't begin to."

"Well . . ."

"And in the second place it really doesn't matter what you want, or what I want, or even what Rae wants, because this has all been decided by the big guy up there." He indicated the clouds that were trying to work into a thunderstorm above us. This time, when I looked back at the house, Rae was taking big strides across the yard to meet us.

"What is this?" she said to me. "What has he been saying?"

The scene had been moving along all by itself until that moment, all the cues taking care of themselves as well, but all of a sudden it was my line and somehow I had missed that part of rehearsal. We call that *going up*, in the theater, and I never knew why, maybe because when it happens you wish you would, up or down or sideways, to anywhere on earth but on that stage.

Get it on its feet, my old acting coach used to say at times like these, and I thought, *That's what I'm supposed to do, I'm supposed to punch him.* Or maybe words, harsh words, "This psychotic asshole seems to think . . . This home-wrecker has just revealed . . . This rich prick . . . This overgrown Nazi . . ." but that didn't seem right either. Or turning the question back on Rae, there was a certain pleasant rhythm to that, "No, I think *you* should tell *me* what . . ."

"I want you to do the thing that makes you happiest, sweetheart. If you think Eddie will make you happier than I will, I think you should go with him."

I didn't know where the words came from, but there they were, just as if I had rehearsed them. Rae looked from one of us to the other, and then she burst into tears.

Rae #7:

I looked out the kitchen window and saw Howard putting his hands through his hair the way he does only when he's really nervous and all of a sudden everything fell into place in my mind like a set of dominoes.

It was *not* my turn for the treats after all. I had been seduced, not by a man, not by a jet, or smoked salmon, or suitcases full of autographed hockey gear, but by my lifelong longing for a safety net, the part of me that wanted to be picked up, sleeping, out of the back seat of the family car and carried into my bedroom, that wanted to be told that no matter what happened everything would be all right. And for indulging this interminable child, for getting rocked in this Eddie-hammock woven of hundred-dollar bills, I was going to lose Howard, and before too long Dante, and possibly even Darlene.

I sat down at my kitchen table and looked at the portrait of Dante in his hunting jacket on the wall. He wasn't dead, not yet, and Howard was still out there, still running his hands through his hair in our yard. I slammed through the screen door, waking Dante and Rose, who leapt to attention and followed me to where Howard and Eddie were standing in front of the barn.

If I had a daughter, I would tell her what a funny thing love is, how it never looks the way you think it's going to, how no matter how old you get, it is love that keeps surprising you. How in the songs sometimes it involves beaches and champagne and chocolate-covered roses, but in real life it is just a prematurely balding man standing in a drought-dried field telling you that he loves you, and that you should do whatever on earth you want.

But I don't have a daughter. I have dogs instead, and they know more about love than anything.

Darlene #4:

When I pulled in the driveway that day I saw Eddie and Howard in the pasture, and Rae sitting next to Dante in the dirt between them, crying and shaking her head.

I got out of my car and suggested we all go for a walk. Motion is your ally, my Dad used to say, and no one knew that better than him. We headed to the back of the pasture quietly, keeping the creek bed on our left. Rae's face was set in doom mode and Eddie was uncharacteristically silent, but nobody seemed to want to tell me what was going on, so I just kept walking, and they kept walking too.

Finally Eddie stopped, pressed the palms of his hands together, and said that something miraculous was about to happen. He said that when we got to the top of the meadow there would be angels coming down for all four of us to catch. If we all four caught them, if none of us let them go, then we'd all see the way through to the other side of this together.

When we got to the top of the meadow Eddie told us to stop walking and stand very still and we did.

"There!" he said, and his line of vision swooped from the sky to the tops of the trees right across the fence in the national forest, and he grabbed at something with his big hockey hands before swooping his vision back up to the sky again.

He said, "Did you see them?"

"Yes," Howard said, but he didn't sound very sure about it.

"You were meant to catch them," Eddie said. "They were meant for you."

"We did," Howard said, "we caught them."

"No you didn't," Eddie said. "I can see them sitting up there in the top of the tree."

"I'm sure I caught mine," Howard said.

"You did not," Eddie said, "you missed your chance," and he looked back at Rae, who walked down to where Howard was standing and took his hand.

"You caught me," she said, "what do you think of that?" and Eddie turned and headed back to the ranch house. Rae and Howard couldn't stop smiling at each other.

"Does somebody want to tell me what the hell is going on here?" I said.

"Grab your angel," Howard said, "and we'll fill you in on the way back to the house."

Seven

·

The
End

Jodi #2:

Rae invited Hank and me down to her Denver apartment. She and Howard were going to spend part of the month of December there, Rae writing and Christmas shopping, Howard auditioning for next year's season of plays. When I moved to the ranch in the San Luis Valley, it was as if a switch turned off in my brain that made me forget all about city life. But once I actually got to Denver I couldn't sit still, dragging Rae to the art museum, the LoDo galleries, every faux-European café I could find.

We had green apple martinis at Kenny Sonoda's, high tea at the Brown Palace, and brunch at the Fourth Story Restaurant above the Tattered Cover Bookstore. We even went to the eleven o'clock service at St. John's Cathedral, where the Very Reverend Peter Eaton gave a sermon that moved even Hank to tears.

"Now there's a man with a collar who doesn't waste your

time," Rae said, on the way out the door. "Let's go find a bar that's showing a football game."

Rae ordered Hank around the way I suppose East Coast girls do, telling him what wine to choose and leaning in when the bill came to see how much he tipped, and Hank gave her as good and more back and we laughed so hard all weekend you would have thought someone else—as Hank likes to say—was picking up the tab.

It felt like Rae and I were continuing a conversation that we'd left off in college, in high school, in grade school maybe, back in geologic time when New Jersey and Nebraska were actually the same place. We would try, in the evenings, just before we'd retire to the guest room, or first thing in the morning before the boys were out of bed, to acknowledge our friendship, and fail. The comfort level, the familiarity, the fear inside each of us that though it didn't feel in the least bit fragile, one of us would probably screw it up.

I've spent my life being just too friendly to ever have to really get to know anybody. I'm a dog in a world where people are more interested in cats; neither difficult, standoffish nor mysterious, and as a result I'd always skimmed the surface with most of the people I knew. I'd never understood what I'd done right to get Hank interested, sang to him probably or some shit like that, and then all of a sudden here was this other person, this second person on earth who seemed to understand that for all my calm Nebraska exterior there was something worth unearthing deep down.

On Monday Dante was due for his three-month cancer scan, and Howard talked Rae into letting him be the one to take him.

"Take Jodi to the Cherry Creek Mall," Howard said. "This is exactly the kind of thing you can start relying on me for." She agreed with him, but I could tell her heart wasn't in it. She spent at least thirty minutes before we left lying on the floor next to Dante with her hand pressed to his chest. "My own special version of reiki," she said. "A masseuse in Santa Fe taught me. I figure it can't hurt."

Dante looked at her long and hard when she went to the door without him and we headed across town to the mall.

"But I thought it was supposed to come back in the lungs," Rae said into her cell phone three hours later, and it shames me now that my first wave of pity was for myself and how completely inadequate I was going to feel for the next several hours of my life.

"What do you need?" I said, when she hung up.

"A mocha," she said, "a big one. Whipped cream," and I went into Peet's and got it for her.

What they had known in advance about this day, was that when it happened there would be no more medical miracles. Dante was going to have his first palliative radiation treatment on the spot, which would take a little over an hour, and then we would meet all of the boys at home.

We wandered around the mall for a few minutes. Rae's face was frozen, with something way more complicated than grief.

"Crying, maybe, would be good," I suggested.

"Yeah," she said "I'll be doing that, at some point."

We sat down on a bench under two giant bronze sandhill cranes. There were a lot of little girls who had evidently just been in some kind of a performance in the mall, sitting around the big empty Christmas box decorations in their leotards and sparkly makeup.

"This is our first weekend together," Rae said. Her voice was small and a little strangled. "I don't want to screw it up."

"No, honey," I said, "don't even think it."

In front of us one of the girls' French braids had come down and her little friend was doing it back up for her.

"Maybe there's a reason," Rae said, "that he waited until now to let down his guard."

I nodded encouragement.

"Maybe he knows that I'm okay now," she said, "because I've got Howard, and I've got you."

For all the look on her face gave away, she might have said a *head cold*, or *herpes,* but I was beginning to understand her, the lack of fanfare when she said something big.

"Maybe he knew that if he waited till you guys went home, I would have tried to go through this without you."

"That's a lot of forethought," I said, "I mean for a dog," but she ignored me.

"You're going to help me through this," she said. "And in the process, I'm going to learn how to help you."

There had been a pit in my stomach since she'd gotten on the phone to Howard, and when she put words to it I felt tears spring to my eyes. Around us the little girls had become languid in the heat, and they were napping in clusters, using each other for pillows.

"I mean," she said, "when the time comes."

"Of course," I said.

"May it be," she said, "a very long way off."

Dante #5:

The cancer has come back, as cancers sometimes will. I tried my best to keep it from her as long as I could. There is a tumor in my rear left leg, a slightly smaller one in the rear right. They've been growing in there for the better part of a year, and only in the last week have I given in to the limp. "Roam about until exhausted and then, dropping to the ground, in this dropping be whole," Buddha said, but it is hard to imagine how I'll ever drop whole without her.

Howard detected it first. All the doctors had convinced my human so completely that if the cancer came back it would come back in my lungs that she put down my lameness to arthritis, which even I might have done had the pain only been a few inches lower, in the joint. That's why Howard offered to take me for my checkup, so he would be the first one to hear the news.

I feel very good about Jodi. I feel good about many things, but Jodi is the missing piece of the puzzle that makes the timing of this as good as it could ever be. My human's education on the subject of choosing a good mate was complete with Howard. But after our recent psychodrama with Eddie, and to a lesser extent Mona before him, I realized we hadn't focused nearly enough on how to find a friend.

In the dog world, friendship is all about the approach, and then the ensuing rhythm, and I can't see how it's much different for human beings. Naturally, it's more important how they smell than what they say, and how it feels to run alongside them bumping shoulders. Mona smelled like winter, like highways and too much wind and adrenaline. Eddie smelled like blood, like bread and water, like those bottles Darlene still finds under the sink in the second bathroom, sanctificated and tri-baptized potion for sinners. I know my sense of smell is a thousand times better than Rae's, but if you can't smell somebody like Eddie coming, you really shouldn't even call it a nose.

If Jodi were a dog, she'd be golden lab/old English cross, loyal, patient, with a slant sense of humor and a lot of hair falling carelessly into her face. She's married, and, I might add, happily, to a human I'd describe as a bull mastiff/newfy cross, gruff and tuff exterior, all feathers and kisses inside.

Since there is no way around the news, I'm glad Rae was with Jodi when she got it. We all arrived back at the apartment simultaneously, me a little woozy from the anesthesia that accompanied my radiation, Howard beside himself with worry that he shouldn't have told her over the phone, Jodi buzzing with usefulness, Rae slow and quiet, her hands clammy from shock. That's how she spent all that first evening, lying beside me on the carpet, and all the other humans let her stare, and then deny, and then hope, and then stare again.

She stayed in bed with me the next morning while Howard took Rose to the off-leash area of Washington Park, and it was there they ran into Malarkey, my full brother from a different litter. He's five years old and healthy as a horse. I took a little offense when Howard told my human he'd met a dog that was "exactly like Dante." Everyone knows that my mother's first litter, in which I was one of thirteen, produced the most handsome, intelligent dogs ever born to her. But I didn't have time to dwell on it, because the next thing you know, we were all in the car on the I-70, heading back to Grand Junction, to the ranch of my birth.

I hadn't expected ever to see my grandmother again, but there she was, still going strong, just a touch of arthritis, at the ripe old age of thirteen. My birth mother, Megan, was look-ing quite well at nine, my Aunt Tifty, much too old for pup-pies now, but acting as a good surrogate mother to a litter of my crazy half-sister Red Sonja's pups. Zelda, the human who had presided at my birth and nurtured me in infancy, stroked my head and marveled at my grace and balance. It felt good to come full circle like that.

Zelda said that Diva, my much younger full sister born to Megan and Baron quite late in their lives, was coming into heat in the spring, and I've got my paws crossed that my human will wind up with one of the puppies. Paperwork exchanged hands is all I'm saying, and I'm hoping part of that was a deposit check.

We both know she'll never replace me. We are both, as Theo would say, clear and secure in that, but what would everything I've taught her add up to, if she didn't believe she could love, and love yet again?

She calls me a perfect being. That's what I hear her say on the phone these days to Jodi, right before she starts crying. *But he is such a perfect being . . .*

Dr. Theo calls me an object (though he won't dare say it while I'm lying on the floor of his office, drinking water out of his proffered little Tupperware and making his job, I might add, easier by half). He says I'm the object she created so she could learn to love herself.

Aren't the humans perfectly marvelous creatures? Doesn't it make you double over with laughter the way they remain committed to the idea that they're the only species that feels deeply, because—what—they have words to talk about their feelings? Has it not ever occurred to them that perhaps the reason they need so many words, the reason their words consistently fail them, is that they are so much poorer at interpreting their emotions than we are, that interpretation, per se, is a step that in the dog world we just skip?

Rae agreed with Dr. Theo, partly to make him happy, partly for a moment's respite from grief. And perhaps I am simply an object. A big grey hairy three-legged object, who knows from across the room when her feet are cold and comes to lay his head there to warm them, who licks and licks the place where her watchband sits so she might understand that to me her sweat is elixir, who puts his head on her shoulder when we are driving because it is her favorite thing in the universe, who keeps it there for hours so she might not feel scared of the dark or the cold or the patches of ice on the highway.

She wasted so much time trying to act perfectly, trying to guard against the loss, always fearful of making the mistake that would lead to it. My job was to love her in her imperfection, and I did. Even when she left me alone in the car for hours, even when she accidentally closed my neck in the automatic back seat window, even when she came home smelling like another dog. She calls me a miracle, but this is the miracle: eventually she believed I loved her, beyond a shadow of a shadow of a doubt.

I wanted her to see that sometimes, no matter what we do, the good thing happens anyway. Sometimes there is a man who lets the occasional hamburger fall from the barbeque. Sometimes there is a friend who wants to be simply that. Sometimes cancer goes into remission, sometimes it stays there. And the fact that it didn't this time doesn't mean it never will. I wanted her to see that the only life worth living is a life full of love; that loss is always part of the equation; that love and loss conjoined are the best opportunity we ever get to live fully, to be our strongest, our most compassionate, our most graceful selves. After all, aren't we all just trying to learn the same things here, about sharing the food bowl with our sisters and brothers, trying to keep crumbs out of the dog bed, remembering to bring the squeaky toys inside in case of rain?

Dr. Evans recommended three radiation treatments so that I might have less pain in the months—or weeks, he said grimly—that I had left. After the second treatment Rae and Howard stopped for take-out and I heard her say, as they were getting out of the car, "It occurs to me, Howard, that you, too, are a perfect being."

Never were words sweeter to my ears.

Darlene #5:

I'm making Rae a quilt for Christmas. When I heard Dante's cancer was back, it seemed like the logical thing to do. I found a part-time job working at the hardware store this winter, and everybody else I know is getting work gloves and tool belts and hand sanders for Christmas, but she's getting a quilt, blue and yellow, an eternity pattern all around the outside.

Rae says the thing she'll miss most is the way Dante puts his chin over the back of her seat while they are driving, the soft hot breath in her ear, the way he'll sometimes—for no reason at all—take a little bite at her earring. But I think she underestimates how much she'll miss him at night. He has this way of turning toward her in the bed—he'll even do it sometimes with me. He'll roll right over and bring his nose to my nose, throw his one front paw right across my chest, stretch out his back legs so they are longer than mine and we're toe to toe. He gives these little grunts of pleasure, and little tiny wet flecks come out of his nostrils and onto my face. Sometimes he'll even nuzzle his chin right into my clavicle, and I've had a few men in my lifetime gone enough on me to want to snuggle like that and none of them ever did it more gently, more lovingly, more romantically than that big dog. You don't get over a thing like that too easily.

However much work you might think making a quilt is, I can assure you it is about three and a half times more work than that. Still, it gives me something to do when I come home nights from the hardware. My cousin Dorice had a T-shirt made for me that says I'VE GOT THE BIGGEST CHEST IN MINERAL COUNTY AND I'M FREE SATURDAY NIGHT. But the fact is, I say no even when they ask me. I'd rather go home, curl up on the couch next to Stanley, put the hockey game on and finish off a couple of squares.

I went out a couple of times last summer with a sweet recovering alcoholic named Herman who caught my attention by telling me he drives sixteen hours every Saturday to see his kid in Salt Lake City for a six-hour visit. He sent roses and took me out to the only real restaurant in town and said all the right things, but there was a darkness there, a void that needed to be filled, and I didn't see myself being the one to fill it. Frank at work is gonna teach me how to drive the forklift, and I'm trading the Unitarian minister ten massages for a slightly used table saw. These are the kinds of deals I like to make for myself, the ones that happen right up here in the light.

What can you say after a three-year remission? I don't think there's a human who would look that gift horse in the mouth. My mother wouldn't have, that's for sure, and I won't either should the same fate befall me. The doctor who comes up here twice a month from Alamosa says I should have been getting annual mammograms starting ten years before my mother was diagnosed, but we've long since passed that deadline. When you've got tits as big as mine, a mammogram might be the last thing on earth you want to contemplate.

I'm leaving at the end of this month. I made the final decision this morning. I've been in this town long enough. I've been in this house long enough. Howard and I are starting to grouse at one another, and I can see it's weighing on her mind. Several years back, some co-workers at the dealership had me a T-shirt made that said DOES NOT PLAY WELL WITH OTHERS, and I wore it until I wore it out, it saved me so much time and explanation. I'm a damn good employee, and to a certain kind of person I can be a pretty good friend, but Rae's always been a little too high-maintenance for me and this was a hard summer on everybody. She's got Howard now and she doesn't need me to handle the practicalities the way she did once upon a time, so I'll be finishing the quilt, staying through the winter, and moving on when spring rolls around.

Rae and Howard have tickets to go to Hawai'i with Jodi and Hank over the holidays and now that the cancer's back she's afraid to go. I told her, *Look, as hard as it is for you to watch him die, it's just as hard on him, watching you watch him*. I was thinking of the look on my mother's face, of her wanting to go, wanting also to make it to my seventeenth birthday. If I'd had the courage then, I would have told her to go on, to get out of the pain; that I would be fine on my own, and was, and am, and always will be. But I was as scared as she was back then, of the dark, of the state and whatever foster deal they'd try to cut for me, of death itself. I begged her to stay and stay and stay, not with words so much as with my eyes, and she stayed, so far into the pain, so much longer than she should have, but still not until my seventeenth birthday.

As if Dante would even consider dying before he knew Rae was back home safe and sound from Hawai'i. She took me down to Denver for a hockey game last week, and when we got back to the apartment he did the most extensive happy dance that I have ever witnessed. If there was a God He'd keep Dante around long enough for Diva's puppies to be born, but when I told Rae that she said it might screw up the master reincarnation plan. I gave her a look that said she might be losing it, but if there was ever a dog that could get himself resurrected into a puppy that Rae has already spoken for, it's this one. There aren't words to describe the way that dog looks at her. It's beyond language. It's beyond anything I've seen in my life.

Rose #4:

They keep telling me that I am supposed to step up. *Step up*, they say, the way the guys on ESPN do, when the Pro Bowl quarterback goes down with a torn ACL, that's what they ask of the rookie. That's me. The rookie. But there are a couple of obstacles they haven't taken into account, and the first one is the bed, which I do not like at all.

I used to like the bed just fine, but there were a few times—I can't tell you exactly how many—when the unsuspecting little Rosebeast came happily down the hall into the bedroom to greet the humans, leapt up onto bed, and just about had her head bitten off by the frail and enlightened one, who until that moment had been in a completely Zen-like state, and therefore horizontal, and therefore invisible to me. I'm not the world's fastest learner, as has been pointed out with some consistency, but I have learned to fear the bed and now the humans want me back in it.

So I try. I get big and brave and surmount my fear of the
bed, hold my breath and leap up there, trust that if they've
invited me it means there is no big angry dog hiding under the
comforter—he's out back on the dog bed because he's woozy,
let's say, from radiation—and they do pet me, and pet me, and
pet me, but then they eventually fall asleep, and after that I just
don't get it. What is the point *then* of being in the bed?

I sleep much better in the dog bed. Let's face it, we *all* sleep
much better when I am in the dog bed. And unlike the
enlightened one, who keeps one eye on Rae 24/7 for the first
hint of distress, I am a girl who both needs and enjoys her
sleep. Sleep is important to those of us who—how can I put
this?—lead with their looks. If worrying oneself to death all
night instead of sleeping leads to cancer, we can all rest
assured the Rosebeast is in for a long and a happy life.

And while we are on the subject, I guess I'd like just a
smidgen of credit for being so easy to please, for not making
her feel guilty every time she drags her suitcase out from
under the bed, for not needing to turn the sleeping arrange-
ments in any given hotel room into some kind of *thing*.

I'm a simple girl, and I like simple things. A big old stain-
less-steel bowl of dry food and then a trip out to the horse
pasture for a few poopsicles for dessert. The trick is to catch
them on a frostbitten morning, somewhere between five and
ten minutes after they've been laid down, when a slight coat-
ing of ice is starting to form on the outside, but on the inside
they are still all warm and soft. Rae says I'm just a tactile girl,
and I guess she's right about that. When people call me stupid she says, no, not stupid, tactile, focused on the present

moment, engaged with her senses, living in her body. Like where the heck else are you supposed to live?

I love running in the snow, especially when it is really deep, exploding through it in a mushroom cloud of white. Or bullrushes, prairie grass, even the surface of a lake. Or the place at the beach where the waves meet the sand, and I'm bounding and leaping and breaking through from one sensation into another, from something thick to something thicker, where one thing ends and another begins.

That's what's coming, the end of one thing, the end of Rae's seven-year love affair, the end of her sitting on the couch trying to work on her computer with his heavy head in her lap. She always gave up, eventually, turned off the computer, put her feet up on the coffee table, and petted the spot between his ears until they both went to sleep.

Howard #7:

So I looked across the park and there stood Dante, only bigger and younger, and restored to four legs. I had left them in bed together that morning, she crying into his salt-and-pepper neck. I hadn't been able to say anything to console her, and I got scared, in a way I have not been scared in a very long time, about what might happen, really, if she couldn't live without him. What if she tried to lean on me and there was nothing there to support her, what if I wasn't quite as sane as everybody suddenly thought?

By that time Rose saw the dog too, and was dragging me toward him. He didn't morph, as I was expecting him to, into a borzoi with a square head, a Dane with an unusually shaggy coat, an Afghan who'd had a nose job. This was an Irish wolfhound, and the closer we got he didn't look less like Dante, he looked like him even more.

"His name is Malarkey," the woman said. "We've met Rose here once before."

And that's what led to us calling Zelda, to the trip to Grand Junction to see Dante's relatives, to meeting Diva, a female so like him that I had to pry Rae's fingers off her when it was time to go, to us putting a deposit on the future Mary Ellen.

It was Mary Ellen I was dreaming of when Dante woke up from anesthesia after his third radiation treatment. I had insisted again that I wanted to be the one who took him, wanted to get an idea of everything Rae had been through during all those months of treatment two years before we met. Dante was pretty out of it, his eyes all wet and dilated, his legs like Jell-O, but he still wanted to give me kisses, insisted on it, in fact.

Here's this dog—a catheter down his throat—in considerable pain from his considerable tumors, and he's just been radiated, on top of everything, and what he wants most to do is to reassure me.

But he couldn't quite get it right. His depth perception was way the heck off, and he would miss my face entirely and lick the air off to the side of it, or he'd ram his nose right up against my cheek so hard he'd stun himself a little so he couldn't get his tongue all the way out of his mouth. There were never any kisses sweeter than those, sloppy and medicinal, and of all the things I'll remember about him, those anesthesia kisses may be what sticks hardest of all.

Dante #6:

I jumped the fence for her when they got back from Hawai'i. I know, it's the last thing I should be doing with the new tumors, the risk of fracture after radiation, my delicate heart and what have you. And though I did nothing but show support for the trip as they packed their bags and left me, it was my secret desire that she'd have her fruit smoothie and her ahi poke and her day or two in the sun, and then decide she missed me too much, and come home. That's what she did, three whole days early, and I jumped the fence for her. I saved up my energy so I'd make it, and I cleared that sucker by a mile.

She had tied herself in knots over that trip to Hawai'i, though I tried to assure her that I would lay low, not put any undue pressure on the leg with the biggest tumor, take my Chinese mushrooms and my vitamin E without complaint.

"Let's try," Dr. Theo said, a week before the trip, "to language both options positively."

"In Hawai'i there will be flowers," Rae began, "and sushi, and sunshine and fresh fruit smoothies, and the lap pool I love and that great yoga teacher, and the sauna that smells like too much eucalyptus."

"That all sounds pretty self-caring," Theo said.

"If I stay I get to sleep with Dante in bed every night and smell his ears and cook in my kitchen and go on hikes in the snow with Rose and look out at the mountain and get some sleep before work starts up again."

"You said you couldn't sleep," he said, "when you were listening for Dante's discomfort."

"Think how much harder it will be," she said, "to listen all the way from Hawai'i."

"You aren't going," Theo asked, "because you are afraid of disappointing Jodi?"

"I'm afraid of everything," she said. "Just like before."

"It's only natural," Theo said, "that Dante's relapse would cause some regression, but you're still a free agent. Why not go for a few days and if you hate it, come home?"

She had stopped looking at him and was focused now entirely on picking the split ends from her hair.

"Rae," Theo said, "can you at least entertain the idea that if you do decide to go to Hawai'i and Dante does die, it won't be because of your decision?"

How can I leave her, I thought, *when this is what she still believes? This is the way the cancer will rob us. There is love now, and the beginning of faith, but the last thing to come is always forgiveness, the last thing to forgive is always the self.*

"You have an opportunity," Theo said, "to see this through until the end, and to see, not only that you can survive his

death, but that your life will be better for it, because you
knew him, because you loved him, because you were there to
help him die."

"Sometimes," she said, "I think the pain will kill me."

"But it won't," he said.

"Why not?" she said.

"You tell me," he said, and she said,

"I can't."

The second hand clicked around at least three times and I
shifted my position so I could rest my head on her foot.

"It's sad," Theo said, "isn't it? To let go of the idea that you
won't survive?"

"Yes," she said. "Why is that?"

"Because it's so useful," he said.

"It keeps you safe," she said.

"From what?" he said, and the second hand started around
again.

"From joy," she said, and he said,

"Bingo."

I gave him a big nudge in the groin as we left the office,
my way of saying that I know I'm leaving her in very fine
hands.

Now another month has gone by. I suppose the tumors are
growing, but since the radiation my limp has not returned.
When I got rediagnosed she promised me salmon, ahi, or
organic stew beef daily, and she has been true to her word.
They even got a new mattress, a Sealy Posturpedic Royal
Windsor with twice the number of coils as a regular mattress,
a pillow top, and three inches of latex foam on top of that.
She laughs it off as a sign of her age, but I know she really did

it on my behalf, and it will please me to think of her from the other side, sleeping in all that comfort.

She told me this morning she was ready. That I shouldn't hang on just for her. I wanted to say it was actually the stew beef that's kept me tethered. We've been courting death for so long now, there's very little left but the humor, and there's no dog on earth that could claim a life sweeter than mine.

Rose #5:

I've heard all the jokes enough times by now, so you can all just spare me. Oh, where did Rose go? Who is this other dog who has come to replace Rose?

The truth is, I could have turned the corner anytime I wanted to, I mean, come on, has anybody ever heard the word puppyhood around here? Just because everybody else within a fifteen-square-mile radius seems to have been denied a joyful childhood, is that any reason for me not to have claimed mine?

Besides, the evolved one was well enough behaved for any three dogs. If I had minded my P's and Q's right from the get-go, my humans would have completely forgotten what a dog is supposed to be.

She's been brushing us a lot lately, and giving us tons of cookies, and last night we had Wagyu beef, which comes all the way from Japan, and I guess it's true what they say about how the cows live in health spas and get massages all the time because the meat is the very most tender and tasty of any meat I've ever had, and I've got to believe that we're talking about some pretty happy cows.

I have noticed that Dante is getting a little more of the Wagyu than the old Rosebeast. I'm pretty sure that last night some of the chunks I got were standard Made in America organic beef stew and the chunks he got had come a long way across the ocean, but this is precisely the kind of unfairness I've grown up with, and it's not like I'm going to say anything about it now.

She cries every day, and sometimes even Howard cries with her. I want to say, *Hey, look at the new snow on the mountain,* or if we are in Denver, *Hey, let's go over to Wash Park and see if we can't rough up some ducks.* But they can't see the snow right now, or hear the stream or smell the poopsicles, so I stay quiet, and wait for the time—I know it won't be long from now—when they'll need me to remind them about joy.

Jodi #3:

I didn't tell you very much about my dog. His name is Misha, and he is half golden retriever, half basset, and whatever mental picture you are conjuring up, my dog looks twice as funny as that. We call him Misha because his little front feet which are actually almost as long as his little front legs are always turned out in the first position. He's got such a big head and a big fluffy golden retriever mane all around it, his legs disappear all together. The worst thing is in the summer when he gets those hot spots and we have to compromise between a cone that is big enough to go around his head and one small enough so he can hold it up and still move forward.

Misha doesn't think of himself as a short dog, which is funny because I'm six-foot-two and Hank is six-foot-seven, and if there were ever a dog who deserves to have short owners it's Mish. That's the first injustice. The second was moving him to Vegas when he's got a fur coat thicker than Celine

Dion's and he's a water dog to boot. When we lived in Manhattan I would take him out to Jones Beach or Coney Island and he would leap over the waves for hours, even in the city I couldn't keep him out of puddles and water fountains; he'd stick his head right in the bucket we kept under the place in our stairwell that used to be a fire escape and leaked every time it rained.

In Vegas every morning after our walk I would take him out to our little slab of concrete that passed for a back yard and shoot him square in the face with the hose on full blast. He would jump up so I could get his chest and his belly with it too, but mostly he liked it right up the nose. Now he's in doggie heaven, with the creek and the mud holes and the buffalo calves to chase around the yard. Hank says we may as well never get any good furniture as long as that dog is alive and I tell him I don't give a rat's ass about furniture and Misha is going to live forever and if I could find two or three more just like him I'd bring them home too.

Howard made up a song for Misha to the tune of "Low Rider," and we sing it all the time now, and Rae knows a place to scratch on the top of his butt that makes him tip his head up with pleasure and gnash his front teeth together like he's eating corn on the cob.

We went up to Rae and Howard's for a Christmas visit. Dante seemed strong and pain-free, and I know that can't last long, but I was glad it lasted for us. Rae had to leave him at home when we went cross-country skiing, of course, so Howard and Hank stayed behind too.

We skied to a place Rae calls Coyote Rock because one time, before they got Rose spayed, a coyote came walking up the canyon talking a blue streak. They had stopped for lunch on a little ledge about fifteen feet off the canyon bottom and they all kept their eyes on the coyote, waiting for him to catch the scent of the dogs and take off, but at some point they realized he had caught the scent of Rose and she was smelling a whole new way, and that was the crux of the problem.

Rae got up and yelled at the coyote and Dante stood and started to growl but it was a big boy, unintimidated, and it was doing a little snarling kind of thing with its mouth which Rae thought was probably just hormones but might have been rabies.

Rose started to whimper a little, as if in spite of her better judgment she was liking the attention, and that's when Dante decided to take control of the situation and he leapt off the rock. He landed right in front of the coyote, who—more impressed with Dante's stature from that angle—turned tail down the trail. The coyote didn't go too far though; they could hear him chattering for another half hour, while Dante patrolled the canyon, ledges and bottom, until the picnic was over and it was time to leave.

It was after that jump, three years ago, that Rae saw the first quiver in Dante's foreleg. She figured at first that he had an impact injury. Then, when it seemed to get worse instead of better, she decided to take him to the vet.

"I've never seen coyote tracks up here, before or since," Rae said, "though I did see some big cat tracks one day, maybe my friend from California has followed me to higher ground."

"Is it hard to be here without Dante?" I asked.

"Everything is," she said, but she smiled as she said it.

It was a warm January day, another year of light snow-pack—one more thing to worry about, Rae had said—even the skis were overkill. We were sitting in the warm sand in the canyon bottom letting the sun hit our faces. We were only a few days away from the shortest of the year, and we needed all the light we could get.

"I don't know if I can stand another summer of fires," Rae said.

I said, "Why don't you worry about one thing at a time?"

"I guess you don't want to hear about the headaches I'm getting that I'm pretty sure are a brain tumor."

"Not today," I said.

"Or the article I read that said people who eat fish are only giving in to their self-destructive tendencies."

"You shouldn't be allowed to read the paper," I said.

"Or watch TV," she said.

"Or buy a newspaper."

"It's going to be strange being at this ranch without him," she said.

"Yes it will," I said. "But if I know him, he'll find a way to check in."

"I'm thinking so," she said. She swiped at her face. "Here's that cry I promised you."

"Well, I think I've earned it," I said.

"I do too," she said.

"Oh shit," she said. "Look at Misha."

My little short-legged superhero had gotten himself up to the top of Dante's fifteen-foot-high leaping ledge and seemed to be testing the waters.

"Don't scream," Rae said, and that's when I realized I had been. "Stay calm," she said, and she got up very carefully and started taking slow steps toward Misha. "Misha, buddy," she said. "You're way too short for the high dive."

Several things came clear to me at once then, that Misha was not actually on the top of the ledge, but on a dangerously angled sub-ledge right below the lip, that he was in a place where his stubs weren't going to get him up or down, and that Rae was going to try to catch him.

"I think he might be committed," I said.

"I think you're right," Rae said. "Misha, buddy, you're okay." She was right under him now. "Just see if you can't drop right into my arms."

He had inched down toward her to a place where the ledge angled even more and his little back legs were losing purchase.

"Should I run up to the top and try to pull him up?" I said.

"I don't think there's time for that," Rae said, and that's when Misha pushed off, like Clark Kent himself, well over Rae's head and out, as if he had somehow convinced himself that he was going to land in a deep pool of blue water.

+ Rae said, "Noooooooooooooooooooo!" and I shut my eyes, but when I opened them again Misha was galumphing toward us. He jumped up into my arms and I checked him for loose parts. Aside from a big old road rash under his chin, which barely clears the ground in the best of times, he seemed to have weathered his escapade brilliantly.

"He's okay!" I said, holding all forty pounds of him up for a victory dance.

"Give him a minute," Rae said, her voice soft, her face pale as death. "To make sure there is nothing internal."

She had told me about a puppy named Jazz, Jackson's puppy, who had gotten hit by a car, run back over to her, seemingly intact, and then lay down at her feet and died. How many dogs, I wondered just then, would Rae watch die in her lifetime?

Meanwhile, Misha was turning happy circles at our feet, and all of a sudden we both were crying.

"You stupid, stupid dog," Rae said, wiping snot into Misha's coat. "I can't believe you didn't break anything. Don't you have any sense?"

But I knew that she knew what really happened. My Misha wanted to fly for her, like Dante.

Dante #7:

The end isn't so far off now. She knows it, and so do I.
We've been staying in Denver all the time now, all of us
together, so Dr. Evans will be close when the time comes.
"Just stay in the center of the circle," Lao-tzu said, "and let all
things take their course."

This is easier, I know, for a wolfhound than it is for a
human being.

They've started to have the quality-of-life discussions,
which I wish I could tell them is unnecessary, for when the
quality of life dips below the practicable point it will do so
fast and unquestionably. It's true, I've had a little diarrhea, but
only because it makes her so happy to see me eat that I've
been eating everything she puts in front of me including the
dog food with all the antioxidants, and between you and me
and the fence post, the dog food with all the antioxidants
gives this old man the shits. I've been trying to convince her,
and perhaps I have succeeded, that a diet entirely comprised

of Wagyu and raw salmon might be the best thing from here on out.

She cries and cries every day now. Howard is doing his best, but he's not a natural caretaker. Rose is trying in her way too, and it warms my heart to see her do it so badly, a hedonist in Joan of Arc's clothes. My human is trying to keep me here, with hundreds of photos, with thousands of words. I know the worrying doesn't do my tumors any good, but what she is feeling now is my responsibility. I convinced her to give me her heart, lock stock and barrel, in a way that she had never given it before, and she gave it. That is a good thing. It is, perhaps, the only thing, but now her heart will have to break. I pray my future niece will have inherited some of my qualities, will demonstrate them even in puppyhood, I whisper her name in my human's ear at night, whether to ease her mind or mine I cannot say.

Last night she lay in bed scratching my face for hours and I knew then how well my mission has been accomplished, that she will let me go with gratitude and grace, that when she cries it will be from the sadness, and not the old fear that if she starts to cry she won't ever stop.

This morning the sun was out for the first time this week and we decided together that a family outing would be a good idea. There's something about when we are all in the car together with the windows open and I'm getting in a little mighty-dog action out the side window up on three legs with my butt pressed against the middle seat for balance, head and shoulders stretching out into the wind and biting at the air like a young dog. Rose has her head on the back of my seat, puff puff puffing her cheeks the way she does. Mom's driving and Howard is making up another song about us, today it was "Rosession," to the tune of Sarah McLachlan's, "Possession" ("... *hold you down, pet you so hard* ...")

It was one of those warm days in February that make you think Denver is the city with the world's best-kept secret and we drove up toward Berthoud Pass, where Howard proposed to my human two years before, and there was still plenty of snow but you could smell spring in the sage and the pine needles melting up from underneath. We stopped at a national forest campground that had been closed up for the winter and walked across the snowdrift to a place where the ground was soft and warm and the little river was melted out and running in and around chunks of blue ice still frozen. The river sand there was the exact same color as my fur, and I could tell that my human liked the looks of it because she took a lot of photos of me and it, close-ups of my nose and neck and eyebrows, one close-up even of my paw.

Rose wouldn't go near the water, she's never gotten over the time Howard pushed her off a rock into the Rio Grande one day and she went under, emerged like a big old beast three seconds later, kicking and pawing like coming up from hell, and that's when everybody stopped calling her Rose and started calling her the Rosebeast.

We spent all afternoon there, she attending to me with pets and chunks of stew beef, me attending to her with a kiss, a roll on my back, or a chin set down onto the thinnest part of her ankle, my lifelong agenda boiled down to today, to loving her every minute. I got in and cooled my chest the way I like to, and there was an osprey way up in the trees above us, and though I think I'm the only one who saw them, three female mule deer in a cluster of ponderosa on the other side of the stream.

She has trusted me, pure and simple, and every one of my actions has been a testament to the legitimacy of that trust. I have let her cuddle me, kiss my nose, smell my ears even when I have been hot or exhausted. I have loved her when she's had to go away and leave me, and I have loved her even more when she's come home. I have happy danced for her even when the pain in my leg urged against it. I would happy dance for her even now.

Dr. Evans #2:

Rae brought him to see me about three months ago, right after his rediagnosis, first time in more than a year. We talked hockey at first. It looks like it might be the Avs and the Red Wings in the Western Conference finals this year. Rae said now when the Wings beat the Avs it's not quite so painful because she thinks of me out there somewhere, grinning from ear to ear.

Most people aren't going to understand this, but I feel like Brendan Shanahan and Steve Yzerman and Sergei Fedorov and CuJo, all those guys who've been with the team these last couple years, well, those guys are practically my friends. I don't have many friends these days, my wife says it's because I make no secret of the fact that I prefer the four-legged variety, but when you spend eighty hours a week on-clinics it doesn't leave you a lot of time for guys' night out and beer.

I told Rae about how Dante's leg has put me on the map, all the conferences I've been to, here and abroad, delivering the paper I wrote about the details of the reconstruction. How all the hoopla got my in-laws and my parents off my back, got the university to give me a year's leave to take my qualifying exam, to get all these miracles into the form of a book.

And speaking of miracles, I've got a healthy baby girl going to be a year old in ten days, a house in the foothills, and a big yard for her to play in. I wasn't sure how I'd do, with her being human and all, but now I can't wait to show her picture around, can't wait till she wakes up from her nap. I don't think it's in my nature to be happy, exactly, but I have to say these are good days. And though there is still the odd moment when my wife doesn't like me all that much, I think she's coming to understand me, and given the choice I'd rather have that. She might have to play second fiddle to a dog in ICU from time to time, but she's figured out that I'm never going to look at another woman, I'm never going to stop trying to make her proud of me, I'm never going to go out drinking with the other surgeons when the alternative is coming home to see Addie and her.

Rae asked me if I could see the new tumor, and I said I wasn't even going to go there. Just let him be a dog, I said. And I know that's what she's been doing.

She called again last Tuesday morning. Said, "I think it's getting to be that time." It was the day before I had to fly to Kansas City to take my qualifying exam. Wouldn't you fucking know it? It's not as if driving over to her apartment and putting that dog to sleep was going to make or break my score. It's not as if the hour or two of studying I'd lose was going to make any difference.

It was just a psyche-out. Like when that one goalie got traded from the Maple Leafs to the Rangers and wouldn't stop wearing his blue goalie pants. He was on a winning streak, forty-four games, and you know how goalie's heads are. Finally the league fined him ten thousand dollars for every game that he didn't change to the Rangers' red pants, which I thought was pretty funny because between the long sweater and the big leg guards, I mean how much of those pants are you really going to see? It still took him three more games to give up those blue pants, and when he did he lost, sure as shit, the very first night.

Maybe it was something like that, or maybe I just didn't want Dante to die. Maybe I didn't want putting him down to be the last thing I did before I took this test that officially married me to veterinary medicine in general and oncological surgery in particular, forever and ever amen. Maybe I didn't want to sit on the plane to Kansas City and ask myself the kinds of questions it would raise.

"I'm sorry about the timing," she said. "I mean with your test."

"This is way more important than any test," I said, and hoped she knew I meant it.

"Let's try some of the harder drugs, and reevaluate the situation when I get back."

On Wednesday morning I prescribed a fentanyl patch for Dante, and headed for the airport. And yes, I did remember how much Dante hated the morphine, how he got dysphoric and how he vocalized, but fentanyl isn't the same as morphine, and in my memory he had done pretty well with it before.

What I knew was that the fentanyl would stop his pain, and what I wanted was to stop his pain. There are a lot of vets out there who will tell you, put the dog down as soon as his quality of life is compromised. But what about a dog who loved his mom so much that his quality of life was totally bound up in gazing at her?

Preserve life, that's the first thing they told us in vet school, and I took them to mean it. I've probably put a thousand animals to sleep in the last fifteen years and a lot of times somebody, usually the man of the family—when it's all over—makes some remark about how much better the world would be if we could do the same thing for people. *Yeah, sure,* I want to say, and that's when I know that it was the woman, or sometimes the kid—who maybe has been spared the death scene—who was the real dog person in the family. When there is life, there is hope, there's no getting around it. And hope is the hardest love we carry, the hardest love to give up of all.

I know what you're thinking, that I'm trying to justify the two days I spent in Kansas City, while Rae and Howard listened to a dysphoric dog howl through the night, but it isn't like that. I'm sorry about the timing, but I'm not sorry Dante got to gaze at her for three more days because of it, even if on two of those days it was through a slightly psychedelic haze.

I came back on Thursday night, and when I didn't hear from Rae I took it as a good sign. The Red Wings played the Avalanche that night, went down to them one to nothing, and I knew she knew I'd be watching the game, but as the last seconds of the third period ticked off I really expected the phone to ring. It did ring the next morning, just after eight o'clock.

"How was the test?" she said.

"Brutal," I said.

"I'm sure you aced it," she said. "Sorry about the shutout."

"Patrick Roy seems to be over his illness," I said. Patrick Roy, the Avalanche goalie, was arguably the greatest that ever lived, though he'd been slumping of late.

"His mental illness?" she said.

"Yes," I said.

There was a second where I thought we might have been cut off.

"It's time," she said. "It's starting to be hard for him to breathe."

We made an appointment to put him down at one o'clock. The patch had worn off to the point where Dante was still getting pain relief, and he was no longer hallucinating, but it was going to wear off further, and he would find it harder and harder to stand. Also, his lungs had started filling with fluid. This could have been disease in his lungs and it could have been the medication finally getting to his kidneys, either way it was going to get a lot uglier before the end, and this time I didn't suggest any last-minute life-extending drugs.

Still, I wanted to be sure, before I went over there, that she was in the right place. There are people, as you might imagine, who change their minds right at the end, and I mean *right* at the end, just as the needle makes contact with the skin, that's when they start shrieking, and you can imagine how I don't do great with situations like those.

So I called her apartment from the hospital. "He's actually having a pretty good day," she said. "Lots of kisses and steak in bed, and he went outside and peed by himself this morning."

"So do you want to proceed?" I said.

He was probably sleeping in the middle of her bed nose to nose with her, his head on her outstretched arm, his fine front paw flung over her chest, his sore back legs pulled up tight to his body, pads resting somewhere around her kneecaps. She'd be crying and trying hard to memorize him, the texture of the big white swirl on his chest, the silkiness of his ears, even the little white patches from the Adriamycin spill on the left one. She'd be wanting so badly to do right by him, holding up all those arguments about *quality of life* against the simple impossibility of a woman asked to sentence the thing she loved most in the world.

"Do you want to proceed?" I said again, thinking of my daughter, not even a thought in the back of anybody's mind three years ago when Dante was diagnosed. I've seen that feral look in my wife's eyes a time or two since Addie was born, and I can't do anything but love her for it, even if its recipient is sometimes me.

People love to talk about irony, and I'm usually the one in the crowd who says, *That's not irony, man, that's life*, but call it what you want, we've got some here. Like how Dante's bone graft was the first truly successful one of its kind in history, but he lost the leg nevertheless. Like how his leg—even after it was no longer attached to him—became the key to my future in veterinary medicine, how it made *everything* better, my reputation, my paycheck, my marriage, my life. How even without his leg he breezed past the critical two-year remission mark, but that bastard disease got him anyway, much too soon, much too painfully, the same week that some board of directors in a big shiny office in Kansas City was going to say I deserved another couple of letters after my name.

"Do you want to proceed?" I said, hating the clinical tone of the words I'd been forced to memorize. Her voice was small when she said,

"What would you do?"

"Quality time is quality time," I said, because it was the only thing that seemed true. "I'll be here all weekend. Call me when it changes, and I'll be right there."

The next call came at seven-thirty Saturday morning. All week her voice had been thick with crying, now it was bright with fear and a little shock.

"He just had some kind of a seizure," she said. "He couldn't breathe for a really long time and he seemed in terrible pain, but then all of a sudden he found his breath and came back. I don't want him to have to go through another one of those."

"I'll be there in an hour," I said, and I was.

They were spooned in bed together, just as I had imagined them. Dante was lying comfortably on her arm. She got up then and left, so I could spend a minute with Dante on my own. I could tell she had thought of this ahead of time. She had great respect for our relationship, more than any pet owner I've met before or since.

When she returned, I said, "I'm going to give him a sedative first, get him nice and relaxed, and then we'll take as much time as you want before I give him the other drug."

She nodded, she looked at me with kindness, as if I were the one in the room who needed to be taken care of. In a time of crisis, I thought, Rae would be the one you would want in the room. Howard came in from the kitchen and put his hand on her shoulder.

I got the catheter in his front leg, that beautiful leg that had carried him so far for so long, that leg that had been pierced so many times by so many needles that the veins didn't want to rise. *This is the last needle,* buddy, I wanted to say, but I was afraid I would tear up, and in vet school that is something they said we should try very hard not to do.

I reached for a syringe to flush the vein.

"Is that the right one?" she asked. "I thought the other one was the sedative."

"Give me a little credit here," I told her. "I don't tell you how to write."

In retrospect, the sedative was probably a mistake. He fought it off, which sent him into another seizure, which she said wasn't as bad as the one he'd had an hour earlier, but this is what I do for a living, and that seizure might have been the worst one I had ever seen. His legs were twitching and he was foaming at the mouth and convulsing and at the same time barking his head off. She hung in there in a way that impressed me, got right down next to his head, telling him she loved him, telling him to let go.

Naturally, with all the thrashing he popped the goddamn catheter, and I tried to get it back in a couple times but I finally had to give up and go to the back leg. That, as it turned out, was my first good decision of the day, because the sedative did have time to take effect and he was peaceful by the time I got the second shot in, and he died, at the very last, quietly.

"That was awful," she said, without a hint of blame in her voice and a kind of goofy smile on her face that told me she could feel Dante in the room just the way I could. His body was lying there, still warm, with no heartbeat, but his presence, his soul—if you don't find that offensive—was filling up that bedroom, filling up the house and maybe beyond that, maybe the whole block, maybe the whole county. She looked up and to the left and closed her eyes for a minute. Our eyes locked again and I knew that she knew that I felt him too.

Rae #8:

It all started in a parking lot in Montrose, Colorado. It ended last Saturday in the middle of our king-sized bed.

It's a difficult thing, to decide when it is time. The secretaries at the hospital handed out their pamphlets with "Let me go" in soft cursive at the top. The vet techs said, "You don't want to see him suffer," and shook their heads like they knew something, anything, about who Dante was or what he was to me. And I had Dr. Evans, on the phone that morning, saying, "Quality time is quality time."

At the time I thought that I waited too long, that I should have done it before he had that first seizure. But after the fact I wondered if I had done it too soon, the way he barked and barked on his way out, the way he ate those last bites of steak so eagerly, it seemed there was still some life left in him, if only we could have figured out a way to help him walk.

Some people throw around words like dignity and compassion. Others say it's too hard, they never could have made that decision, but how easy is it to watch a dog die in his own time, in his own spit and piss and vomit, how easy is it to watch the one you love struggle without breath, foam at the mouth, how many hours, how many days should you keep him with you when he's got nothing anymore but fear in his eyes?

I don't know the answer, and I never will. What I know is that I did my best, and I tried my best not to put myself before him, and I was loving him with every fiber of my being when he had the second seizure—and then when he took his last breath.

There are moments when I think that because he's not here anymore I have no real purpose in life. It's a funny thing to say about a dog, even a dog as wonderful as he was, but I'm tired of believing that feeling this way is some kind of a deficiency on my part.

Dante is still with me, sort of up and to my left. I'll never hear that big tail thwacking again, never feel his big grey chest roll toward me in sleep, but what I have instead is everything he taught me, like how without loss, life isn't worth a hill of beans. And without love, life is nothing more than a series of losses.

When I've lost people in the past, my mom or Jackson, Jonathan or Esther Robinson, or even people who didn't die but just left, it was different. Because once they were gone it felt like there was nothing left of me, or maybe there was, but I didn't know it. I thought that if the people I loved disappeared I would disappear too, and now I see that's why Dante was always looking and looking at me, so I'd know that I really do exist, and could keep on existing after he was gone. And the funny thing I found out is that when you really love somebody, and they love you—no holding back—it is just like what we learned in school about matter: it changes form but can't disappear entirely, which is hard to believe until you see it for yourself, inside your own little Bunsen burner of a life.

When Dante used to run to me across a field—even when he'd already gone as far as three legs could take him, even those last weeks when the pain in his hips had gotten so bad that he couldn't quite stand up straight, even in the days when he was starting to find it hard to breathe, and he would just tear across the grass at about a hundred miles an hour, his eyes locked only on mine—I'd always think, *This might be the last time I ever see this, this might be the last time I ever feel this,* and then came the day when it actually was.

What I didn't understand then, what I couldn't have understood until I watched him breathe his last breath, is that nothing could take him away from me, not cancer, not an amputation, and not even sodium phenobarbital; that only in his dying could I truly understand the way I would have him forever, the way I'd had him forever all along, the way I will see him, whenever I need him, running across that big green pasture into my arms.

I remember those days three years ago, sitting on the grass with Dante and Brooklyn Underhill, as some of the finest hours of my life. That grass is gone now, to make way for the new oncology wing. In Brooklyn's presence, as in Dante's, I felt I had everything to learn. And dear Dr. Evans. I don't want to take anything away from Howard, but if anyone understood Dante's gift as well as I did, it was that strange and silent man.

When we carried Dante's body out of the 4-Runner for the last time, and left him at the hospital to be cremated, Dr. Evans gave me a hug and called me "love," which sounded so strange in his mouth I nearly startled. It took me a moment to realize that the word wasn't so much a term of endearment as a statement of what we were in the midst of. *There is love here,* he might have said, *all the way around.*

Letter #1 (Brooklyn to Rae):

Dear Rae,
Greetings from the country of Bahrain, where I am currently stationed. These are dangerous times in this part of the world, to be sure, although in this particular corner of the region I have been made to feel both safe and welcome. I have found the accommodations comfortable, the local food to my liking, and the people utterly fascinating, extremely well educated, and warm. I'm learning more about camels than you'd ever dream possible, as well as other desert-dwelling types, all in all this has been a rich and rewarding experience.

I have written and rewritten my quick response back to you. I finally decided to trash my first response and start all over. I am not having an easy time expressing my feelings. Normally, I am not troubled by death. I see it as a transitory separation and nothing to be sorrowful about.

However, Dante's death made me sad. Not sad for him, or because I think he is gone forever. I know that death is not the end of our existence, and I feel strongly that our relationships continue beyond this life. However, Dante filled the world in a unique way that cannot be replaced. Even though I haven't seen him in several years, I feel a loss at his passing unlike anything I have felt over any other death in my life. It is strange and I cannot explain it.

Dante has a very unique and special spirit. He filled the world in a remarkable way, certainly much different than any human or nonhuman being I have ever met. My heart goes out to you, because I think I would be very sad at his loss if he had been my companion. I am still not getting this out very well, and the only excuse I have is that vet school robbed me of my ability to write.

Even though Dante is gone, I do hope we run into each other again at some point. You are one of the amazing people I have met in my life. I guess you are like Dante in that you seem to have a profound effect on the people you meet. You both blessed my life, and I am grateful for the impact that knowing you has had on me.

Take Care,
Brooklyn Underhill

Letter #2 (Dante to Sophie):

Dear Sophie,
I've been meaning to write you for a couple of weeks now, but I've been putting it off because I'm afraid what I have to tell you is going to make you sad, and the last thing I want to do in the world is make you sad. But I also don't want you to think I've forgotten you, because I haven't, not for one minute, and I never will.

In December I started limping again, just a little bit, and I went to the doctor, and, sadly, my osteosarcoma has returned. I have three small tumors, one in each of my remaining legs, but luckily not in my lungs or any of my other vital organs. My mom was very sad when she first heard, and you might be too, so I'm going to tell you what I told her to try to cheer you up.

Three years of remission is a very long time for a wolfhound. They say the average human year is equal to seven dog years, and since an Irish wolfhound's life expectancy is shorter than normal dogs, seven and half years if you believe the books, then one human year is equal to at least nine years for an Irish wolfhound. So you see, my three years of remission actually felt like twenty-seven years to me, and these two months since December are like another year gone by. In any case, wolfhounds don't measure life in terms of days and years, because for a wolfhound, every minute is right now, and every minute lasts forever.

Today my mom took Rose for a little walk and left me sitting with Howard in the grass of a park I like. We've been spending a lot of time on the grass there, since I can only go for short walks these days, and when they came back over the hill from their walk . . . it was only a short one . . . I gathered all my strength and went racing over to her, ignoring the pain in my legs, running as fast as I could so she would see how happy I was to see her, because for me, and I hope for her, that moment of me running to her will last forever. I want her to see it forever, every time she is sad, every time she is scared, every time she feels alone, I want her to close her eyes and imagine me flying toward her across a big field of new spring grass.

I bet you have a million of those moments, with your mom or dad or sister or Scruffy, that are pure and perfect like that one, and what I want you to know—what I want my mom to know too—is that once you've had those times together, they become like a present you can open again and again. Humans call this memory, because they can't open their eyes wide enough to see around time, but real love isn't any less solid than picture frames and colored pencils, and a great deal more durable. Death can't take it from you once you've held it in your hand.

I wish you a hundred people years of happy healthy living, my little friend.

Dante

Eight

·

The
Future

Howard #8:

Here's the funny thing. It turns out I was sane from the very beginning. Sanity is a relative term you say, and I say, you can say that again. Like when all the people who have told you you were crazy your whole life turn out to be crazy themselves, then it starts to be like one of those Tom Stoppard plays where reality just keeps collapsing, and that's all very exciting on the stage, but not so much fun in real life.

Rae's friend Jonathan was always talking about the lunatics running the asylum, which always made me laugh until last summer when Jonathan put a bullet through his heart.

Look. I'm not trying to say I'm without a bad day now and then. But could I have walked up to the front desk of a Howard Johnson's, asked for and paid for a room, taken some kind of big-ass gun out of my briefcase, put the cold barrel of that thing against my chest in the approximate location of my heart, and fired? Never in a hundred billion years.

Rae says I acted crazy because my family needed me to, which may be true because now that I don't act that way anymore, they sure don't want anything to do with me. She says now I act sane because she needs me to act sane, and it's hard to know where the real me might stand in all of that, but I have to say I like this version better than I did the last one.

About two weeks after Dante died, Jonathan's friend Gene gave Rae a call and asked her if she wanted Jonathan's books—he had over ten thousand of them up at his cabin, and she said they ought to be donated to a library in his name, and Gene said he didn't have time to deal with that, the new owners were moving in over the weekend, so Rae asked me if I would hook up the little box trailer to the 4-Runner and drive out to California and pick up the books.

Rae had to make a speech in Denver that Friday night, but it seemed too close to Dante's death to leave her alone, and when I stopped to think about it, I wasn't all that eager to be poking around Jonathan's cold cabin all by myself. We decided to go as a family, and loaded Rose into the 4-Runner early Wednesday morning for her first solo road trip.

The fastest way from the ranch to Placer City, California, is across Utah and Nevada on Highway 50, the Loneliest Road in America. We had a good drive out there, singing dog songs, and telling stories about Dante and Jonathan. There's nothing like an all-night car ride to sink right into a good talk about the dead. Rose was stepping up like a champion, putting her nose up on Rae's shoulder just like a certain gentleman we used to know, and I wrote a new song for her, "I Love the Rosey-Ro" to the tune of "I Love Rock and Roll," that kept us both singing.

After the Loneliest Road leaves Delta, Utah, that's when you start to think about alien abduction. It's classic basin and range topography, five miles of tight curves on either side of a pass and then flat as flat as far as the eye can see until the next pass, with curves so tight you better pay attention. A hundred miles from Delta you hit the Border Motel, where the sign says, PAY FOR YOUR ROOM IN NEVADA, BUT SLEEP IN UTAH! as if that's some kind of big treat. Ninety miles later you get to Ely, where you'll find the last all-night gas station for 250 miles. The tiny towns of Eureka and Austin divide the next 250 miles into three equal segments. The next lighted sign after Austin is the Salt Wells whorehouse with its little stick-figure go-go dancers clad in black bikinis. The sun rose that morning between Fallon and Fernley, which was all for the best, I thought, given the nature of our outing.

We got to Jonathan's cabin just after ten.

"Eddie said Jonathan died because of the darkness in my soul," Rae said, before the first box of books was filled and loaded.

"Eddie should know," I said. "Being Satan's spawn."

"Isn't it strange how when somebody says something like that," she said, "there's that particle of truth that sticks?"

"But you don't have darkness in your soul," I said.

"Rivers of it," she said.

"And oceans," I said, "of light." She leaned across the top of the box and kissed me.

It took us all day, seventy-five boxes and forty dollars' worth of bungee cords (five boxes would have to ride on the roof of the trailer), but we were going to make some library in Colorado very happy. Rae looked at the sun and then looked at her watch.

"Okay," she said, "if it takes us seventeen hours to make it home, with the time change, that leaves me two extra hours to shower, change, and get over to the Denver Center. Let's hit it."

I'd never seen anyone who could go like Rae. She'd been in high gear since Dante left us, doing three, four, even five all-nighters in a row, and I'm guessing this was also how she lived before his first diagnosis. Dante had taught her how to slow down, how to sit still, and she hadn't done either since the day Dr. Evans came over to the apartment to give him the shot. I was worried about her, but maybe even more afraid of what would happen if she stopped.

I'd done a fair job of staying awake on the way to California, but one all-nighter is what I've got in me at best, and we both knew Rose and I would be asleep before she got the 4-Runner up to sixty. She gunned the engine and before too long we were back in Nevada, back on the Loneliest Road. I came to seven hours later as Rae was easing the car into the parking lot of the Border Motel.

"Howard, honey," she said, "we have a flat tire on the trailer. Do you remember where you put the spare?"

I may be sane, but that doesn't make me handy. I'd left the spare at Jonathan's cabin, to make room for all those god-damned books.

"Please tell me you didn't leave the spare in California," but she already knew that I had. "I have never met a man anything like you," she said, and this time it didn't sound like a very good thing.

From behind the motel desk a man with dark curly hair watched us. I was squeezing my face together the way I used to right before one of my faux-panic attacks.

"This is your mistake," she said. "Think of a way to fix it, Howard. Now."

"Okay," I told her, "okay. Go ahead and unhook the trailer. You go on to Denver and make your presentation. I'll figure out a way to get home from here."

"Howard, for chrisssake, I can't leave you out here in the middle of the desert with an overloaded trailer and no vehicle," she said. She looked around at the dark empty desert. "Is this place a whorehouse or what?"

"It's a motel, honey," I said, "just go, or you'll be late. I'll figure this out on my own, swear to God, I really will."

"Howard, I love you," she said. "But let's face it, problem-solving isn't really your thing." The man behind the desk had opened the door now, and was leaning against it, listening.

"You guys need help?" he called from the doorway.

"There's no time like the present," I said, "for things to change."

Rae called me every five minutes for the first hour she was on the road.

"You're going to get killed in that place," she said, and I could tell that she'd been crying, "all for me and my stupid schedule."

"All for me and my stupid packing," I said.

"Either way," she said. I could hear the long black highway rushing outside her windows. She was going faster, I knew, than she let herself go when I was in the car.

"I've talked to Hector," I said, "and he said he's going to help me in the morning."

"Who?"

"The night manager, Hector, he says his boss has some tires maybe he can sell me."

"And then what?"

"Then we'll see," I said. The first problem was tires; if my trailer actually rolled, my options increased exponentially.

I paid for my hotel room in Nevada, and I slept in Utah. I had a dream that I found Dante's fourth leg. I was running through a forest looking for someone, though it escapes me now who. It was a Snow White kind of forest, colors and shapes exaggerated, animals stopping to look, and smiling as I went by. The leg was encased in glass, not unlike Snow White herself, mounted with little gold clips above folds of red velvet. It was not bloody or decayed, and in the dream I couldn't wait to tell Rae that there was part of Dante that was still intact. Hector pounded on my door, as I had asked him to, at six A.M. Nevada time.

"First we take my *niña* to school," he said, "then I help you."

School was a tiny building sunk down into a couple of cottonwood trees.

"Mormons who got kicked out of Salt Lake City," Hector said. "They have too many wives." He laughed. "One wife is more than I can handle, you know what I mean?"

I could only imagine what he was thinking when the trailer dropped off its hitch last night and Rae roared off in the 4-Runner without me.

"My *jefe,*" Hector said, "he no mind if I sell you the tires, but we can't tell this other guy, the one who might be there. This other guy, if he find out, he go to my *jefe* and say, 'Man, Hector is no good, you turn your back and he is selling your stuff.'"

I bought Hector's *jefe* two brand-new tires over the phone from a mail-order catalog. The old rim was so warped from sitting without rubber all night that Hector had to cut it off with a hacksaw. His *jefe*'s tires fit my trailer like a dream.

"There is this guy," Hector said, as we took turns tightening the bolts, "who want to kill me. So I go to his house and I say, you want to kill me, you kill me now. Here I am, go ahead and kill me, because if you kill me then I kill you." Hector had a lot of stories that involved other men and killing.

"Maybe I drive you all the way to Denver," he said, when the trailer was finished.

"That would be wonderful," I told him, "but Delta is good enough."

He took me to the U-Haul place in Delta, and waited to make sure the hookup was going to work out all right. I filled his gas tank, bought him lunch, and gave him a hundred dollars for his time and an unchewed plush dog toy for his *niña*.

I didn't make it in time for Rae's speech at the Denver Center, but I was home before midnight.

As we got in bed I said, "I can imagine being sad enough to kill myself, really I can. But then I would think about whatever I was going to eat next, and that would pull me through the moment every time."

"You're my hero," Rae said, and she rolled over and put her head on my shoulder. "I'm going to go to sleep now," she said, "for a very long time."

Rae #9:

It has been a warm March in Colorado. Warm enough to keep all the windows down on the drive to Grand Junction. This weather is worrisome on the one hand, hardly any snow again this winter and temperatures already high enough to melt what little snow there is, but it's hard not to love the tiny new leaves on the cottonwoods, or the smell of the river as it breaks through the ice.

Howard and Rose are on a mission to get me to stop worrying in advance about the coming summer and the fire danger. It's what Dante would have wanted, they say, because they know that always works, and I tell them it was Dante's cancer that got me into the habit of worrying, and they say, no, you were in the habit long before that.

"PUPPPIIIEEEE!" Howard shouts, and Rose perks up her ears. Howard is now officially Rose's person and so she pays special attention whenever he makes an unusual noise.

Howard says that Rose is not misbehaved. He says she has a perfectly valid worldview that is equal to our worldview, only different. He says that it is ethnocentric of us to feel that our worldview is superior, just because Rose's worldview leads her to act, occasionally, in ways we don't like. She likes to pick up a big mouthful of her dog food, for example, and walk with it from the kitchen into the living room, drop it, covered with drool, onto the rug, and then eat it up again. She also likes to wipe her butt on that same rug—a Gabbeh—leaving a brown smelly smudge on the creamy white. She is the loudest snorer in the house, especially during allergy season. She loves to lie in the back seat of the 4-Runner and rest her head on the open window casing so the breeze coming in runs right up her nose. She loves bursting out of the pussy willows that line the creek bed at the ranch, or running straight through the middle of a mud puddle and feeling the droplets cling to the short hairs on her belly, getting a little wetter with each step.

She's a sensory girl is how I see it, like Howard that way, who is a big fan of pleasure, and they're both good for me, the only member of the family who spends too much time in her head. Last weekend Jodi and Hank came to visit, and we walked back up to Coyote Rock, only this time we left Misha at home with the boys.

"Can I ask you a favor?" Jodi said when we got there. "When you call me and you get my machine, could you not say, *Jodi, this is Rae*?"

"What would you like me to say?"

"I'm embarrassed to tell you," she said.

I thought for a minute. "Hi, it's me?" I said.

"That would be great," she said.

"Because *Jodi, this is Rae* doesn't properly convey . . . doesn't fully represent . . ."

"It makes you sound like my real estate agent."

"You crack me up," I said.

"If it's not too much trouble," she said.

"Hey," I said, "it's the least I can do." And it was, for this woman who drove two hours through the snow when Dante died with a car full of wood scraps and oil paints so we could make our own cross, who regularly gets on the Internet in the San Luis Valley to help me get out of Denver rush-hour traffic, who hates scenery and early mornings and loves Cornhusker football and bison, her strange brilliant husband, her short-legged stunt dog, and me.

That night I cooked a fancy dinner and broke out all the pretty plates I hand-carried back from France. I made the first fresh Alaskan halibut of the year in a lemon and chive butter, baby turnips with sea salt, and a huge salad with avocado, Sweet 100 cherry tomatoes, hearts of palm, scallions, and fresh pea sprouts, finished with a big mound of blue cheese crumbles in the center that I brought to the table for Jodi to toss.

Rose had been eyeing the blue cheese from the moment I took it out of the refrigerator. As Jodi lifted the big salad forks to start tossing, Rose was suddenly at her side.

"No, Rose," I said.

"No, Rose," Jodi said.

"No, Rose," Howard said.

And then came the *harrrrunk* of Rose's nose diving straight into the center of the salad.

"Rose, no!" Howard said, with his version of urgency, and Rose looked up, pea sprouts pointing every which way from her muzzle.

Jodi forced Rose's big jaws open and the mound of cheese fell back into the salad. Jodi blotted it dry with a paper towel for several seconds, put it back in the bowl, and went ahead and tossed the salad, shooting me a look like she'd just stuck the landing. *For life,* that look said. *Let's see you doubt it now.*

Grand Junction has the lowest altitude in the state, and as we get closer, the buds on the cottonwoods get bigger and bigger. Howard is making up another dog song, "Rosebeast, I'm Calling" to the tune of Tom Petty's "Free Falling," and Dante is here, hovering in the place he seems to have chosen for himself, right up and to the left of my left shoulder. I'm breaking out the liver treats which have piqued Rose's interest, and forest fires be damned when the 4-Runner feels like home and we're all in it together and happy. I pull my feet out of my boots and put them up on the dashboard and admire my shiny green toenails. I told Howard it was getting to be that time of year again, but I was too exhausted to paint them myself, so he volunteered to do it last night, *after* I had fallen asleep.

I had a dream last night that I was walking along the gravel road to the west of the ranch. A large animal leapt out onto the road near me, and then two equally large but slightly less grand versions of the same animal came loping along behind. Too big for a coyote, I thought. Too graceful for an elk. They were silver, nearly the color of mercury, and there was something vaguely translucent about them when they moved. Then the first one, the big one, turned his big head sideways to look at me. His face was round, and decorated with long dark whiskers. What was a tiger doing on Middle Creek Road?

I stood my ground, remembering what Jonathan had said about mountain lions and prey, and the big cat padded slowly, but confidently, toward me. His two companions, females, I was pretty sure, hung back and waited to see what he'd do next.

The big cat circled me, sniffed the hem of my shorts, and butted me, playfully I thought, in the side. I held my ground but didn't butt back. He butted me twice more, once hard enough to make me lose my footing, then he yawned, turned, and walked back to meet his companions, and they loped off across the pasture toward the trees.

Just as they disappeared into a stand of ponderosas, two Mongolian men in full uniform and carrying bayonets came running up the road from behind me.

"You okay?" one asked.

"Yeah, fine," I said. "Who are you?"

"We are sorry," the other said, "we didn't make it in time. Are you sure you're okay? He didn't hurt you?"

"No, no, I'm fine," I said, and, satisfied, they raised their bayonets to their shoulders and trotted off in the same direction as the cats.

The next thing I knew I was in Common Grounds, the coffee shop in town. They were open for dinner, which they never are in real life, and though Jill said they were full, she said if we wanted we could sit at one of the picnic tables out back. I was with Howard and Darlene, and as we set our own table I told them about the big cats on the road.

"What," Jill said as she carried a platter past us, "you don't know about the paper tigers?"

"The what?" we said.

"The rare Siberian paper tigers," she said. "They've been transplanted here as an experiment, because their habitat is so threatened overseas. They sent guards with them, to protect us from the tigers they said, but if you ask me, it's probably about protecting the paper tigers from us."

Now, on the way to Grand Junction, a couple more miles go by and I start worrying that if Howard pays too much attention to the puppy, Rose will have her feelings hurt. She's been a little depressed since Dante died, and she has done an admirable job of stepping up, and I imagine her looking up at Howard with her big golden eyes and saying, *Daddy, why wasn't I enough?* The next thing I know my head is full of Eddie saying I needed an exorcism and Jonathan raising a gun to his chest, and another smoke-choked summer on the way. But there are big grey clouds building over the desert to the west, and on the Weather Channel they're calling for snow tonight, maybe a whole lot of it, and this is a day for joy, because this day marks the end of the twelfth week of young Mary Ellen's life, and the first day of her life with us.

Mary Ellen, of the dark face and the large paws, I call her, from the photos we've received, but within the hour those photos will morph into a real live dog. The daughter of Dante's sister, and if I'm allowed to hope, a chip off the old man's block.

On our camping trip to Utah, when Mona told me her dreams, she said that after I buried her and our baby beside the Green River—in that life that came before—I moved to Grand Junction, a frontier town in those days, built to supply the railroad and the miners, and I became a very successful entrepreneur. I had lots of women, she said, over the years, but before I bedded each one of them, I took them to a room off the back of my house where I'd made a little shrine to Mona. I showed them her picture and said, "This is the only woman I will ever truly love."

People will lie about anything, about love and dreams and even God, and until you learn to forgive both them and yourself, it's too damn easy to believe them. I see my mother staring into that mirror that made her flaws so much bigger than they actually were. I think about how sometimes when I stand in front of the mirror I'll look only at the clothes I'm in and not at myself. Before long I'm making a list of all my failures, all of the things in my life I have run from, all the things I couldn't save.

Fat wet flakes start to hit the windshield and Howard puts his arm across my shoulders. Rose sets her chin down on top of his arm and I put my other arm out the window to catch the big spring snowflakes and again I am reminded: this is a day for counting blessings, and so I do, all the rest of the way to Grand Junction.

SIGHT HOUND

Pam Houston

Before *Sight Hound* was published, a reporter from a major newspaper asked me what it was about. "It's about faith," I said, surprising myself completely. "Wow," I added, "I'm glad I didn't know that until right now." This is the kind of question that writers tend to keep from themselves, the kind that would scare us into paralysis.

For the four years that *Sight Hound* was in process, I said, "It's about a dog and a girl," a much safer answer. Only when I was finished was I willing to admit that each of the major narrators in *Sight Hound* is, consciously or not, searching for what the character Jonathan would call a "reliable system of belief." Rae tries to believe that painting her toenails green will keep the Colorado wildfires from destroying her ranch. Jonathan, who writes letters to rock stars, both hopes for and fears their replies. Brooklyn Underhill believes in salvation through service to God and country. Eddie Kominsky believes that God talks to him, that God gave him a hockey championship, that God tells him who is ready to be saved. Dante is a Buddhist; Rose, a hedonist; Mona believes in reincarnation; and Dr. Evans believes that the Detroit Red Wings are his friends.

I was also interested in writing about what happens when faith fails us, when no matter how hard we hope or pray or cross our fingers and toes, the thing we most fear happens anyway. Also what happens when we lose faith, when we fail to stand strong in the face of fear, or when we use our belief systems to manipulate the people we love.

Now, months after publication, I can see that I was trying to wrestle with some pretty basic questions. Are we capable of loving completely when loss is inevitable? How can we maintain equanimity when we know that the only constant in our lives is change? How can we relinquish our attachments to the pain and fear that "keep us safe from joy"? How can we learn to savor—on a minute-by-minute basis—how much we love the world?

Maybe dogs are savvier about the answers to these questions than we are. Or maybe dogs just know how to accept these questions with grace.

A few months ago, another reporter commented, "It seems that in this novel, the dogs are nearly always the teachers."

"Pretty much," I said.

"And the humans are nearly always the recipients of the lessons."

"More or less," I said.

He asked, "Wasn't it kind of human-centric to have it come out that way?"

I thought about this for a moment. "Well," I said, "I guess if *Dante* had written the book for a canine audience, most of the lessons would be directed toward the dogs. But as *I* wrote it primarily for a human audience, I hope its human-centric slant might be excused."

DISCUSSION QUESTIONS

1. This novel is told in the first person by twelve different narrators, nine of them human, two of them canine, and one of them feline. What do you think the author was trying to accomplish by changing point of view so many times? What does she risk?

2. In Dante's first monologue he says, "It is funnier how love is both harder, and easier, without language." What does he mean by this? In what way does the novel explore the difference between spoken love and love as represented in action?

3. Much of Rae's personal history is narrated in the voices of Jonathan and Darlene, rather than in Rae's own voice. Why do you think the author made that decision?

4. If Dante is the primary teacher in the book, what is Rose's role?

5. Howard spends a lot of time making up stories, most significantly Oprah Fantasies #1 and #2. Does this bode well or poorly for Rae and Howard's marriage? What are the chances that Jonathan and Eddie's grim predictions for the marriage might come true?

6. Jodi arrives in the novel quite late, but Dante calls her the missing piece of the puzzle. What does Dante mean when he says this? Do you think he's right?

7. There are three things that Rae is afraid of in this novel: that Dante will die, that the wildfires will destroy her home, and that Eddie

Kominsky will destroy her marriage. In what ways are these threats different from one another? In what ways are they all the same?

8. The author makes the decision to let the usually laconic Dr. Evans narrate the scene of Dante's death. Why do you think she chose him over narration by Howard or Rae?

9. Darlene decides, near the end of the novel, to leave the ranch. What motivates her? In what way will Rae's life be different after she is gone?

10. In the final pages of *Sight Hound*, Rae recounts a dream of paper tigers. What is the metaphorical function of these paper tigers? To what moments in the novel do they ask you to return?